SAVING GRAYSON (SPECIAL FORCES: OPERATION ALPHA)

SAVING SEALS, BOOK 5

JANE BLYTHE

This book is a work of fiction. Names, characters, places, and incidents are products of the author's imagination or used fictitiously. Any resemblance to actual events or locales or persons living or dead is entirely coincidental.

Cover designed by TRC Designs

Dear Readers,

Welcome to the Special Forces: Operation Alpha Fan-Fiction world!

If you are new to this amazing world, in a nutshell the author wrote a story using one or more of my characters in it. Sometimes that character has a major role in the story, and other times they are only mentioned briefly. This is perfectly legal and allowable because they are going through Aces Press to publish the story.

This book is entirely the work of the author who wrote it. While I might have assisted with brainstorming and other ideas about which of my characters to use, I didn't have any part in the process or writing or editing the story.

I'm proud and excited that so many authors loved my characters enough that they wanted to write them into their own story. Thank you for supporting them, and me!

READ ON!

Xoxo

Susan Stoker

DEDICATION

I'd like to thank everyone who played a part in bringing this story to life. Particularly my mom who is always there to share her thoughts and opinions with me. The wonderful Cat Imb of TRC Designs who made the stunning cover. And my lovely editor Lisa Edwards for all her encouragement and for all the hard work she puts into polishing my work.

CHAPTER 1

January 17th

8:53 P.M.

RAIN WAS POURING DOWN.

Grayson "Chaos" Simpson navigated through the storm with ease. He'd always loved storms, there was something about the power of nature that called out to him. As a child, he drove his parents crazy because he would always go outside and stand in the middle of the pouring rain and howling winds. It didn't matter how many times he tried to explain that being out there in the midst of nature at its roughest that he felt his strongest, they never got it.

Tonight's storm had cut short a barbecue with his teammates and their families. The barbecue had ended up being a cover for Logan "Shark" Kirk and the woman whose life he'd saved four months ago to announce to their SEAL family that they were engaged. Chaos couldn't be happier for the two. They had been through so much, and he knew that Claire was far from healed physically or emotionally, but they deserved their happy ending, and he was praying there would be no more bumps in the road for the two of them.

Despite the fact that he was thirty-two and had grown up with parents who were happily married and had just recently celebrated their thirty-sixth wedding anniversary, Chaos hadn't given much thought to finding a partner or falling in love. Four of the six guys on his team were now either married or engaged, and three of them had kids. While he liked women and definitely wasn't opposed to the idea of love, he just hadn't met anyone who he felt a connection with.

Lightning streaked the sky as he pulled into his driveway, and thunder crashed loudly enough that it felt like the entire world trembled beneath it. As he parked the car in the garage, he stood for a moment at the open roller door watching lighting dance across the dark sky. The air was cold, and even though he was standing inside the garage the squalling winds sent raindrops swirling around him. The cold had the rain partially frozen, and each drop felt like a tiny little knife stabbing at the exposed skin on his face and hands.

Although it wasn't late and he was home a little earlier than he'd been expecting, Chaos was looking forward to some time alone. Hanging out with his team had changed over the last few years. There were three little ones now ranging in age from six months to twenty-one months, so inevitably the focus of attention was now more on the kids than on the adults just talking and chilling.

Dragging in a last breath of icy air, Chaos hit the button on the wall to close the door and headed through the garage to the interior door that led into his kitchen. He had no idea what he would do for the rest of the evening, but probably video games. He was a bit of a gamer, while the guys on his team would play with him none of them were really into it, so he was hoping that when one of their kiddos grew up he could get one of them hooked.

He was dropping his keys and cell phone onto the counter when he heard something.

His brow furrowed when he realized what it was.

The washing machine.

Only he hadn't thrown in a load before he'd gone over to Shark and Claire's place this afternoon.

The wind continued to howl outside, rain drummed down loudly, and Chaos stood there for a moment, confused.

Maybe he had put the washing machine on earlier?

He'd come back from PT and gotten distracted playing video games. It was late when he'd glanced at the clock, and he'd hurried to shower and change and get to Shark's place on time. Maybe he had thrown something in before heading out.

If he hadn't, who would break into his place just to do a load of laundry?

Snatching his phone back up, he quickly sent a group text to his team telling them that there was a situation at his place. He knew they would drop everything to come rushing over, despite the storm, same way he would if one of them called needing help. It was the way his team worked, they weren't just friends, they were family, and family was always there for you when you needed them.

Slipping his phone into his back pocket, he grabbed his weapon from the lockbox in the kitchen and began to clear his house. His place was semi-remote, his nearest neighbor over a mile away, Shark and Claire's place was closest to his but that was still a fifteen-minute drive. For now he was on his own.

There was no one in his living room or the formal dining room he never used. He headed up the stairs, cleared the two spare bedrooms, one of which he had set up as a home office, the other as a gaming room. He moved on to the bathroom, and while it was empty, there were drops of water on the glass door of the shower and the tiled floor and walls as well. It was obvious someone had taken a shower in here because he used the master bathroom ensuite. The last person to take a shower in here was his teammate Ryder "Spider" Flynn after he'd had the guys over one night and their gaming session had led to dares, which had ended with Spider covered in ketchup. Not wanting to go home and explain to his wife Abigail why they'd thought trying to squirt ketchup across the room and catch it in their mouths was a good idea, Spider had showered here before going home.

That only left the master bedroom.

The door was closed, but that wasn't out of the ordinary, Chaos always closed the door to a room when he was finished in it. There were no lights on, but when he eased open the bedroom door he immediately noticed the lump in the middle of the bed.

A human-sized lump.

Whoever had put the washing machine on had obviously decided to go take a nap, and Chaos couldn't help but feel like the bears in Goldilocks and the Three Bears as he approached his bed, wondering who he was going to find. The fact that the person had washed their clothes, taken a shower, then climbed into bed made him think they were probably homeless and trying to hide out from the storm, but there was no way to know for sure, so he approached the bed as though this were a worst-case scenario.

The person didn't stir as he crept across the room. They were right in the middle of the mattress and from the impression under the blankets it looked like they were curled into a ball.

Wanting to move quickly to get the intruder restrained and get this whole mess sorted out, Chaos held his weapon in one hand, and with his other, he reached toward the covers. Grabbing the blankets, he snapped them out of the way, then grabbed the wrist of the person in his bed just as they woke up. He yanked them out of the bed and shoved an arm up behind their back, causing them to cry out in pain. Without pausing, he slammed them up against the wall, grabbed flexi-cuffs from his nightstand, and bound the intruder's hands behind their back.

Without releasing his prisoner, Chaos grabbed their bicep and pulled them along with him as he went back to the door and switched on the lights. Only then did he notice that the person who had broken into his house was a woman.

A beautiful woman.

A beautiful *naked* woman.

She had long light brown locks hanging right down to her backside and stunning green eyes that were currently staring up at him with unveiled terror. There was a smattering of freckles across her nose, and the fact that he could count her ribs hinted that she was indeed living on the streets and half-starved.

This woman was no threat to him, and he'd bet his entire gaming system that it was the storm that had her breaking in here.

Obviously terrified at being caught and her state of undress, the woman attempted to curl in on herself, angling her body away from his as best as she could. While he wouldn't uncuff her before she explained herself, Chaos did take mercy on her and released her, crossing to the bed to collect a blanket, then draping it over her shoulders.

It wasn't until then that he noticed that his entire bedroom had been tidied up. The clothes that were usually strewn about were now nowhere to be seen. The haphazard piles of magazines that usually sat on his nightstand had been straightened, now sitting in a perfectly neat pile centered to perfection in the middle of the nightstand. The collection of action figures that usually stood on top of his dresser had all been placed an equal distance apart. The few that had fallen over that he hadn't found time to right were now standing in line with the others.

Looked like his little cat burglar had a neat streak a mile wide.

Chaos threw back his head and laughed.

9:09 P.M.

HE WAS LAUGHING AT HER.

For some reason that irked her.

Juliet York was self-conscious about her OCD. It was one thing to keep it to herself, do her best to hide it from everyone else, contain her compulsions to her own space, but right now her obsessive-compulsive disorder was well and truly on display to the man whose house she'd broken into.

Broken into.

What had she been thinking?

She hadn't.

That was her only excuse. She'd been wet and freezing cold and couldn't stomach the thought of spending hours in the storm. Then she'd seen his house, the lights were out, there was no car that she could see, and the next thing she knew, she was picking the lock.

Her only excuse was that desperation made you do crazy things.

"Answer me one question, cat burglar. How did you think you were going to slink in here and then back out again without me knowing it when you cleaned my bedroom?" the man asked, clearly amused. He was a good-looking man, tall, muscles on his muscles, a full head of sandy blond hair, and green eyes.

He was too sexy for his own good.

And he was mocking her.

Her offense at him laughing at her morphed into embarrassment, and she dropped her gaze to the floor. It had been stupid. She'd known that even as she was folding his clothes and putting them away in the drawers, and hanging his pants in his wardrobe that she may as well be painting a sign across his wall advertising the fact that someone had been in his house.

She just hadn't been able to stop herself. "I was hoping that either you'd think you had tidied up, or you had a girlfriend or mom who might have done it for you."

He threw back his head and laughed again, and it annoyed her how he just assumed she was no threat to him. Yeah, so she was naked, and he had caught her in the first good sleep she'd had in weeks and got her restrained, but she wasn't some helpless little girl, she would have fought him if given the chance.

"You're out of luck, cat burglar, my mom told me long ago if I wanted to live in filth that was my problem not hers, and there's no girlfriend to clean up after me."

"Would you stop calling me cat burglar? I didn't steal anything," she said through clenched teeth. For some reason this man had the ability to irritate her like no one else ever had. She knew she was being ridiculous. He was the victim here, she'd broken into his home, used his washing machine and his shower, and gone to sleep in his bed. He had every right to cuff her and call the cops to have her arrested, which he would no doubt do despite the fact he seemed to find her amusing.

"Because you didn't get a chance, I came home before you woke up." His green eyes were twinkling, and she was pretty sure he didn't think she was actually here to rob him.

"Are you going to call the cops?" she asked, her irritation bleeding away as fear took its place. If she was arrested then they'd know where she was and everything she'd gone through the last few weeks would have been for nothing.

The man grew serious, and he stood before her, leaning over so they were eye to eye. "You in some sort of trouble?"

Juliet gulped and then nodded. She was definitely in trouble, trouble she had no idea how to get out of.

"Drugs? Alcohol? Gambling? Trouble with the law?" he asked.

"No!" she blurted out, appalled at the thought. She had never done drugs. She didn't drink, had never seen the fun in wasting money on gambling, and had never so much as had a parking ticket. The only crime she'd ever committed was breaking and entering tonight in this man's house.

"You running from someone who wants to hurt you?"

She dropped her gaze to the floor, ashamed that she'd been blackmailed into this situation. She hadn't realized it was as bad at first, but the first time he put his hands on her, she knew that blackmail or not there was no way she was staying with him.

The man hooked a finger under her chin and gently nudged. "If someone hurt you it's not your fault."

Why was he being so nice to her?

She had broken into his home, used his things, and yet his touch was soft, his eyes were kind, and she sensed that he was more likely to offer to help her than he was have her thrown in jail.

"It was my fiancé," she said quietly. "He's my dad's business partner, I work for my dad, I couldn't stay so I ran. I've been living on the street." Juliet lifted her gaze and met the man's squarely, completely prepared to own the massive mistake she'd made tonight. "I'm sorry. I was wet and cold and scared of the storm, but that's no excuse. I swear I didn't take anything of yours. I didn't even put any washing powder in with my clothes, and I only washed myself with water, I didn't use your soap or shampoo or anything. I was just tired of being cold and wet and just … tired … I broke down. I was only going to sleep for a bit then I would have left. I'm really sorry, I know it doesn't fix anything, but I am."

"Apology accepted."

Juliet gasped and stared into his eyes, searching to see what angle he was playing and what he was trying to get out of her in exchange for not handing her over to the cops. It hit her that she was naked despite the blanket draped over her shoulders that didn't really cover much of anything.

Was he going to ask for sexual favors in return for not having her arrested?

"I'm not sure I want to know what your life was like if the look on your face right now is any indication of what's running through that pretty head of yours," the man said. "You were desperate, it's storming out, you were just looking for somewhere warm and dry to wait it out. I can understand that. I'm not calling the cops, at least not yet."

"Not yet?"

"My team is on their way here. You can explain to all of us what's going on."

"Your team?" Just who was this guy? Trust her to take a bad situation and manage to make it worse.

The man simply nodded.

"Why do I need to explain to all of you what's going on?"

"Because we might be able to help."

Help?

How?

Juliet didn't want to be pessimistic, but nobody could help her with her current situation. And even if they could, why would this man even want to? Surely she'd caused him enough problems. She would have thought he couldn't wait to see the back of her.

"Why would you do that?" Juliet asked, completely dumbfounded.

"Because you need help."

He made it sound so simple, but he didn't even know her name. Juliet had never met a man like this before, and it made her feel completely out of her depth. Over the years, she'd learned how to handle her family, learned the hard way that it was easier to comply than it was to fight, but how did she handle this man?

Tears burned her eyes, and she felt weak all over. When in her life had anyone ever offered her such unequivocal support? Never. The answer was never.

Yet here was this stranger forgiving her criminal behavior and offering his assistance.

Her heart had never felt this full, and it made her feel weird.

The man moved the blanket so it was draped across her front rather than her back, then his large fingers circled her wrists, and he cut through the zip tie binding her. Juliet rubbed at her wrists then startled when the man reached for her hand.

"I'm Grayson, but my friends all call me Chaos," he announced as he shook her hand.

"I'm Juliet."

"Nice to meet you, Juliet."

Grayson went to move, but she tightened her hold on his hand. "Grayson, I'm really sorry, I knew it was the wrong thing to do but I did it …"

"Shh," he said softly, touching a finger to her lips. "I already accepted your apology. I'm going to go rewash your clothes with detergent this time. My team will be here soon, so you'll have to wait to take a bath till they're done, but I can get you something to wear." He went to his wardrobe, laughed as he looked at how she had organized it, then returned and gave her a pair of sweatpants and a t-shirt. "I'll go make you something to eat."

With that, he disappeared out of the room leaving her staring open-mouthed at his retreating back.

This man was so calm and easygoing, so completely unrattled about finding an intruder naked in his bed. She had no idea what to make of him, but as she pulled on his clothes the one thing that stuck most in her mind was the feel of his finger touching her lips. She definitely wasn't thinking about kissing him though.

Definitely not.

~

9:21 P.M.

. . .

CHAOS GRABBED some leftover homemade fried chicken he'd made the night before and set it on a plate, he had fresh vegetables steaming on the stove, and he poured Juliet a glass of milk and set a bottle of water on the table. There. That covered most of the food groups. He'd felt how frail she was when he'd dragged her out of the bed and cuffed her. He'd been able to feel each one of her ribs, and her hipbones had been way too prominent. When he'd left her to get dressed and come to cook her some dinner, he'd checked his fridge and his pantry and seen that she hadn't taken anything, despite the fact she was no doubt starving.

He didn't believe that Juliet had broken in here for any other reason than to find a safe and warm space to hide from the storm. The flare of fear in her eyes when she'd mentioned her fiancé was enough to stoke his protective side, and he wanted to help her get free of her past.

"I hope it's okay, but my feet were cold so I put on a pair of your socks," Juliet said as she padded quietly into the kitchen.

Not able to hold back a smirk he turned to face her. "Did you have to pair up all the socks in my drawer?" It was clear to him in the fifteen minutes or so since they'd met that Juliet had obsessive-compulsive disorder, and he knew that his sock drawer where all his socks were just shoved haphazardly inside would have driven her crazy.

Juliet huffed, her cheeks blazing red, but she nodded. "I tidied it up for you, and, umm, I might have also tidied the rest of the drawers in your dresser too," she admitted.

"So you went through my underwear drawer?" he asked because teasing her was so much fun he couldn't resist riling her up.

"It wasn't, uh … sexual … or anything," she stammered, but the way her gaze darted to him and then the floor made him think that sex was exactly what she'd been thinking about as she organized his dresser.

Interesting.

His pretty little cat burglar was attracted to him. Well the feeling was absolutely mutual. Juliet was a beautiful woman, and once he helped her fix whatever problem with her fiancé and her father that had her living on the streets, he wouldn't be opposed to asking her out.

"Sure it wasn't, princess," he said as he dished up the vegetables onto her plate.

"So it's princess now is it?" she asked, hands planted on her hips.

"I can go back to cat burglar if you prefer." He shot her a grin and set her plate on the table.

"But I didn't steal anything," she reminded him.

"Well, nothing but water to run the shower and washing machine," he couldn't help goading.

She rolled those stunning green eyes at him. "There's plenty of water outside at the moment, you want me to go outside and catch you some?"

Chaos laughed, bantering with her was more fun than he'd had in a long time. "Sit down and eat, princess."

"You cooked me dinner?" she asked, dropping down into the chair he'd pulled out for her.

"I told you I was."

"You said you would get me something to eat. I assumed that meant you'd like pour me a bowl of cereal or make me some toast or something. Not actually cook me dinner."

He made a face. "Cereal and toast is not dinner."

The smile she gave him had an air of vulnerability. "You're one of those, huh? Those people who eat healthy all the time."

"What gave you that impression?" he teased.

"You're … umm … well … you're really … you know … hot," she said with a shrug.

"You been checking me out, princess?"

Her cheeks went red again, then she looked from the plate of food he'd cooked for her to him. "You're not eating?"

"Ate at my friend Shark's place earlier, my team and I had a barbecue." Realizing she was waiting for him to eat too out of politeness he nodded at her meal. "Dig in, princess. When you're done you can have some ice cream."

Her eyes lit up at the mention of ice cream, and having been given permission to start eating she began to hungrily devour her food. He could tell that a sense of manners had her trying to slow herself down, but it was plain to see that the woman was starving. Chaos hated that, hated knowing that she'd been so afraid that she had thought living on the street was her best option. He itched to fix her problems for her, and while she hadn't protested the idea of him helping her, she also hadn't accepted his help.

She would, though.

Whether he ended up asking her out or not, he'd make sure that she was safe and had a place to live before he bid her farewell.

There was a knock on his door, and Juliet almost jumped out of her skin.

She eyed the backdoor, and he was sure she was contemplating taking her chances out in the storm versus dealing with whoever was at the door. He had no doubt that she believed her fiancé had managed to track her here. Chaos knew that Juliet had no idea that she was in the house of a Navy SEAL and she was perfectly safe. He knew dozens of ways to kill a man with his bare hands, and he wouldn't allow anyone to hurt her.

"It's okay, princess, it's just my team," he said gently. His words didn't seem to soothe her much, but at least she stayed in her seat. "I'm just going to go let them in," he told her. He spoke to her as he would a spooked animal, attempting to keep her calm because if he didn't she was going to bolt and run right back into whatever danger she'd fled.

Leaving Juliet in the kitchen and praying she was still there when he returned, Chaos headed through the living room and to the front door.

"Everything okay, man?" Owen "Fox" LeGrand asked.

"Fine," he assured them.

"So false alarm? No one actually broke in?" Eric "Night" McNamara asked.

"Oh no, someone broke in," he replied.

"What the hell, dude," Charlie "King" Voss said, looking confused.

"My little cat burglar didn't break in to steal anything, she's on the run from an abusive fiancé and has been living on the street, she broke in to get out of the storm," Chaos explained. "Come meet her, she's in the kitchen. She was starving, guys," he said softly, hating that Juliet had been forced into such a situation.

Half expecting Juliet to be gone by the time they returned, instead he found her still at his table. She'd finished her dinner, but she was watching the kitchen door nervously, wringing her hands together. Her eyes widened when she saw his team, and he knew they were an intimidating bunch, especially if you didn't know that they were the good guys.

"Juliet, this is my team. Meet Fox, Spider, Night, King, and Shark. Guys, meet Juliet, my little cat burglar," he said, making the introductions.

The nickname made her roll her eyes, but at least she relaxed a little. "Hey," she said softly. "I'm sorry, I know I shouldn't have broken in here, I apologized to Grayson already, and I really am sorry. It was a stupid thing to do, but I was … desperate."

His team looked from her to him, and when they saw that he was obviously not angry with her, they all nodded and softened toward the scared woman huddled in a chair at his kitchen table.

"Nice to meet you, Juliet," Fox said. "Chaos said you're running from an abusive ex."

She nodded and sipped at her water.

"You can tell us, Juliet, we all want to help," Chaos said as he joined her at the table.

For a moment, she studied him and then the rest of his team, clearly weighing up her options. She must have decided she had nothing to lose by telling them so she gave a single nod and then started talking. "I don't even really know him. My father blackmailed me into marrying him. I only just met him at Christmas, and then at my father's New Year's Eve party, he hit me. I told him I was leaving that no matter what my father said I wouldn't marry someone who hit me. He uh … didn't like that and he beat me up pretty badly. I didn't know what to do, but I knew I wouldn't marry him, so I just ran. I couldn't take my credit cards or car because I was worried my father would be able to track me, so I've been living on the street."

Chaos stared at her, anger at both her father and the man he was forcing her to marry coursing through him. What kind of man blackmailed his own daughter into marrying a man who would abuse her?

"What's your fiancé's name?" Spider asked.

"Dimitri Fedorov," Juliet replied.

His brow crinkled. Surely she couldn't mean *the* Dimitri Fedorov, the only son of a Russian crime boss.

"How do you know Dimitri Fedorov?" Night asked, and he could see his teammates had also recognized the name.

"I don't. All I know is that Dimitri's father became my father's business partner after my dad got into some financial trouble last year. I don't know why he wanted me to marry Dimitri. Even if he didn't know the man was violent, he knew I didn't want to do it. Why would he blackmail me like that?" The last was said quietly as though she were asking herself.

Did Juliet know who the Fedorovs were?

What did her father do?

Was she involved in something illegal?

No.

The pain on her face as she wondered how her own father could blackmail her into marriage said she was more upset about that than anything else.

"What's does your father do, Juliet?" Fox asked.

"He's a dealer in diamonds and other precious stones. He also designs and sells high-end jewelry," she replied.

"Your last name is York," he said. "Your father is Arthur York."

Juliet nodded. "He's going to be so angry that I ran."

Interesting, she was more worried about her father being angry with her than running from the Russian mafia. If he hadn't already been convinced that she had no idea who her fiancé was that would have sealed the deal.

"Do you know who Dimitri Fedorov is, Juliet?" Night asked.

"Some rich Russian businessman," she said with a shrug. But then she took in their faces and fear slowly bled into her features. "He's not just a Russian businessman, is he?"

"No, princess, he's not," Chaos told her.

~

9:38 P.M.

"Who is he?" Juliet asked, wondering just what kind of mess her father had gotten her into. It was clear that Grayson and his team of scary-looking friends all knew who Dimitri was, but she didn't and she was the one who might be forced to marry him.

"Dimitri is the son of a Russian mobster," Grayson told her gently.

"He's what?" she screeched a little too loudly. Sure she must have misheard, Juliet looked to the faces of the other men, but each one of them only confirmed what Grayson had told her.

Her father had blackmailed her into marrying a Russian mobster.

Well, he'd tried.

If she hadn't run from Dimitri that night then she might be his wife by now.

She had a feeling that beating her up was the least of what he would have done to her.

Still could do.

"What will he do to me when he finds me?" she asked, terrified beyond anything she'd ever felt before. She'd run away from the Russian mafia, that couldn't be a good thing.

Although the question had been more wondering aloud, Chaos leaned over and gripped her arms. "He's not going to get his hands on you."

He said it so firmly, so unflinchingly, that Juliet believed him in spite of herself. She nodded her thanks. "I don't understand how any of this is happening." Juliet knew her father didn't love her, that she disappointed him at every turn, but this seemed so … extreme.

"What was your father blackmailing you with?" the man with the gray eyes—she thought he was the one called Night—asked.

She could see on their faces that they thought she'd done something wrong, something criminal, and that was what her father used to control her. Indignation mixed with humiliation and she huffed. "It's not what you think. I'm not into anything illegal, breaking in here was the first time I've ever broken the law. I … went through a rough time as a teenager. I was depressed, I tried to kill myself," she said softly. "My parents sent me to a treatment facility, it really helped. My therapist was great, and I learned to understand the things that used to make me hate myself. I haven't had any suicidal thoughts since I was sixteen, I swear I haven't, but my father paid off this doctor, and he has documents that recommend that I be committed for my own safety. He said if I didn't agree to marry Dimitri, he'd have me locked away and keep me there. I swear, Grayson, I'm not suicidal." She turned pleading eyes on him, for some reason it seemed important that he believe her.

His hands landed on her shoulders, and he gently kneaded. "I believe you. If you were suicidal you wouldn't have run from Dimitri when he hit you."

Juliet let out a relieved breath. She wasn't sure about his friends, but Grayson believed her and that helped. She'd felt so alone ever since her father dropped his bombshell on her, and then these last few weeks living on the street, sleeping in alleys, or the park, or anywhere else she could find had been pure hell.

"We'll figure this out, okay?" Grayson said, his green eyes holding steady as he met her gaze.

She had no idea how they would do that, but his air of authority again convinced her that it was true.

"You're not alone anymore," Grayson told her.

"Why are you doing this? After what I did you should have just handed me over to the cops and washed your hands of me. So why are you helping me?" It made zero sense, but in Juliet's experience people rarely did anything nice for others out of the goodness of their hearts. So what was Grayson going to want in exchange for his help?

"We're doing it because you need help," he replied simply.

"All of you?" Her gaze met the other men's, but there was no hostility there, none of them seemed fazed by Grayson's declaration that they were going to find a way to help her get out of this situation her father had gotten her into. She kind of felt like a stray that had been adopted by a bunch of well-meaning—albeit a little scary—men who looked like maybe they possessed the skills to fix this for her.

"We're not just a team, Juliet, we're a family, and we help one another," Grayson told her.

"You guys are military aren't you? Special forces?"

"SEALs," Grayson answered.

"I'm not surprised, you're all so big, and built, and kinda menacing, but you're so confident."

The guys all laughed, apparently amused by her description of them. When they all started to move like they were getting ready to leave, Juliet realized her reprieve was over now. Grayson had said she could take a bath before she left, but she'd really rather just grab her clothes and go now, she'd imposed enough already, especially after his promise to help her.

"I should go," she said, pushing back from the table.

"You can have your ice cream after your bath," Grayson said.

"No, I mean I should leave," Juliet corrected him.

"It's still storming," Grayson said like she couldn't hear the howling wind and torrential rain.

"I'm aware, but …" Juliet trailed off and shrugged, not sure what he wanted her to say.

"Don't fight it, Juliet, Chaos has adopted you now," the blued-eyed man—Spider—said with a laugh.

The guys exchanged goodbyes, and before she knew it she and Grayson were alone in his kitchen.

None of this made sense to her.

It was like she had entered some alternate universe.

"What does it mean when your friend says you've adopted me now? Am I some sort of project?" She didn't quite like the idea of being Grayson's newest pet project. She knew that wasn't fair, she should be grateful—and she *really* was—but maybe for once in her life she just wanted someone to actually care about her.

"I like to help people," Chaos replied. "I wouldn't call you a project, you're a person who needs help, and I'm in a position to help."

"So I'm just going to stay here now?" Surely that wasn't what he meant. He was just going to let her take a bath, eat ice cream, and wait out the storm, right? Anything else was just pure crazy.

"Yep." Chaos smiled warmly.

"For how long?"

"Until you're ready to leave," he said.

He was being too nice to her, and she didn't have a lot of experience with people being nice. Juliet chewed on her bottom lip to keep from bursting into tears and further embarrassing herself in front of this man. "But you can't just …"

"Juliet, relax." Grayson put his hands back on her shoulders and massaged just like he had earlier. "I can invite you to stay here, and I have. If you're uncomfortable with that then tomorrow we'll set you up at a hotel. I'm here to help, I don't want anything in return, so just relax and accept that sometimes people just like to help others."

Not in her experience.

In her experience everything came at a price.

But it seemed like Grayson was the exception to the rule.

He seemed to be a genuinely nice guy who just wanted to help someone in need. While she didn't quite know how to deal with someone like that it was nice to be able to let her guard down a little. Her father had controlled her life from the minute she was born, and she had to constantly be on the lookout for ways he was going to manipulate her, but maybe with Grayson she could just … be.

"I don't know how to thank you for all of this," she said.

"You already have. Now, are you having ice cream first or a bath?"

Her hands twitched uncomfortably on her lap. She was feeling out of her depth from everything that had happened with her father, her fiancé, and what she'd just learned about them. And from the way too sexy for his own good man who was still touching her.

When her world felt like it was spinning out of control she had to find a way to get it back.

Cleaning and organizing were her go-to's. Keeping what she could completely under her control was the only way she had been able to deal with living in her father's house and having her life micromanaged.

Grayson glanced down at her twitching hands. "You need to clean something, don't you?"

Juliet studied his gaze carefully searching for any signs that he was mocking her, but she didn't see any. He seemed to have just accepted that her compulsion to clean was as much a part of her as her green eyes, freckles, and brown locks were. That easy acceptance, something her own family hadn't been able to give her, helped her to relax. Grayson was a nice guy, he'd shown her more kindness than she deserved given how they'd met, and he truly didn't seem to want anything from her in return.

A part of her soul uncurled as she smiled up at Grayson. "Let's do ice cream, and then I'll clean your kitchen like it's never been cleaned before."

~

10:11 P.M.

HIS DAUGHTER HAD RUINED EVERYTHING.

Just like she always did.

Juliet had been a disappointment from the moment she'd been born.

Arthur York had wanted a son. A boy he could mold in his own image, train to take over the family business, and pass along everything he had built from scratch. Instead, he'd gotten a girl who had almost cost her mother her life during childbirth. The doctors had been forced to give his wife a complete hysterectomy to stop the bleeding, ending any chance he could ever have to have the son he wanted.

As if that wasn't bad enough, Juliet was nothing like him. Absolutely nothing. The girl didn't have a ruthless bone in her body, there was no way she would cut it in his world. Add to that the fact that she was odd, and he knew there was only one use she would ever serve him.

He had grown up in poverty. He'd had nothing, no house, barely enough food to remain alive, clothes that were dirty and didn't fit, but he'd had the one thing he needed to get out of that life and make something of himself.

Drive.

A burning drive to be better, to have everything that he wanted, to never want for a single thing. And that was the life he'd built for himself. He'd learned poker, won the money he needed for college, studied hard, and graduated top of his classes. His business had started small, a simple jewelry store that did most of its business selling engagement rings and pretty charm bracelets on Mother's Day. From those humble beginnings, he was now the number one dealer of diamonds and other precious stones in the entire country. The jewelry his company designed and made was all one of a kind and sold to the rich and famous for millions. Every time he saw royalty or a celebrity wearing something that he had made pride flushed through him.

He'd done it.

He'd made it.

He owned a mansion in America, as well as homes in Paris, London, and Rome. He bought a new car every year, he had a yacht and a private plane, he could buy anything his heart desired.

And Juliet held the power to ruin all of that.

There was no way he would allow that to happen.

There wasn't anything he wouldn't do to maintain the lifestyle he had so carefully built. Not a single thing. If Juliet thought that being his only child somehow meant she was set in a different category and that he wouldn't use her for his own personal gain, then she was sorely mistaken.

Tipping back his head, he downed the last of his whisky then leaned back in his leather wingback armchair. This room was his favorite in his house, the dark colors, the furniture, the large fireplace, his study was his own personal sanctuary and he came here when he needed to relax.

After Juliet's stunt, running after the New Year's Eve party he'd thrown, he hadn't had a single moment to relax thanks to the angry Russians breathing down his neck.

It had probably been a mistake going to Alexi Fedorov for help, but at the time it had seemed like the only option. The man was wealthy, well versed in the international diamond trade, and had seemed to be only too happy to step in and pay off Arthur's debts in exchange for a fifty percent share of his company. He hadn't been pleased to sell off half the business he'd built from the ground up to someone else, but at the time, he'd been desperate, and it had seemed like a good deal. Besides, he'd always thought that he could buy the share back once he was out of debt.

Arthur hadn't been expecting the Russians to offer him an exchange.

He gives his daughter to be married to Alexi's only son Dimitri, and he gets his company back.

Simple.

The daughter who had done nothing but disappoint him, who embarrassed him with her little obsessions and crazy rituals, who had humiliated him when she attempted to take her own life and got herself committed, she would finally do something good. Not only would he get her off his hands, but joining his family to the Russian mafia meant opening up a whole new world of possibilities.

At least it had until Juliet had fled.

His phone rang and Arthur's heart sunk when he saw Dimitri's name on the screen. He'd avoided his future son-in-law's calls for the last two days, but he knew the longer he put it off, the angrier the man would get, and the last thing he needed was for the Russians to take out their anger at Juliet on him.

"Do you have her?" Dimitri snapped the second Arthur answered the phone.

"Not yet."

"What is taking so long?' Dimitri demanded.

"She knows that she's being hunted. She never stays in the same place for more than a few hours."

"But you are tracking her, yes?"

"Yes, but she's twenty-five, the tracker isn't as accurate as one made today would be. It merely gives me her general location. She hasn't gone far, and I have all my men out looking for her, but she knows that I'll do that. She's making sure to be as unpredictable as possible. Never stay in one place long, constantly change direction, don't go places where CCTV cameras will catch her image. She's playing this smart, but I will find her," he promised. He had to, if he didn't he would be the one to suffer and he wasn't about to take his daughter's punishment on her behalf.

"You better." If he wasn't already afraid of the Fedorov family, the cold malice dripping from Dimitri's voice would have done it.

"I will," he insisted, trying not to let his fear make his voice quiver. He might have spent years toeing the line between right and wrong, edging around the law, even outright breaking it to earn more money and make his business known around the world as the premier name in jewelry, but he'd never gotten his own hands dirty. He had men who did his dirty work for him. He brokered deals, they broke kneecaps when necessary, he sat in his office, sipping whisky and making deals, his men worked in back alleys and abandoned buildings putting holes in those who dared to cross him.

If he didn't find his daughter and produce her to her fiancé, then he would be the one getting his kneecaps broken, he'd be the one who would be shot or tortured or whatever it was the Russians were into these days.

"She is a beautiful woman and I want her as my wife. I always get what I want, Mr. York," Dimitri said. "But you have not taught Juliet her place in this world. It will be time-consuming to train her how a Russian mafia princess bride is to behave, but I find myself looking forward to her lessons."

The threat behind the words was clear as day. Dimitri was not only reminding him what would happen to Juliet once she was found, but also reminding him what he would suffer in her place if he couldn't get her back.

"Juliet is stubborn, but I have always found her to be logical and to acquiesce to the path of least resistance," he told the younger man. "I am sure once she realizes that her options are limited and that she belongs to you she will follow your rules to avoid further … uh … problems."

At least he hoped so.

Did he love his daughter?

No, not really.

In his mind she was, and always had been, a chess piece that could be maneuvered and used to get him to checkmate.

Now her role was to link him to the Russian mafia and get him his company back. If she failed to do that, then she deserved whatever punishment her soon-to-be husband metered out.

The idea of her being physically harmed didn't sicken him as he supposed it should. After all, she had brought this on herself. If she had just given herself over to the man he had sold her to then she wouldn't be punished. In fact, if she welcomed her new role with open arms she would live out the rest of her life in the lap of luxury, a princess in her very own castle, she would have everything her heart desired.

As far as he was concerned it was a fairytale she hadn't earned, she should be thanking him instead of disappearing and causing him all this stress and aggravation.

"I should hope so, Mr. York. Juliet belongs to me, and I want her soon. If you are unable to produce her, then I will simply eliminate you from the equation. Don't disappoint me, I promise you that you will not like the consequences."

"I will find her," he vowed, but the line had already gone dead.

Frustration and anger bubbled inside him. Despite what Juliet thought, he had been a good father. She had lived in a mansion all her life, she had attended the best schools, she had everything she asked for, clothes, toys, a pony, her own car, she had never gone hungry, never worried about how she was going to survive. He'd paid for her college, given her a job designing jewelry that she was good at, bought her a place to live, and found her a husband who could take care of her. And he had done all that despite her humiliating quirks and ungratefulness.

Juliet would do what she had been born to do, further his position in life and earn him more wealth, and she would do it by marrying Dimitri Fedorov.

CHAPTER 2

January 18th

6:03 A.M.

"I WONDERED if you'd still be here this morning, cat burglar."

Juliet shrieked at his words, spinning around from the pantry, the can of soup she'd had in her hand clattering to the floor. Her hand flew to cover her heart, and she tossed a glare his way. "You did that on purpose to scare me," she accused.

She was stunning when she was annoyed. Sparks danced in her green eyes and her bottom lip stuck out making it hard to think of anything but kissing her. He also liked how it wiped away the fear and weariness from her face.

"A little jumpy this morning, princess," he said with a smirk as he closed the back door behind him and rubbed his cold hands together. He'd spent the night downstairs on the couch, woken at five to find the storm had stopped sometime throughout the night. Before going for his customary early morning run he'd gone upstairs to check on Juliet, finding her tossing and turning in his bed.

It had taken every molecule of his self-control not to join her in the bed, tossing and turning together as they made wild, passionate love. Chaos didn't have to have kissed the woman to know that sex with her would be explosive. She was a tightly coiled spring, and he wanted to be the one to unravel her.

"Well, I'm going to be jumpy if you're going to sneak up on me and scare me," she muttered as she bent to pick up the can then turned her back on him and returned her attention to her task.

"Whatcha doing?" he asked, grabbing a bottle of water from the fridge and crossing the kitchen to the pantry.

"Oh, I'm uh … fixing your pantry for you."

Her cheeks were that adorable shade of red again, and he couldn't help but laugh. She said it like it was some sort of secret, like he wouldn't know the first time he opened the pantry door that it didn't look the way he usually kept it. "Fixing it?" he asked, amused.

"Well, you didn't have everything organized … like at all," she added as though the very idea was utterly foreign to her. "Everything was just kind of thrown in there, and I don't know how you could even find what you were looking for."

Although she was talking about food, he couldn't help but agree with her in a completely different sense. He hadn't been able to find what he was looking for. Every woman he dated ended up falling short of his expectations, but somehow he felt like this spunky, quirky, brave woman could be exactly what he'd been searching for.

"Is that right?" he asked, propping his shoulder against the pantry door, slightly crowding into her personal space but not enough to make her feel threatened. That was the last thing he wanted. He hoped that Juliet would feel safe and comfortable here. He had no intention of pretending he wasn't attracted to her or interested in her, but he also wasn't going to push her into anything she wasn't ready for or didn't want, she had enough on her plate as it was.

"Yep, totally right. You see it's easier if you group all like things together. You had all-purpose flour all the way up on the top shelf, but your self-raising flour was down on the second bottom shelf in the back corner. What you should do is keep them together, that way when you go looking for something you know exactly where to go and don't have to waste time searching for it. When I'm finished with your pantry I'm also going to do your other cupboards. Do you know it took me three minutes to find a glass this morning because you didn't put any thought into where you put everything."

"Three minutes, huh?" Chaos asked, fighting back a laugh. If he laughed, Juliet would think he was laughing *at* her, when really he found this side of her sweet and endearing. He got the feeling that in the past her OCD had been a barrier between her and other people, they'd used it against her, not understood her, mocked her for being a little bit different. That wasn't how he saw it at all, but they'd only just met, and she wasn't going to believe him if he told her that. Instead, he'd have to *show* her.

"Yep," she agreed, barely sparing him a glance as she continued to rearrange things in his pantry. "And you know what you need?"

"Nope, but I'm positive you're going to tell me."

She threw a quick glance over her shoulder and rolled her eyes at him. "You need a label maker and glass jars. It's so much neater to have things like the flour and sugars in glass jars, and then we label them and you'll never ever have to go looking for anything ever again."

Her enthusiasm for reorganizing his kitchen was the most endearing thing he'd seen in a long time. "You're enjoying this aren't you?"

"Of course," she said it like it was obvious.

"Okay, after breakfast we'll go get you your label maker and glass jars, and you can fix up my kitchen the way you think it's supposed to be."

"Oh." She spun around to face him, the spark of excitement fading from her eyes. "I'm being rude. Sorry. Sometimes I get a little carried away when it comes to organizing things. I just … I feel more in control when I can control my environment. But that's no excuse. This is your home and you've been kind enough to not only not have me arrested last night, but to help me and let me stay here. I shouldn't have taken over your kitchen like this, I'm really sorry."

"Hey." He caught her shoulders as she tried to brush past him. "I think it's cute how excited you are to tidy up my kitchen. I'm not offended or upset with you, nor am I angry with you. My job means I'm away a lot, but this place is my home, I love hanging out here, I love having my friends and their families over to hang out here. This is a home not just a house, and while you're staying here, I want you to feel as though it's your home too. If reorganizing my kitchen helps you to feel more comfortable here then I don't mind at all. Okay?"

For a long moment she studied him, her gaze serious, and he hated that when he looked into her eyes he saw a soul so much older than a mere twenty-five. "I still don't quite understand why you're being so nice to me."

"Because helping others is what life is all about. We all need a little help sometimes, Juliet."

"You don't look like you've ever needed anyone's help. You're so big, and strong, and capable, you look like you have the whole world figured out."

"Sometimes looks can be deceiving."

Her eyes widened like he'd just told her that Superman sometimes got scared. "You've needed help before?"

"Of course, everyone does. There have been times when I had to rely on my team to keep me alive, and when I was a kid my family went through a really tough time, and we had to rely on our neighbors and friends, and sometimes even strangers, to help keep us going. It's not a weakness to use a support system, it's what smart people do."

"I guess you're right," she agreed hesitantly.

"Course I am. Princess, I work with hardheaded, alpha, stubborn SEALs who don't mind relying on their team on a mission but think their personal lives should be handled all on their own. If I can convince them to let their friends help in things that don't have to do with life and death then I can certainly convince one very pretty but equally stubborn cat burglar."

"I keep telling you that I didn't steal anything so I'm not a burglar," she said, but he'd managed to get a half-smile out of her. It wasn't enough, he wanted to see her let go and laugh like she didn't have a care in the world, but he'd take what he could get for now.

"I'm not so sure about that, princess," he said. It felt like Juliet had the power to steal the most important thing he had. His heart.

She cocked her head. "You mean something else but I don't know what."

"I know," he said, giving her a warm smile. She didn't understand but she would in time.

"I don't know what it's like to have someone be this nice

to me without wanting something in return," she said, and he was pleased that she at least felt comfortable enough with him to give him honesty. "You make me uncomfortable, you're so … nice."

Chaos tossed back his head and laughed. "You say that like it's a bad thing."

"Not bad, just confusing," she corrected.

"Go take a shower and get dressed, your clothes are clean and waiting for you in the laundry room, I even folded them for you," he added because he knew it would make her smile. "After breakfast we'll go shopping. You need clothes and whatever other hoopla women need to make themselves all pretty, and we'll get you your label maker."

"Trust me, once you start using a label maker you'll never go back," she said as she walked through the kitchen.

He agreed, he had a feeling that once he got used to this little label maker he wouldn't be able to let her go.

11:36 A.M.

"I CAN PAY you back for everything, I swear I can, I have more than enough money to compensate you for everything that you're doing for me," Juliet said as they loaded the bags into the back of Grayson's car. He'd seemed happy enough to walk around the store with her for the last couple of hours, making sure she got everything she needed. He'd actually encouraged her to get way more than she'd intended, pointing out anything he thought would look nice on her.

"I'm not really worried about it, Juliet," he said as he went to open her door for her.

"Well, I want to. You've been so nice, buying me all this stuff and letting me stay with you, I want to pay you back," she said firmly.

"If it makes you feel better," he said, shooting her a smile that clearly said he never intended to take a dime from her.

"I mean it," she warned.

"Positive you do, princess."

She rolled her eyes as she climbed into the car and buckled up, once she had, Grayson closed her door and circled the car to get into the driver's seat. She'd had doors opened for her plenty of times before, anytime she went with her parents to attend some event or other they always took a chauffeured car. And even when she'd lived at her father's house one of his staff would always get her car out of the garage for her and open her door as she came down the front steps. Juliet had always hated it, it had made her feel weird to have people waiting on her, but when Grayson opened doors for her it made her feel special, and gave her a fluttery feeling in her stomach.

Grayson Simpson was the exact opposite of everyone she'd ever met.

He seemed to want to help her just to be nice, didn't seem to expect or even want anything in return, and she could swear that when he looked at her, he was thinking about kissing him.

Or maybe that was her projecting her own thoughts onto him.

Because Juliet definitely wanted to kiss the sexy SEAL.

As they drove to his friend Shark's house, he told her all about his friends and their families, but she was finding it hard to concentrate. Juliet wouldn't say that she was a shy person, she enjoyed hanging out with the few friends that she had, but this made her nervous. She wasn't just meeting a couple of Grayson's friends, she was meeting his family, the team who watched his back and kept him alive when he was on a mission, and their wives and kids.

It was a lot of pressure.

She didn't do well under pressure.

In her lap, she tented her hands and began to tap her fingertips together starting with her thumb and working her way down to her pinkie finger then restarting the cycle again.

She didn't always make a good first impression. Sometimes she could keep her OCD tendencies under control but not always, and that made people look at her funny. Then she got self-conscious and awkward, and then they felt bad, and then she felt like she had to avoid them.

"Relax," Grayson said, reaching over to clasp her hands in his. "It'll be fine, they'll like you."

"You can't know that. I don't always make a good first impression, Grayson, and these people are important to you. Plus, I have to make up in their mind for my first impression with you, and it's just a lot of pressure," she explained. She didn't like talking about this kind of stuff, but Grayson was doing a lot for her, and she owed it to him to make sure he knew she wasn't going to mess up with his friends on purpose, it just happened sometimes.

"You're overthinking it, I promise. They understand you broke into my place because you were desperate, they're not going to hold it against you."

Juliet wished she could believe him.

Five minutes later they were pulling up in front of a pretty white colonial with cute dormer windows and a wide porch. There was a nice front yard, and the neighborhood was just the kind she wished she'd grown up in. It looked like the kind of place where everyone knew each other, where there were street parties and kids played in each other's yards, and everyone was happy. Nothing like the cold, empty, lonely mansion where she had spent her childhood.

"You like dogs, right?" Grayson asked as he opened her door for her. "Because Shark's fiancée Claire went through a traumatic ordeal a few months back and she has an assistance dog. Goldilocks is a golden retriever and as sweet as can be, but if you don't like dogs I can ask them to leave her in the backyard or put her in another room."

"I like dogs," Juliet assured him. If she was just going to meet a bunch of dogs she wouldn't be nervous at all.

He didn't pause at the door to knock, just opened it up and strolled inside, guiding her along with him with a hand to the small of her back, and yelled out, "We're here."

"In the back," a voice yelled back. She recognized it as belonging to one of the men she'd met last night, but she wasn't sure she remembered which one.

Grayson led her through the house and into a bright, airy living space down the back. There was a kitchen on one side, a living area on the other, and a large kitchen table in between. The five men from last night were all there along with a woman with the most amazing eyes Juliet had ever seen. One was a golden brown and the other a silvery gray, a woman with long red hair, one with wild blonde curls, and a pretty brunette who was sitting at the table patting the dog's head. The blonde had a baby on her hip who was babbling away, and two toddlers, a boy and a girl, were building with blocks on the floor.

Juliet grimaced, if there was one thing she was not good at it was interacting with small children.

She never knew what to say to them, what to do with them. If adults made her anxious then kids did a hundred times more.

"Everyone, this is Juliet," Grayson announced, already

heading off to kiss his teammate's women on the cheeks. "This is Spider's wife Abby," he said, indicating the woman with heterochromia. "Night's wife Lavender," he said as he kissed the redhead. "Owen's wife Evie and their son Sullivan," he said as he kissed the blonde and then tickled the baby, making him giggle. "And Shark's fiancée Claire," he said, indicating the brunette. "The two munchkins over there playing are Spider and Abby's son RJ, and Night and Lavender's daughter Anastasia. They're only six months apart those two, and already best friends."

"Hi," Juliet said, giving an awkward wave. Her gaze was already roaming around the homey room and noting all the things that weren't aligned with precision at tidy right angles. She didn't mean to do it, it wasn't like she expected everyone else to set up their home the way she did hers, but when she was nervous she couldn't seem to stop herself.

"Hi," Abby said, coming over to give her a warm hug.

"Welcome. Can I get you something to eat or drink?" Claire asked. As she went to stand, the largest man in the room, Shark, put a hand on her shoulder, holding her in place.

"I can get her something," Shark said, then looked at her expectantly.

"Oh, I'm, uh, fine, thanks though," she said. Her hands moved back together as though they had a will of their own. She began to tap her fingertips again, it was an obsession that calmed her when she was anxious, but she knew she looked silly doing it.

"We'll have whatever you guys are having," Grayson said as he took a seat at the table and took the baby from Evie, swinging him above his head and making the little guy giggle. "Come sit down," he said to her when he noticed she was still standing awkwardly in the middle of the room.

No one seemed upset with her over her breaking into

Grayson's house, they all looked welcoming, the guys and their wives, but still she worried. She knew what she'd think in their place, and that was that someone who broke into another person's home had to be up to no good.

"It's okay, Juliet, none of us bite, promise," Evie said with an easy smile.

"I know it can be intimidating to meet so many people all at once, especially those guys," Claire said, waving a hand at the SEAL team. "They scared me when I first met them, although that was probably because they thought I betrayed Logan so they weren't too pleased with me."

She didn't know the stories of how the SEALs had met their partners, but she was intrigued by what Claire had said, and she tentatively moved toward the table and sat down. Without thinking, she arranged the placemat and coaster so they were perfectly aligned with the edge of the table and each other, and were facing so the floral pattern was the right way up.

Juliet could feel eyes on her, watching her movements, and she felt her cheeks burn. They probably thought she was crazy now, her father had, and had never missed an opportunity to berate her when she performed any of her little rituals.

Before she could make an excuse or anyone could comment on it, Juliet felt a tug on her leg and looked down into a pair of bright blue eyes.

"Read," RJ said, thrusting a book into her hand.

"Oh, I'm not …" she trailed off, intending to send him to his mother or father, sure that someone would come in to claim the little boy, not wanting him to be too close to the stranger who'd committed a crime.

But no one came to get him.

She looked over at Grayson, but he was smiling at her and

clearly didn't intend to rescue her from the adorable toddler who was trying to clamber onto her lap.

"Umm, here we go," she said, picking him up and setting him on her lap. "I … I guess I could read you a story."

"Gummilo," RJ said firmly as he smacked the front cover of a book called The Gruffalo.

Anastasia came running over, not wanting to be left out, and before she knew it, Juliet had two toddlers on her lap, a picture book in her hands, and an audience listening to her read, but surprisingly she felt accepted, part of the group, and like no one was judging her.

~

4:49 P.M.

JULIET SET the stack of plates in the cupboard, and Chaos could tell that she was itching to rearrange it so it was organized her way, but she refrained, instead straightening and grabbing a cloth, she proceeded to wipe down Shark and Claire's kitchen sink. He kind of liked knowing that while she had controlled her OCD need to organize his friends' kitchen, she'd had no such qualms about organizing his. Chaos hoped that because she felt comfortable enough with him, she didn't have to hide part of who she was.

He found her OCD fascinating, but suspected that it was only because of the stress that she was under that had her struggling to control her obsessions and compulsions. If he had met her any other time, she probably would have been able to hide that side of herself, at least for a while, and despite the very real danger she was in he found himself pleased that he knew all of her from the beginning.

"There," Juliet said as she folded the cloth perfectly in half then set it down and turned to find all the adults in the room watching her. Immediately her cheeks heated as she realized she'd been obsessively cleaning the kitchen sink, but before he could, Claire shot Juliet a genuine smile.

"Thanks for cleaning up. If you hadn't, Logan would have had to, and then I'd have been stuck listening to him complain," Claire said, giving her fiancé a teasing poke in the side.

Shark's lips quirked up in a rare smile—although his smiles were becoming more frequent the longer he spent with Claire—but he nodded his head agreeably. "Hate doing dishes."

"Oh, well then, you're welcome," Juliet said, relaxing as she realized that his friends weren't going to mock her.

Walking over to her, he slung an arm around Juliet's shoulders. She tensed slightly, but he didn't loosen his hold, and she didn't pull away, which was good because he liked touching her. "Thanks for lunch," he said to Shark and Claire.

"You're welcome, thanks for coming," Claire said.

The guys with kids had already packed them up and left a couple of hours ago, but he and Juliet, and King, had all hung around a while longer. King had a date tonight, and Chaos wanted to take Juliet home and spend a bit of time alone with her, so the party was definitely broken up.

Claire walked them to the door. She was still moving a little slowly, but he was pleased to see more color in her cheeks and a calmness about her that said she was slowly starting to heal from her ordeal. At the door, Chaos kissed Claire's cheek, and she gave him a hug before she turned and hugged Juliet too.

"It was great meeting you, and please know you're welcome here any time, especially if the guys get called away," Claire told Juliet, who looked surprised and a little uncomfortable by the warmness with which his team and their families had embraced her.

"Umm, thanks," Juliet said.

It was cold out, and it looked like more rain was on the way, so Chaos quickly bundled Juliet into his car, then joined her. He noticed that even though she'd already clicked her seatbelt into place her hand lingered on the buckle, tugging on it over and over again as though confirming in her mind that it was truly done up. Not wanting to embarrass her, he didn't let on that he knew, instead he asked, "Why don't we pick up takeaway on the way home? What do you like?"

She shot him a sheepish look. "Just so you know, I'm a really picky eater."

"How picky?"

"Worse than a toddler. I bet RJ and Anastasia have a more eclectic palate than I do."

Chaos would be eternally grateful to the little boy for managing to break the ice and get Juliet to relax and enjoy hanging out with his friends, because he wanted them to become her friends too. Whether she said yes when he asked her out or not, you could never have too many friends, and Claire, Evie, Lavender, and Abigail were all wonderful people, and Juliet would be lucky to have them in her life.

"So, what don't you like?" he asked.

"I don't really like when my food is mixed together or is touching each other. The vegetables that you made for me last night I separated so that the carrots, and broccoli, and cauliflower weren't touching." She looked over at him, waiting to see if he would admit that he'd noticed her do it.

Seeing no reason to lie, Chaos nodded. "I already picked up on the OCD when I saw you'd cleaned my room. You don't have to be embarrassed about it around me."

"My dad hated it," Juliet said softly. "He used to punish me if he caught me performing any rituals."

"Your dad is a …" he trailed off, insulting her father wasn't going to help either of them.

"I know he's not a good man, Grayson. Even before I found out he was involved with the Russian mafia. But I don't know how to not be embarrassed about my OCD, it was such a big deal to my dad, and the more he got angry about it, the more self-conscious about it I became. I didn't understand why I was like that at first, I thought there was something wrong with me. I'd never heard of obsessive-compulsive disorder, and I didn't know there were other people like me out there. It made me feel very alone."

"Is that why you attempted suicide?" he asked gently, reaching out a hand to brush a fingertip across the pale pink scar on Juliet's wrist.

"Yes. It turned out to be the best thing I ever did. My doctor diagnosed me with OCD, and I learned a lot about it, including the fact that there are lots of people with it, and that it doesn't make me crazy. I learned how to control my impulses through cognitive behavior therapy, and I was able to accept the fact that I could have a completely normal life because I am a normal person, I just have OCD."

"I'm sorry it took something so drastic for you to get the answers you needed, but I'm glad you know that having OCD doesn't mean there is anything wrong with you."

"I like pizza," she announced.

"Pizza for dinner then," he said, fighting back a smile. She'd opened up to him more than he thought she would have given they'd known each other less than a day, and she was legitimately scared for her life and wary of anyone.

"I only like cheese pizza," she added.

"Of course you do, little cat burglar," he said with a laugh.

"Are you ever going to stop calling me that?" Juliet demanded, but he could see she was fighting a smile and Chaos found himself wanting to get more out of her than her usual half-smile. He wanted to see her entire face light up with delight, and hear her laugh with all the innocent joy of a baby.

"Nope, you better get used to it, princess."

She rolled her eyes, but her hand left the seatbelt buckle to settle in her lap, and he noticed that she didn't do the finger tapping thing he'd noticed she did when she was feeling anxious. Counting that as a win, Chaos reminded himself to take baby steps. It sounded like Juliet's life hadn't been a happy one. She'd been made to feel like something was wrong with her, and had her own father blatantly not accept her. Add to that the fact she'd been sold to a Russian mafia prince and had spent the last three weeks living on the streets, and she really didn't have anything to smile about.

They'd get there though.

Making people smile was who he was, who he had always been. Anyone who had known him as a kid would have been shocked to find out that he had joined the military and become a SEAL. But despite the horrors he'd witnessed and experienced, nothing could kill that part of him. There were a lot of horrible things in the world, but you could undo a little of that evil with a smile.

"Okay, we'll get a half cheese, half meat lovers pizza," he said as he took the next left and headed toward his favorite pizza place.

"Actually, that will mean that my half will taste all meaty and icky," she said, scrunching up her cute little nose.

Chaos laughed heartily at the look on her face. "Okay,

princess, we'll get two separate pizzas and we'll make sure we don't put one box on top of the other so none of the icky meat smell gets into your precious cheese pizza. Do I even want to ask what you want to have for dessert?"

"That's easy," Juliet said.

"With you? Why do I get the feeling that nothing is easy with you?" he teased.

"You keep calling me princess, just gotta live up to my name," she said with a smirk, making him laugh again.

"Okay, princess, what's for dessert?"

"Anything chocolatey," Juliet replied.

"My princess' wishes are my commands."

CHAPTER 3

January 19th

8:54 A.M.

"I COULD HAVE STAYED at your place this morning," Juliet said as Grayson parked his car outside his friend Spider's house. She hadn't been alone once in the last thirty-six hours, and she needed some time to herself.

It wasn't that she wasn't grateful for everything Grayson was doing for her because she was—she absolutely was. Nor was it because she didn't enjoy his company because she did—way more than she should—she was just used to being on her own. As a child, her father controlled who, when, and how she spent time with other kids. He even managed to find ways to control her while she was away at boarding school. Now she had a few friends of her own, a girl from boarding school who also had a controlling father who she'd remained close with, and she was friends with her personal assistant, although of course, the fact that she was the boss put a barrier between them. Another single woman lived in the same building as she did who had also become a friend. Besides that, there were acquaintances she'd spend time with at formal functions, but nobody who she spent this many hours straight with.

The more time she spent with Grayson, the more she liked him, and the harder she knew it would be to leave. But at the same time, the pressure of trying to control her OCD was wearing her down. If this hadn't come on the back of three weeks running for her life, barely eating, sleeping outdoors in the elements, she would have done a much better job, but the truth was she was exhausted. A kind of bone deep weariness that left her feeling vulnerable.

"Until we get a handle on your situation I'd rather not have you be alone," Grayson told her.

"Oh." It was hard to argue with that. And in light of how lonely and scared she'd been while she lived on the streets, maybe she shouldn't complain about being around people twenty-four-seven. Given a choice, she would pick Grayson and his friends every time. Although she'd been anxious and nervous about meeting them and knew she hadn't made the best first impression, they had all gone out of their way to make her feel comfortable and accepted. "I don't want them to feel like I'm intruding though."

"They don't feel that way," he assured her.

He was no doubt right, didn't mean her anxiety melted away. "I really like your friends."

"*Our* friends," he corrected.

Juliet scoffed at that. "They barely know me, they're your friends."

"They'll get to know you."

Would they?

She had no idea how long she'd be around. Why should his friends make any effort to really get to know her?

Grayson rounded the car to open her door for her, but his large body blocked her from walking down the front path to Spider and Abigail's front door. "Have lunch with me today?"

"Sure, if you're done with your PT we can get lunch on the way back to your place," she said distractedly, trying to mentally prepare herself for hanging out with his teammates' wives without the comforting and reassuring presence of the man standing before her.

"No, princess," he said, gently grasping her chin between his thumb and forefinger. "I mean, can I take you out to lunch today?"

She gaped at him when she realized what he was asking. "You mean like on a date?"

"Yes." The corners of his green eyes crinkled in amusement.

"But you don't even know me. Why would you ask me out?"

"I believe it's customary to go on a date to get to know a prospective girlfriend," he said, clearly finding her hilarious.

"Prospective girlfriend?"

"Unless you're opposed to the idea," he said, giving her the chance to gracefully decline. Juliet knew that if she did, he wouldn't hold it against her and would still help her with the situation her father had gotten her into. And that made the answer easy.

"No," she said slowly. "I'm not opposed to the idea." Juliet didn't date a lot, it was hard when your father still tried to micromanage every aspect of your life. The few times she'd gone out with men her father hadn't selected, she'd had a nice time but she hadn't felt that spark. Grayson gave her the spark just by being in the same room as her let alone when he touched her.

When he touched her Juliet felt alive. She felt excited about her future. She felt like energy was running through her veins like she could do anything, like she was invincible. It was an intoxicating feeling and she didn't want it to end.

"Good, I'll be here to pick you up at one, have fun." He leaned in and for a moment she was sure he was going to kiss her, and he did … on the tip of her nose. Then he was gone, and Juliet found herself staring after him, watching until his car disappeared around the corner.

There was something so light about Grayson Simpson, it was hard to believe he spent his life working to rid the world of evil as a Navy SEAL.

Shaking her head, she turned and walked toward the house. Apparently the women of Grayson's teammates were close and liked to hang out together whenever they could. From what she'd learned yesterday, Abby was a ballet teacher, Lavender worked as a receptionist at the same dance studio where Abby taught, and Evie was an emergency room nurse. Claire was a psychologist who was a civilian contractor for the military, although she was currently taking extended leave as she recovered from injuries she'd sustained in Afghanistan when she'd become a target for a terrorist cell. From what she'd gathered, all of the women had been through traumatic events, and yet they all seemed so … normal. And nice. She admired them and it was kind of nice to have them welcome her into their circle, even if she and Grayson weren't together.

At least not yet.

That thought had her smiling as she knocked on the door.

The door swung open a moment later, and Abigail's

nervous face met her. The sight of the woman looking so uncomfortable made Juliet immediately uncomfortable.

"Umm, sorry," she stammered, "Grayson said you knew I was coming, but I can leave if you want."

"What? Oh, no, of course not, come on in. Evie isn't joining us today she had to work, but Lavender and Claire are in the kitchen." Abigail offered a smile. "Sorry, we knew you were coming, it's not that, it's just …"

"Abby might be pregnant," Lavender said, sticking her head around the corner.

"What? Oh, that's … exciting?" Juliet wasn't quite sure if the woman was pleased or not about the possibility of being pregnant, and she didn't want to say the wrong thing.

"She's kind of in shock about it," Lavender explained.

"Not kind of," Abigail corrected with a grim smile as she closed the door and led Juliet down to the kitchen.

"You don't want another baby?" she asked as they joined Lavender and Claire.

"I do, but we were going to wait until RJ was two before we started trying," Abby explained.

"He's nearly two," Claire said, "he's twenty-one months already."

"I know, I don't know where the time has gone." Abby smiled at RJ who was busy playing cars with Anastasia. "If I'm pregnant I will be excited, it's just, two kids is a big responsibility."

"Does Spider know that you think you might be pregnant?" Juliet asked.

"No, he doesn't, I didn't want to tell him until I knew for sure one way or the other, but I couldn't take the test alone, I needed my girls here with me," Abigail replied. "Ugh, the suspense is killing me."

"Well, you're going to find out in one minute now," Claire said, glancing at the large clock hanging on the wall.

"I just took a pregnancy test before you got here," Abby explained. "Evie was on a break at the hospital so she's on the phone. We were hoping you'd get here before we get the results."

"You were?" Juliet asked, surprised that they'd care one way or the other, they'd only met her one day ago.

"Of course," Lavender said like it was obvious.

"But I'm not, you know, one of you," she said with an awkward shrug.

"Not yet," Abby said with a grin.

"What do you mean?"

"Well, you and Chaos are a couple, right?" Claire asked.

"No."

"Not *yet*," Abby corrected. "He definitely likes you."

"I haven't seen him this excited about a woman since I've known him," Lavender said. "And that's going on seven years now."

"He did ask me out," she admitted, the words out of her mouth before she'd even thought about it. She liked these women and could actually see herself becoming good friends with them, and while she still felt like a bit of an outsider, she could see that changing if things did get serious with Grayson.

"I knew it," Abby said delightedly.

The others were grinning at her as well, and Juliet felt herself blush. These women seemed genuinely enthusiastic about the idea of her and Grayson as a couple. She could tell how much they respected and cared about him, and if they liked the idea of her as Grayson's partner then maybe that meant they kind of respected her too. That was a nice thought, she wasn't sure that anyone had ever respected her like that before.

"We only just met, there's no way to know if it will work out," Juliet said, more to remind herself than for the other women's benefit.

"It's time," Evie's voice floated up from the phone that was sitting on the kitchen counter.

Abigail dragged in a deep breath and then picked up the pregnancy test sitting on a towel on the counter beside the phone. She looked at it then gave them all a shaky smile. "It's positive. Ryder and I are going to have another baby."

From the look on her face it was hard to gauge if she was excited or not. Apparently, Juliet wasn't the only one who thought so because Lavender reached out and touched Abby's hand. "And you're happy?"

A grin broke out on Abigail's face and her unusual eyes twinkled merrily. "I'm thrilled."

"Then yay!" Lavender threw her arms around Abby.

Claire joined the hug and Evie was cheering and clapping from the phone, but Juliet stood back, not wanting to intrude.

The others were having none of that though. Claire reached out and pulled her into the circle, and Juliet felt that right down to her soul. They hadn't just included her in the hug, sharing Abby's joy with her, they had welcomed her into their family, and for the first time she felt like she actually had people who cared about her instead of wanting to use her.

~

12:36 P.M.

. . .

"I JUST HEARD BACK FROM EAGLE," Chaos announced to his team as he slipped his cell phone back into his pocket. They'd just finished PT, and if he didn't hurry, he was going to be late picking Juliet up for their date, but he needed to keep his team up to date because if things went bad he'd be relying on them to help him keep Juliet safe.

"He have any intel on the Fedorovs?" team leader Fox asked. They were all friends with Eagle and his siblings who owned Prey Security, the best private security and black ops company in the country, and they all knew that there wasn't anything that the man couldn't find out. He had contacts everywhere, in every country across the globe. He was the man to go to if you needed information.

"You really need to ask that?" Chaos asked with a grin.

"So, what did he say?" Spider asked.

"He said that word on the street is that the Fedorov family wants to expand beyond Russia, they want to put roots down in the US," he explained.

"What better way to do that than to marry an American citizen, get yourself a green card," Night said.

Chaos nodded. "It looks like the Fedorov family bailed Arthur York out of some financial trouble about a year ago and now own half of his company."

"You think he offered them his daughter to get his company back?" King asked.

"That would be my guess," he agreed. "If they're serious about expanding into the US then they're not going to back down. They need Juliet if they want to stay here legitimately. Of course they could just move here anyway, but the Fedorov family as always made a point of appearing legitimate on the surface so I'm guessing they're not going to let Juliet go."

"She's definitely in danger," Fox said.

"If they find her," Night added. "So far it doesn't look like they know where she is."

"How long can we keep it that way though? Juliet isn't going to want to give up her life and stay in hiding. I don't know if she plans to go back to designing jewelry, but if she does, she's going to have to use her name and experience to get a job, and even if she wants to do something else she's going to need to use her real name. Plus, she's going to want to get her stuff from her house eventually, and get access to her bank accounts, drive a car, and use her license. She can't run forever, we need to figure out a way to face this problem head-on," Chaos said. Juliet deserved the chance to finally get to live her life the way she wanted, to get out from under her father's thumb. He was going to do everything within his power to make sure she got that opportunity.

"We'll figure this out," Fox assured him, and the rest of his team nodded their agreement.

"Now go, get your girl, take her on your first date," King said with an encouraging smile.

"And don't let this mess with her father ruin the mood," Night added.

"Nothing is ruining our first date," he assured his friends.

Saying goodbye, Chaos grabbed his gear and headed for his truck. He had a simple first date planned. From the time he'd spent with Juliet so far he'd learned that she hated how pretentious her father was, and that she'd disliked having to get all dressed up for events or dates with the men her father set her up with. So he'd decided to do the exact opposite, he hoped she liked it.

It had been a long time since he'd been nervous on a date. While he didn't date as much as their resident ladies' man King, he loved women, not just sex, but hanging out and having fun, but the only woman he'd ever been serious with turned out to be married. That was almost two years ago, and after being duped like that it had taken the shine off relationships, and he'd been keeping things casual ever since.

Lavender and Claire had already gone back to their respective houses, so he was the only one other than Spider to head to Spider and Abigail's house. He got there second because he had to stop by his place to grab some things, and Juliet was already waiting on the porch, making him frown as he got out of the car. He couldn't see either of his friends kicking Juliet out, but he couldn't think of another reason she wouldn't be waiting inside.

"Abby is pregnant," Juliet squealed when he was halfway to her. She was smiling, and her green eyes were twinkling in a way he hadn't seen before. "She's telling Spider right now, that's why I said I'd wait outside for you."

"Abby's pregnant? That's awesome," he said, grabbing Juliet and pulling her in for a hug. "I didn't even know they were trying."

"They weren't. Abby said they weren't going to try until RJ was at least two, but I guess things didn't work out that way," Juliet said, a conspiratorial smile on her face, and he could tell she was tickled pink about being included in the women's circle. "She's pretty excited though, and I wanted her and Spider to have that time alone to share together without having me hanging around."

"I'm thrilled for all three of them. RJ is going to be an amazing big brother, he already loves taking care of Anastasia and Sully. If Abby has a girl I think RJ is going to be one overprotective brother," he said, already imagining it. "And I think Spider will lose it if it's a girl. He was thrilled to have a boy, said he didn't think he could cope with a daughter who would one day be a teenager who'd date."

"It must be nice having siblings, I always wanted a

brother or sister, I didn't care which, just someone to hang out with," Juliet said with a wistful smile.

"Siblings aren't all they're cracked up to be, I can tell you," he said with a grimace. "I have two sisters, the older one mothered me all the time, and the younger one is the sassiest, most annoying little thing ever."

"And you love them both to pieces, don't you?"

"Guilty as charged." Chaos snagged her hand and led her down to the car. "For you," he said, grabbing the bouquet of flowers off the passenger seat when he opened the door.

"Oh, so pretty," Juliet said, gifting him another smile. "How did you know daisies are my favorite?"

Because they were beautiful, and simple, and sweet, just like Juliet was. Instead of telling her that he said, "Lucky guess."

"So, where are we going for lunch?" Juliet asked once they were both buckled in and he'd started driving.

"Ever had fish and chips before?"

"Like English fish and chips?"

"The very same."

"No, I've never had that before. Any time I've been to England we've always stayed in some fancy hotel in London, eaten at five-star restaurants." She made a face as she said it and it was clear Juliet was a camping, picnic, jeans and a t-shirt kind of girl, yet her father had clothed her in glitz and glamor refusing to let the real Juliet spring free.

"Do you eat fish? And fries?" He knew Juliet said she was picky, but he hoped she'd be happy to eat that because he wanted to share something from his past with her.

"I like both," she said.

"Great, this place we're going to is one we used to go to a lot when I was a kid. It's right near the beach, and my family always used to take our fish and chips over and sit on the sand and eat. Then we'd make sandcastles and go swimming. I know it's too cold to swim today, but I thought we could still hang out on the beach for a while, maybe build a sandcastle, watch the sunset."

"That sounds wonderful. I've never been to the beach before," Juliet admitted.

"Never?"

"Nope. I mean, I grew up in Orange County, but my dad didn't like the beach, thought it was too common, so I was never allowed to go. I've always wanted to run my bare toes through the sand and to stand in the ocean, feel the waves, it must feel so wonderful and refreshing."

"There's nothing like the ocean," he agreed. Even as a kid he had been drawn to the water and when he decided to join the military it had seemed only natural for him to join the Navy and eventually become a SEAL.

"You and your family went to the beach a lot?"

"No, not a lot. Actually, usually it was kind of a special treat," he said.

Noting the sadness in his voice, she turned to look at him. "Why was it a special treat if you lived so close to the beach?"

"My little sister had leukemia. She was first diagnosed when she was four, I was six, and my older sister was eight. My little sister, Lizzie, didn't go into remission until she was thirteen, so most of my childhood was spent being shuffled around between babysitters and school and relatives. My parents weren't around much, their focus was Lizzie, and Tillie and I were okay with that, at least we were healthy. Lizzie was so brave, and our parents gave us every spare second of time they had, they just didn't have a lot to give, so yeah, we missed out on some things, but in the end, Lizzie recovered and that's all that matters."

"You were a good son, a good brother."

"I used to make it my mission to make Lizzie laugh. Sometimes she was so sick she couldn't get out of bed, couldn't eat, couldn't play, but if I could make her smile then I counted that day a win."

"Your family was lucky to have you."

"And I was lucky to have them," he said. While his childhood had been difficult, and a seemingly endless black cloud had hovered over them, he'd learned to find joy and pleasure in the small things. A simple joke, a harmless prank, anything he could do to ease his sister's suffering made a little sunshine shine into their lives. In the end, his family had loved one another, and that was more than he could say about Juliet's family.

~

1:42 P.M.

"Do you trust me to order, or do you want to look at the menu?" Grayson asked.

Juliet looked over at him, his face was so open, so honest, and he'd shared so much with her about who he was and what his life had been like, and she'd only known him two days. That openness inspired in her a mirroring of trust, instead of guarding her heart and her personality so closely, knowing the people around her cared little about either, she felt herself wanting to lay everything bare.

"I trust you."

Grayson shot her one of his easy grins, and she found herself smiling back. "Perfect. There's a coat for you in the back, scarf and beanie too, and a blanket, grab them and go wait on the sidewalk. The store is tiny and there's not much space to wait inside. Don't go onto the sand yet though."

"Why not?"

"Because I want to be there to see the look on your face the first time you experience the beach," he replied.

Thinking that was sweet, Juliet rugged up and grabbed the picnic blanket while Grayson disappeared inside a tiny shop. She watched as an elderly man rounded the counter to drag him into a hug and she couldn't help but smile. Of all the houses in the area she could have broken into, she was so glad that it was his. Well, really she wished she could take that back so his first impression of her wasn't as a criminal, but he seemed not to care, so she should probably stop worrying about it.

Juliet had seen the ocean many times, but it had always been from a distance. Her father hadn't thought it high class enough, and her mother had hated anything even remotely messy, which included sand and salty water, but she'd always been intrigued by the power of the water, the endless blue that met the sky at the horizon.

She crossed the street to stand on the sidewalk, itching to put her feet on the sand but determined to wait for Grayson. She wanted to share this experience with him. Actually, she wanted to share a whole lot more with him, but the old fear inside her that she wasn't good enough for a man like him had her holding back.

"You ready?" Grayson asked, appearing beside her with a box wrapped in paper.

"Yep." She took the hand he offered and stepped out onto the sand. It was a little awkward to walk on because it was so soft and moved beneath her feet, and she couldn't wait to yank off her socks and sneakers and sink her toes right into the white, silky-looking sand.

"So?"

"It's wonderful, I can't wait to pull my shoes off and run my fingers through it," she replied, beaming up at him.

"First rule of the beach, sand gets everywhere. And I mean *every*where. It's also almost impossible to get rid of, so no touching till you're finished with your food."

"Good to know. I definitely don't want to eat sand with my fish and chips." She made a face and Grayson laughed as he spread out the blanket for them.

They both sat down and Grayson unwrapped the food. There were thick, crunchy-looking fries, two large pieces of fried fish, and big circles, battered the same way as the fish, but she wasn't sure what they were.

"What are these?" she asked, picking one up.

"Potato cakes. It's a thin slice of potato, covered in batter and then deep-fried along with the rest of the food. Try it, they're really good."

Juliet loved potatoes, so she took a big bite and then moaned in delight. "You're right, this is amazing."

They ate in companionable silence. There was so much to look at that Juliet was focused on taking it all in. The sky was cloudy and gray which reflected back in the water giving it a gray-blue look. The waves crashed consistently against the sand with a swirl of white foam. Despite the cold day there were still plenty of people about, some like them were eating, others were walking along with dogs or kids, some were tossing balls or frisbees. There were a couple of kids building a huge sandcastle, and a dog that was running around frantically, barking at the waves, running at them, then backing off before the water touched him, and wagging his tail like the ocean was his new best friend.

It all felt so real and raw, experiencing nature at its finest and she couldn't wait to become a part of it.

"All done," Grayson said as he handed her the last chip.

"Can I take my shoes off now?" she asked as she ate it.

"Yes, you can." Grayson was smiling at her affectionately, obviously amused by her enthusiasm.

As she undid her laces and pulled off her sneakers, then her socks, sticking them inside her shoes to keep them clean, Juliet felt like a child as she moved first one foot and then the other off the blanket and into the sand. The sand was soft on her feet, and she dug her toes in then lifted them and watched as the sand slid down her skin. A few grains stayed on her skin and when the sun broke through the clouds they seemed to sparkle like glitter.

"Want to go put your feet in the ocean?"

"Is that even a question?" she said as she scrambled to her feet. The sand moved with each step she took, and her feet sunk into it, but the closer they got to the water the firmer the sand became until it was almost like walking on solid ground, except for the fact that each footprint was clearly marked.

At the water's edge, she paused to roll up the bottoms of her jeans and kind of wished they were here on a warm day so they could jump into the waves and swim. Still she could come back whenever she wanted. Now that she had finally broken free of her father's hold on her there was no way she was going back. Let him try and get her committed with his fake doctor's notes, she'd fight him with everything she had, and for the first time that included a group of friends who would have her back.

"Whoa," Juliet said, throwing out a hand to rest on Grayson's forearm as she stepped into the water. "The sand moves out from under your feet," she said, surprised that she needed to try to keep her balance. She'd never felt anything like this before. The only time she'd ever been in the water was a swimming pool, but that was so contained, and the ocean was so wild.

"The water gets sucked back out and takes the sand with it," he explained as he moved his arm so they were holding hands.

"It feels so weird," she said with a startled giggle as the sand beneath her feet disappeared and she wobbled precariously. She looked over at Grayson who was watching her with an odd expression on his face. "What?" she asked, self-conscious now.

He reached out to tuck a stray lock of hair behind her ear, his knuckles lingering on her skin in a gentle caress. "It's the first time I've heard you laugh. You have a pretty laugh."

Her cheeks heated but she smiled at his words. That was very possibly the sweetest thing anyone had ever said to her. Her parents hadn't been big on sentiment, and they'd never told her that they loved her, although that was no doubt because they didn't. In fact, Grayson had shown her more care and affection in two days than her parents had in twenty-five years.

"Thank you," she said softly.

"You're a beautiful woman, Juliet, and I can't wait to kiss you." He leaned down, and she sucked in a breath as she waited for his lips to meet hers, but instead he kissed her forehead, then tugged her over to where the sand was half wet, half dry.

"Are we going to build a sandcastle?" she asked, fighting disappointment at the non-kiss kiss. Grayson had said he wanted to kiss her, that he would be kissing her, so she had to trust that he was waiting until the timing was perfect.

"Better, we're going to build a ball run."

"A ball run?"

"My sisters and I used to do it all the time. We used to try to outdo each other, make the biggest ball run with the most twists and turns, bridges and tunnels, it was so much fun," he gushed.

She couldn't help but laugh again at the look of enthusiasm on Grayson's face. "Okay, then. And do we actually have any balls?"

Grayson winked at her, and she blushed as she realized that she'd unintentionally been flirty. Then he reached into his pocket and pulled out two tennis balls. "Yeah, we do."

She laughed again when he went straight to work, scooping up huge handfuls of sand and piling them up high. Juliet watched him for a moment before she dropped to her knees in the sand and began to make her own large pile of sand. It didn't take her long to realize just how sticky sand could be, it got under her nails, it caked the knees and bottom half of her jeans, she had smudges on her cheeks, and the cuffs of her sweater and coat, but she didn't care, she wasn't sure she'd ever had this much fun in her life.

Juliet lost all track of time, and she had no idea what she was doing, but she watched Grayson and she soon got the hang of what he was doing. When they both stood up a couple of hours later, her ball run was nowhere near as good as Grayson's, which was huge and intricate and clearly showed he'd done this before.

"Let's do yours first," Grayson said, handing her a ball.

"Okay, but I wish mine looked more like yours."

"You'll get better at it. Not as good as me, but better." Grayson gave her a smirk that had heat firing through her body. He better be planning on kissing her soon because the more time they spent together the more desperately she wanted him to.

Her ball run might not be as fancy as Grayson's, but she'd put in a couple of loop-de-loops and a pretty cool tunnel, and it took her ball at least a full minute to get to the end.

"That was pretty good, you have a designer's eye."

"Thanks," she said with a grin. It was so nice to get a compliment even over silly fun stuff. "Your turn."

Grayson's ball twisted and twirled around his run for almost five minutes before it finally got to the bottom.

"Wow, that was amazing. I have no idea how you managed to get so many turns like that. And that bridge is super cool, I don't know how you got the sand to stay up like that. And your tunnel has to go for like a whole two or three yards," Juliet gushed.

"Practice, princess, practice makes perfect."

"I always hated that saying," she said with a mock shudder. "Do you know how many hours I had to spend practicing the piano, or the violin, or the harp? Or learning Spanish, and Chinese, and Latin? Or painting and drawing so I could perfect my skills?"

"And I bet now you can do all those things."

Juliet shrugged. "I'd rather have spent a lot of that time having fun."

"We're making up for lost time now, princess," Grayson said, reaching out to cup her cheek in his sandy hand.

"Yeah, we are," she agreed.

"The sun sets in an hour or so. You want to hang out here, watch it?"

"I couldn't think of a more perfect way to end this date."

Grayson took her hand and led her back to their picnic blanket, and they sat down side by side. He must have brought another blanket with him because he wrapped it around their shoulders and she snuggled against him, resting her head on his shoulder. Neither of them spoke, they didn't have to, they were both content to just be and soak up the other's company.

The wind swirled around them, people laughed and talked and enjoyed the atmosphere, and Juliet just watched everything happening and felt like her entire being was unraveling into a state of relaxation she hadn't realized existed. She'd been so tense her whole life, struggling to live up to the expectations of people who were going to find fault with her regardless of what she did.

But sitting here on the sand, watching as the sun slowly sank into the ocean streaking the sky with pink, purple, and gold, with Grayson's arm pleasantly heavy against her shoulders, Juliet felt like she might have actually found her place in the world.

A place where she could be happy.

CHAPTER 4

January 20th

7:27 A.M.

ARTHUR PACED NERVOUSLY around his study.

Okay, so he was way past nervous.

He'd definitely reached the stage where he was one step away from full-blown panic.

It had been three days since he'd last spoken with Dimitri Fedorov, and he still hadn't been able to get his hands on his daughter.

At least Juliet seemed to have stayed in one place this time. Maybe she thought she was safe now, she'd been gone for almost three weeks and he hadn't found her, so perhaps she thought he had stopped looking.

If that was the case, she was going to be sorely mistaken.

There was no way he wasn't going to find her and bring

her back. He couldn't. There was no way he was sacrificing himself for the child who had disappointed him and embarrassed him for the last quarter of a century.

Juliet *would* marry Dimitri.

It was the only way he could get back the company he had poured his blood, sweat, and tears into. And with the position as Dimitri Fedorov's father-in-law, there wouldn't be any height he couldn't climb to. People would scramble to do his bidding when they found out he was connected to the Russian mafia, and he couldn't wait to start exerting that position for everything he could get out of it.

Desperation was clawing at him, he could feel it like it was a physical being on his back, wrapping its hands around his neck and squeezing the life out of him. He had to get Juliet, there was only so long the Fedorovs were going to be patient with him, and if he got them off his side he would pay for it with a pound of flesh.

Literally.

The Fedorovs had risen to power because they were cold, heartless, and ruthless. They demolished anyone who got in their way without discrimination, young, old, male, female, innocent or not, it didn't matter to them, if you found yourself in their path, whether by your own doing or someone else's, you would be shown no mercy. While threats usually accomplished their goals, he knew they wouldn't hesitate to follow through if they didn't get the result they wanted.

One of their favorite ways of doing that was to remove a pound of their victim's flesh.

"Where are you?" he muttered. He'd narrowed down Juliet's general location, she was in San Diego, and she was in the same ten miles or so that she had been in for the last three days. On paper, it sounded easy to find her, send men to the location, search for her, and bring her back here. But in reality, there were a lot of places where she could be in that ten mile radius that made locating her time-consuming and tedious.

The opening of his study door had him whirling around about to lay into whichever of his staff had thought it was okay to interrupt him. They all had strict instructions that he was never to be disturbed while he was in here, this was his sanctuary and he didn't like it to be breached.

The insult that was about to be flung at the intruder died on his lips when he saw who was standing there.

Alexi and Dimitri Fedorov.

Both were dressed in matching expensive suits in dove gray, their dark hair was combed neatly into place, and both sets of dark brown eyes were fixed on him with a lethalness that made him squirm. He was used to being the one who delivered those death stares at the men or women who failed to live up to his expectations, but being on the other end of one made him both uncomfortable and fearful.

"You have not yet produced my future daughter-in-law," Alexi said, strolling across the study like he owned the place. The older man stopped in front of his liquor cabinet and helped himself to a glass of Arthur's favorite whisky.

He fought against the urge to tell Alexi to take his hands off things that didn't belong to him and pursed his lips together to keep silent. Further antagonizing either Fedorov right now wasn't wise. Instead, he watched as Dimitri strolled around the room, stopping in front of the only photo of Juliet. Just because he couldn't think of a family he would rather marry his daughter into, didn't mean he appreciated them strolling into his home like they owned the place.

"I know she's in San Diego," he replied, sinking into his favorite chair and pretending that he was relaxed and uncaring of the two intruders.

"If you know where she is, why haven't you gone and gotten her?" Alexi demanded.

"I have men down there, but as I was telling your son the other day it's not that simple. The tracking implant is old, it tells me approximately where she is but not her exact location," Arthur explained.

"And why did you not replace the tracking device with a newer one when the technology became available?" Alexi asked, bringing his drink with him as he took the leather armchair on the other side of the fireplace.

"Because there was no way to do that without her knowledge. And I never expected that Juliet would run, she's always been fairly obedient, and I believed the threat of having her forcibly committed meant she would take the obvious choice." He honestly had no idea what had possessed his daughter to behave like this. Despite her embarrassing behavior and the humiliation of her suicide attempt as a teen, Juliet had always been one to take the road of least resistance, and he didn't understand why she would risk his wrath—and that of the Fedorov family—and the possibility of spending years in a psychiatric facility drugged out of her mind, by running.

"Obviously, you do not know your daughter as well as you thought you did," Alexi said, and Arthur had to bite back another retort about the man stating the obvious.

"As I said, I have men looking for her, they will find her and bring her back here. Then your son can take her and do whatever he deems necessary to make sure she doesn't run again."

"I have grown weary of waiting for you to produce my fiancée," Dimitri said, speaking for the first time. "She is a beautiful woman, and I wish to take her back to Russia with me and make her my wife. I feel like we have been patient with you, given you plenty of time to find Juliet on your own, but our patience has now run out. If you don't produce Juliet by the end of the day tomorrow we will be forced to take matters into our own hands. Do you know what that means, Mr. York?"

Arthur swallowed audibly and nodded.

Yes.

He understood.

All too well.

Unless he found Juliet and brought her back here, handing her over to the Fedorovs, he would be the one who would suffer.

"I will find her," he promised. He wasn't sure how he would do that, but he would rally every single one of his men and send them all to San Diego. He'd go there himself as well, surely between all of them they'd be able to find where his daughter was hiding.

"You better," Alexi said, those cold, empty eyes staring unblinkingly at him.

"I will," he vowed. It wasn't like he had a choice. There was no way he was taking a beating and losing a pound of flesh because his daughter was acting like a teenager attempting to exert her independence. Juliet should have known her place, and if she didn't, when she was sent to Russia with her fiancé and his family she would certainly learn it. It would be tortured into her until any thoughts of independence fled her mind and she became the perfect Fedorov wife.

"We will wait to return to home until we have my son's bride in our possession," Alexi said. The threat hung ominously in the air, what he hadn't said as clear as what he had said.

If he didn't procure his daughter and hand her over to the

Russians, they would not return home until they had made sure he had suffered for his failure and for bringing disrespect to the family by ruining Dimitri's upcoming wedding.

"I think we will stay here while you go and find my fiancée," Dimitri said with a smile as he took a seat on the couch. "It is so much nicer to stay with family, and I would love to spend some time getting to know my future mother-in-law better."

If there was one thing in this world that Arthur York actually cared about besides money, power, and himself, it was the wife who had stood by him for the last thirty years. It was one thing for the Fedorovs to hurt his daughter, one thing to threaten him, but quite another to bring his wife into it.

Maybe it was time he started considering a solution to the problem of the Fedorov family.

Perhaps once Juliet wed Dimitri, and he had a claim on the family name and business, he might find a way to eliminate Alexi and Dimitri. At the helm of one of the world's most notorious and wealthy crime families he would be unstoppable.

11:52 A.M.

"IT'S SUCH A NICE DAY, it's almost hard to believe it's winter," Juliet said as she stared out the car window.

Chaos watched her with a smile on his face. Sure she was right about the weather, it was a gorgeous winter's day, but his attention was focused firmly on the passenger in his car. He couldn't seem to get enough of looking at her, it wasn't just that she was beautiful, it was that the more time they spent together, the more he saw her barriers start to slip away. She was starting to trust him, and he knew for a fact that there hadn't been many people to trust in her tightly controlled life, and that she was letting her guard down for him made him feel ten feet tall.

Yesterday at the beach she'd been like a kid, so excited about everything from walking in the sand, to standing in the shallows, to watching the sunset. Seeing that twinkle in her eyes, the smile on her face, hearing the sound of her laugh, had touched him deeply, and he knew that Juliet had the power to make him fall hard and fast.

He was trying to go slow, keep things simple, but also make it clear that he was interested in her. If she didn't reciprocate those feelings he would never hold it against her, he'd still do everything he could to make sure she was safe and help her get back on her feet, but he only had to see the way she looked at him when she thought he wasn't watching to know that she felt the same spark between them that he did.

The spark went deeper than mere attraction, she pulled out the same protectiveness from him that his sisters did. He wanted to keep her safe, wanted to wipe away every bad thing that had ever happened to her so she never had to feel sadness again.

"What?" she asked, turning to look at him. "Why are you staring at me?"

"Because you're nice to stare at," he said.

"You're driving though, shouldn't your eyes be on the road," Juliet said, but he saw the delight in her eyes.

He saw the hunger there too, she wanted him to kiss her, but he had been trying to keep things casual for now. She was under enough stress without feeling like he was pressuring her. It wasn't like they had to rush anything, they had the rest of their lives to explore this thing between them. They didn't have to jump into the deep end.

"Haven't crashed the car yet, princess." Chaos winked at her but then did return his full attention to the road.

"Yet," she muttered, but he heard the humor in her tone.

He wanted to keep her like this forever, lighter, freer, no longer under the control of her father. "Can I ask you a question?"

"Of course," she sounded surprised. "You can ask me anything."

Chaos caught the fact that she began doing her finger tapping thing again and knew she was worried he would ask her something about her OCD, possibly in a derogatory manner, but she should know by now he had already accepted that side of her. "If you could do anything in the world, what would you do?"

"Oh." The surprise hadn't gone from her tone, but her hands relaxed. "Well, I don't mind designing jewelry for my father, I like being creative, and it is kind of cool to see a celebrity or royalty wearing something I made. But if I could do anything I always thought I'd be good at helping people organize their homes or offices. I like organizing things, it's fun for me, but all my things are already organized, so helping others would be like a win-win. I get the fun of doing something I love, and they get help organizing all their things. I'd be my own boss so I wouldn't have to take orders from anyone, and I'd be able to set my own hours so I'd actually have time to maybe have some hobbies or something." She shrugged like maybe he'd think her idea was stupid. "Anyway, it's just my dream job, I don't know if it will ever come about."

"I think you would be amazing at that." He reached out to grab her hand, holding it in his then resting their joined hands on his thigh. “Dreams are important, they give you something to strive for, something to focus on.”

“What's your dream?”

“Well, I already have my dream job, and I love my friends and my family. I think the only thing I'm missing in my life is a family of my own.”

“You want to get married and have kids?”

“Always have. I knew once I decided to become a SEAL that it could be tough. I'm gone a lot, and most of the time I couldn’t tell my partner where I was and what I was doing. That takes a toll on a relationship. Plus, it's not always easy dealing with the things I see and do, whoever I was to marry would have to be able to deal with it too. I guess it takes a special kind of woman to be married to a SEAL.”

“Abby, Lavender, Evie, and Claire all seem to be able to handle it.”

“They're all special women,” he said. “It's why I love them all like sisters, they’re good for my brothers and they make our team stronger. They’ve all been through ordeals, and while I hate that they suffered, I think it gave them a bit of an understanding of what we do.”

“Do you think they wouldn’t be able to deal with your jobs if they hadn't been through those ordeals?”

Sensing she was feeling him out to see if he believed she had what it took to marry a SEAL, he smiled at her and squeezed her hand. “Not at all. They’re all strong women, and I know that they could handle the lifestyle regardless, it just gave them unique insight they wouldn’t have otherwise had. But each one of those women is strong, capable, and independent, they can take care of themselves, which means my team isn’t distracted worrying about them while we’re away. We can be gone for months at a time. Sometimes for the people left behind it can feel like they’ve been abandoned, like our job is more important than them. Wives have to be almost single parents, and kids have to help carry the load, this lifestyle isn't for everyone, but the women who are married to my teammates know one thing without a shadow of a doubt."

"What?" Juliet asked, somewhat breathlessly.

"That they are the center of their husband's world. That there isn't anything their husbands wouldn't do for them, and I know that my friends, when they're home with their families, try to make sure they are one hundred percent there and involved. Somehow they all manage to make it work."

"And you want to find someone to make it work with."

Unsure if that was a question or a statement, he replied anyway. "Definitely. I want a marriage like my parents have, still happily together thirty-six years later. They fight, but they also love each other enough that they were able to weather the storms a sick child brought. I want that kind of marriage, always have. I just want to make sure I have it with the right person."

Parking the car in the parking lot beside the park where they were having a picnic with his team and their families, Chaos met Juliet's gaze squarely. He wasn't sure if she was the one, it was way too early to tell, but he knew she was strong, he knew she was a survivor, and he knew that she was the sexiest woman he'd ever laid eyes on.

He took his time unbuckling his seatbelt, never breaking eye contact, and watched as Juliet's pupils dilated as he leaned toward her. He'd wanted to kiss her yesterday at the beach but the timing hadn't felt right, he wanted to do this properly, earn her trust, woo her, then when it felt natural he'd kiss her.

It felt natural right now.

Framing her face with his hands, she sucked in a breath as he moved closer. He went slow, grave her time to pull away if she didn't want this, but the way her gaze dropped to his lips told him she wanted it every bit as much as he did.

Finally, he touched his mouth to hers, keeping the kiss light and gentle, but Juliet immediately parted her lips. She struggled against her seatbelt, and he reached over and unsnapped it, drawing her into his lap as he curled an arm around her waist, holding her close against him as he kissed her like he'd wanted to ever since he'd found her naked in his bed.

She hummed her appreciation, and the taste of her was driving him wild. He wanted so much more than to kiss her, he wanted to lavish attention on every inch of her body, showing her what it felt like to be loved.

Reluctantly, Chaos ended the kiss, pulling back so he could see her face, her cheeks were flushed, her lips swollen, her breathing heavy. She was a vision of sweet sexiness, and he loved that she was as into him as he was into her.

"Why did you stop?" Juliet asked.

"Because we're sitting in my car, in a parking lot, about to go meet our friends," he replied with a grin.

"Oh, right," she said like she'd forgotten where they were.

He liked the idea that their kiss had temporarily scrambled her brain. "What I want to do to you needs privacy and time."

Heat flared in her green eyes. "When are we doing that?"

Chaos threw back his head and laughed. It was clear she was into him physically, but he wanted more than sex from her, and she was just running from a marriage her father arranged. She might want time to find her feet, discover who she was without her father's interference. She might want independence and time alone, not jump right into a relationship. Until he knew what her long-term goals were, he was content to take things slow, get to know her, make out a little, go on some dates, but he wouldn't sleep with her until he knew they were after the same things.

"When we're both ready," he replied, brushing his fingertips over her cheek in a gentle caress.

~

12:15 P.M.

GRAYSON HAD KISSED HER.

And promised her more.

Juliet wasn't sure which one excited her more.

She stole a glance at him as they grabbed a picnic blanket and some snacks from the back of his car, she wished she knew what he was thinking right now. While she hadn't had a lot of lovers, she felt like she was able to satisfy them. Sex for her had always been okay, she'd been satisfied, but at the same time it had always felt like something was missing.

Now she realized it was a connection with her partner. One kiss with Grayson had been so much better than the sex she'd had so far.

He said he was looking for love and a commitment, that he wanted a marriage like his parents had, but did he mean he was thinking about her when he thought about his future, or was he just interested in some kissing and sex until he helped her get away from the Russian mafia and then it was over between them?

She wanted to ask, but he'd already locked his truck, taken her hand, and was heading toward the park where they were meeting up with his friends for a picnic lunch.

Maybe she'd ask later when they were alone at home.

If she was brave enough.

When she'd fled her father and Dimitri, finding a man had been the last thing on her mind, all she'd been thinking about was surviving. But Grayson made her want so much more out of life than she'd had so far, he made her want … everything.

Grayson was right about one thing though, they should wait to have sex until both of them were ready, and as much as she liked him and was attracted to him, she wasn't sure she was ready to take that step yet. It wasn't like they were in any hurry, they had all the time in the world. They could hang out, get to know one another, date and make out, and then when they both felt like the timing was right they could move their relationship to the next level.

It felt so nice to have options, to not feel pressured to do what someone else wanted, to have someone actually care about what she wanted, and she had Grayson to thank for making her feel special like she mattered.

Perhaps she was a little closer to being ready for more with Grayson than she thought she was.

"Hey, everyone," Grayson said as they reached the others.

"Ready to get destroyed?" Fox asked, tossing a football at Grayson.

"Ready to destroy you," Grayson shot back.

Juliet rolled her eyes and shook her head. Guys were so competitive when it came to sports. Personally, she'd never seen the hype of sports, and even when she had competed in show jumping with her horse she'd never been very driven to win, much to her father's annoyance.

But her father had no place in her mind today, she was here to have fun, relax, and get to know Grayson's friends better. "I hope you beat him," she said to Grayson.

"Don't worry, princess, he doesn't stand a chance," he told her, giving her one of the grins that made her heart flutter. "We're just going to be over there," he told her, pointing to a large field over on the far side of the park.

"Okay, have fun."

"We will." He leaned in close and said so only she could hear. "And then tonight when we get home you and I will have some fun of our own."

Heat rolled through her body, settling between her legs, and as though he could read her mind he laughed, dropped a quick kiss to her lips, and then he took off at a run, his teammates taking off after him.

"So you two are officially together?" Evie asked from where she was sitting propped up against the trunk of a tree, six-month-old Sullivan in her arms, drinking from his bottle.

"Umm, yeah, I guess so," she said as she set the box of cookies down and went to spread out the picnic blanket. "We haven't discussed it, but …" as she flicked out the blanket she frowned as something seemed to puff out of it, raining down around her. "What the …?" She held out her hand and was surprised to find glitter covering it.

"Is that glitter?" Claire asked.

"Yeah, it is. Why would there be glitter in the picnic blanket? We used this same blanket yesterday at the beach and there was no glitter on it then," she said, thoroughly confused.

"Chaos," Claire, Evie, and Lavender said in unison.

"Grayson," Abigail said with an amused nod. Juliet noticed that while the other women called all the guys except their own by their nicknames, Abby called all of them by their first names.

"Why would Grayson put glitter in the picnic blanket?" she asked, even more confused now.

"Because of that," Lavender said with a poorly smothered laugh as she waved a hand at Juliet.

"Am I covered in glitter now?" she asked.

"Like you took a shower in it," Abby said, clearly amused.

"So he did it on purpose, knowing I'd have to walk around covered in glitter now for as long as we're at the park?"

"Yep," Lavender agreed.

Juliet glanced over to where the guys had gone and found Grayson watching her and laughing hysterically. "He's a dead man," she vowed.

"Welcome to the world of Chaos," Evie snickered. "You have now been initiated into his universe of pranks and jokes, and I hate to tell you, but there's no getting back out."

"He does this kind of thing often?" she asked as she started to brush off the glitter covering her arms, legs, and body.

"All the time," Claire told her. "You'll get used to it."

"I need a cookie," she said as she gave up on trying to rid herself of glitter, the stuff was virtually apocalypse survivable anyway. She opened the box of Oreos, Thin Mints, and oatmeal raisin cookies, and picked up an Oreo before passing the box to Abby.

"I remember the first time Chaos played one of his pranks on me," Evie said. "It was not long after Owen and I moved in together, and somehow Chaos got a hold of my keys. I had them all cut in different colors so I could easily tell which key opened which lock, but he took them and had them recut with the colors all different. I came home one day and it was pouring rain, but I couldn't get the key to go into the lock. I had no idea why, and I kept trying over and over again. In the end I got back into my car and called Owen to come home and let me in."

Juliet couldn't help but laugh as she pictured Evie standing there in the rain, drenched to the skin, trying to figure out why her key no longer fit in the lock. "Yeah, that's mean, but kinda funny."

"Chaos certainly thought it was funny," Evie said. "When Owen finally got home and let me inside and we figured out that it had to be one of Chaos' jokes, I called him and yelled at him for ten minutes while all he did was laugh."

She laughed again and then took a bite of her cookie, only to grab a napkin and spit it straight back out. "What the …?" she said, looking at the cookie then lifting it to her nose to sniff it.

"What?" Lavender asked.

"It tastes like toothpaste," she said, brow crinkled in confusion. Then it clicked. "Grayson," she growled. He must have pulled apart the Oreos, scraped off the cream filling, and then replaced it with toothpaste. He was diabolical.

"He's on a roll today," Claire said with a giggle.

"I wonder what else he has planned," Lavender added.

"I'm not sure I want to know," Juliet said. "You guys have to help me figure out a way to get him back, turn the tables on him, see how he likes a taste of his own medicine."

"Ooh, I like that idea," Abby said. "It would serve him right to get pranked himself."

"Between the five of us, I'm sure we can come up with something really good, something he'll never see coming," Lavender said.

"Yeah, we can," Claire agreed.

"I know I'd love to teach him a lesson," Evie said, a wicked smile on her face and they all laughed.

"Jewet, swing," RJ said, leaving the ball he and Anastasia had been playing with to come and tug on her arm.

"You want to go play on the swing?" she asked, and he nodded eagerly. Not wanting to just step in and take him over to the playground if his mom wasn't comfortable with that, after all Abby and the others had only known her a few days now, she glanced at Abigail. "If it's okay with your mommy I can take you over to the swings."

"You can take him if you don't mind," Abby replied. "Now I'm craving cookies but since Grayson ruined the ones we have I'm going to run to the store and buy some more."

"I can go," Claire offered.

"No, it's okay, stupid pregnancy cravings have to be satisfied, and they're my cravings. When Grayson gets back here I'm going to ream him out, messing with a pregnant lady's food is not okay," Abby said with a mock growl.

They were all laughing as Abby snatched her purse, and Juliet stood and took RJ's little hand in hers, but she hadn't gone more than three steps toward the playground when something loud cracked through the air, and a moment later she felt a burning in her arm.

Gunshots.

Someone had just shot at her.

Someone had hit her.

When a second shot was fired, Juliet grabbed RJ and rolled him beneath her as she threw herself to the ground.

12:31 P.M.

"I CAN'T BELIEVE you glitter bombed your own woman," King snickered as Chaos watched Juliet spread out the picnic blanket then stop in shock as glitter rained down around her.

"Hey, it's nicer than some of the pranks I could have pulled," he shot back. "Remember the time I stole all the condoms from your place and replaced them with tissues?" It had taken him hours to open all the condom packets with painstaking care, replace them with rolled up pieces of tissue, then glue them all closed again. King's reaction had definitely made it worthwhile though. "You brought that woman from the bar home, the one you'd been hitting on for weeks who finally agreed to go home with you, and then the two of you couldn't do anything because you didn't have any protection." He threw back his head and laughed at the memory.

"Yeah, I remember," King said with a glower. "She thought I was pulling some kind of prank and she left in a huff. I tried to explain that it was my idiot friend trying to be funny, but she didn't believe me. I missed out on hot sex with a gorgeous woman thanks to you."

Chaos shrugged. "Not like you don't have plenty of other options." King was their team's resident ladies' man, not that any of them had ever struggled when it came to attracting attention from pretty women, but King went through girls like he changed his underwear, none of them ever lasted past a single night with the man who had vowed that commitment didn't run through his blood.

"That's true," King said, laughing and throwing him one of those charming smiles that had any woman within a hundred yards turning into a puddle of goo at his feet. "But I would have loved to get some of her, she was hot."

"Guys, are we standing around congratulating Chaos on his weird sense of humor, or are we playing ball?" Night remanded, tossing the ball in the air and catching it again.

"Playing ball," Chaos replied, "although I wish I was going to be there when she finds out what I did to the Oreos."

His friends rolled their eyes at him, but he knew they all understood that his pranks were meant to be harmless, just a bit of fun, a chance to make someone smile, to remember not to take life too seriously.

They were halfway to the field when the unmistakable sound of gunshots filled the park.

Juliet.

That one thought ran through his mind as fear took hold. Not fear for himself, but fear for the woman who had already captured a part of him. Fear for the women he loved as sisters, and the children he loved every bit as much as his niece and nephew.

He and his team did what came naturally to them, they sprang into action. So many years working together meant they didn't need to hang around and work out a plan, they all knew what to do, and they didn't hesitate to do it.

People were screaming, kids crying, parents were trying to get to their kids, it was pure pandemonium. With practiced eyes, Chaos looked past the chaos and focused on where he'd heard the shots come from.

There.

Two men.

Both dressed casually in sweats, looking like every other jogger or walker who was out enjoying the pleasant winter afternoon.

The men were moving closer to someone, ignoring the commotion around them, they were focused on something, he recognized the signs of a predator with prey in their sights, and that was exactly what these men looked like.

Leaving King, Shark, Spider, and Night to deal with the shooters, he and Fox headed straight for their families.

Chaos was halfway there when he saw that Juliet was lying on the ground.

He couldn't see the others, but he assumed—hoped—that they had grabbed the kids—and the dog—and gotten somewhere safe. They'd set the picnic up under the shade of a couple of large trees, the trunks of which would provide cover, but for some reason not only had Juliet not been able to get to cover she was out in the open, unprotected.

Possibly already shot.

Was she the target?

He had thought that her father would send people after her, he had to if he didn't want to get on the Russians' bad side, but he hadn't expected him to have someone shoot at her in the park.

But if he'd managed to find her, this was a good way to stage an abduction. Shoot a gun in a park filled with families, kids, walkers, joggers, and then in the ensuing commotion grab your victim and disappear. People were too busy trying not to get shot to worry about anything or anyone else.

The shooting had stopped, and Chaos didn't need to look to see that his team had the two shooters contained. Keeping his focus on Juliet, he skidded to his knees when he reached her, pressing one hand to her neck to check for a pulse.

"Juliet?"

He felt her pulse, and she moved at his touch, lifting her head to look up at him. Her eyes were wide with fear, her bottom lip trembling, and as she levered herself further up he saw that RJ was tucked underneath her. Immediately he snatched the toddler up, pinning the little boy against his chest and covering as much of his body as he could. He pulled Juliet into his arms as well, standing and bringing her up with him and half-carrying her as he moved them both around behind one of the large trees.

Abby's terrified face met his, and he dropped down behind the same tree she had taken shelter behind. "RJ?"

"Right here," he said soothingly, handing her the toddler who immediately clung to his mother and began to cry. "Are you hurt, Abs?"

"No," she said, burying her face against her son's head. "Juliet, thank you so much, you saved his life."

"Juliet?" he asked, turning his attention to the woman who huddled against him. She didn't answer, and he gripped her shoulders and gently eased her back so he could get a look at her. There was blood streaking her left arm and he tightened his hold on her. "You were shot," he said, somewhat accusingly.

"I … no … I …" Juliet stammered, shaking her head in denial.

"Yeah, princess, you were," he said softly. Taking her face between his hands, he leaned down to touch his lips to her forehead, then because she was staring at him silently begging him to make her feel safe, he whispered his lips across hers before hauling her back into his arms.

"Chaos?" Fox asked as he joined them. His teammate had his son snuggled in one arm, his other was wrapped around his wife. Lavender and Anastasia, and Claire and Goldilocks the dog, were behind him. "Everyone okay?"

"Abby and RJ are fine, but Juliet was hit," he replied. Quickly he ran his gaze over the others but didn't see any blood. "You guys all okay?"

"Fine," Lavender said, but her voice wobbled betraying her fear.

"He was shooting at Juliet," Claire said, dropping to her knees and hugging the dog to her. He could see she was shaking and he hated that she'd been further traumatized by what happened today when she hadn't yet healed from her ordeal in Afghanistan last September.

"The shots came as soon as she stood up," Evie agreed, resting her head against her husband's chest.

"No." Juliet shook her head wildly, as though that could somehow eradicate what had just happened. "Why would he

…? My father? No … no … no …" the last was a sob, and she struggled out of his grip backing away from them all. "If he … RJ … I'm so sorry. I'm so sorry." She sobbed, continuing to back away.

"It's not your fault," he said firmly, following her and pulling her back into his arms.

She fought him. "If my father did this, then it is."

"No. If your father did this then it's his fault and his alone. You saved RJ's life."

"But—"

"No buts. No buts, princess. The guys have the shooters, if your father sent them then no doubt they're going to take a deal and talk. If he did this then it's all on him, not you, you're not responsible for his actions."

"If it's him then he knows where I am," she said, her small body trembled in his arms.

"I won't let him hurt you, Juliet. I promise you, he will not lay a hand on you," he vowed. He meant it too. He was already developing feelings for Juliet, he could see them building something real, having the kind of relationship that lasts a lifetime, and he certainly wasn't going to let anyone snatch her away from him when he'd only just found her.

"You promise?" she whispered, seeking his reassurance.

"I promise."

She nodded once, and then she wrapped her arms around his waist and snuggled against him, holding on to him like he was her anchor in the storm her father had created. As he tucked her closer and pressed his cheek against the top of her head, he felt his heart rate start to slow. For a moment there he thought he'd lost her, but she was alive, safe, here in his arms, and he didn't intend to let her go.

~

7:44 P.M.

"WHY DON'T you go take a shower, and I'll make us some dinner," Grayson suggested gently as he led her inside his house.

He'd been treating her carefully all afternoon like she might shatter into a million pieces if he didn't handle her with kid gloves. While his attentiveness had been appreciated those first couple of hours after the shooting, now it was making her feel like she really was about to fall apart.

"I'm not hungry," she said dully, wrapping her arms around her middle.

"You need to eat," he reminded her, reaching out to trail his fingertips across her temple. "You're cold, go take a hot shower."

She was cold, and soothing her tense muscles with steaming hot water did sound like heaven. Reluctantly she nodded. "Okay, I won't be long."

"Be as long as you want, but be careful with your arm, the doctor said to try to keep it dry."

Juliet nodded again, she remembered what the doctor had told her. He'd told her that she'd been lucky, that if the bullet had gone a little to the left it would have gone through her chest instead of grazing her arm. Instead of a trip to the morgue she'd taken a trip to the emergency room, despite her protestations that she didn't need to go. Her arm had six stitches in it, and even though the doctors, and the cops who took her statement, told her how lucky she was she just didn't feel it.

Grayson stopped her, grabbing hold of her hand. "It's going to be okay, princess. Your dad didn't figure on you having an entire team of SEALs at your back."

Because she didn't know what to say she merely gave him another nod as she gently tugged free of his hold and headed up the stairs. She might have a team of SEALs prepared to have her back, but what would it cost them?

RJ could have been killed today.

Any of her new friends could have been.

How would she have felt if someone had died because of her?

Was it fair to stay here? Risking her father hurting one of the people she was growing to care about?

For now, she was too exhausted to come up with an answer to that question, so instead she just dragged herself up the stairs and into the bathroom. Despite the heavy weight of exhaustion pushing her down, she removed her clothes and folded them neatly, placing them in the hamper. Being tired was no reason to be messy.

Besides, she needed all the reassurance she could get right now, and when she was anxious she needed to maintain control of her world.

Absently she flicked the light switch five times.

Five.

She liked the number five.

Juliet turned the shower on, and while she waited for the water to heat, she fiddled with the edges of the bandage wrapped around her arm. She wasn't sure how she would keep it dry because she needed to feel the soothing heat of the water on every inch of her skin.

Was it really that bad to get her stitches wet?

Right now she wasn't sure she cared.

Stepping beneath the spray, she let out a shuddering breath and then the tears came. They streamed down her cheeks, she didn't try to fight them, but she held back her sobs, not wanting to alert Grayson and worry him any more than he already was.

On autopilot, she shampooed her hair and then conditioned it. With her hair clean, she reached for the body wash, held the loofah underneath the pump and pressed one, twice, three times, then four, then she froze.

Four.

It was supposed to be three pumps of body wash.

It was always three.

It had to be three.

Three.

Only three.

That familiar sense of panicked horror washed through her, she'd gotten it wrong, there was no way to undo it.

"Juliet?" The shower curtain was ripped aside, and Grayson stood there staring at her, concern evident on his handsome face. "What's wrong? What happened? Are you hurt?" His eyes scanned her naked body, but there was no heat there only affection and worry.

That hit her hard.

He was worried about her, and she was standing here freaking out over four pumps of body wash instead of three.

She didn't deserve a man like Grayson, and if he knew what she was crying about he would agree with her.

Gently, he tugged the loofah from her hand and proceeded to wash every inch of her. When he was done, he positioned her back under the spray until the soapy suds had washed away. Then he turned the shower off, grabbed a towel, and wrapped it around her, lifting her out of the shower and setting her on the counter.

He tugged the towel down enough to reveal the now-soaked bandage, but instead of reprimanding her for getting it wet he simply removed the dressing, carefully patted dry the wound, and then rebandaged it. Then he carried her into his bedroom where he released his hold on her long enough to set her on her feet, grab a pair of his sweatpants and one of his sweatshirts, and dress her in them.

Then she was back in his arms again, and he carried her downstairs, turned on the electric fire, and set her on the couch, wrapping her in a blanket before sitting beside her. He didn't ask again what had happened, didn't speak at all, just put an arm around her shoulders and held her.

Slowly her heart rate slowed back down, and the terror clawing at her skin receded, with a small sigh she sunk further into his embrace.

"Can you tell me what happened?"

She didn't want to … and yet maybe part of her did. He already knew about her OCD, and he seemed to accept that side of her. Maybe it wouldn't hurt for him to know about her little freak-out. "I accidentally put four pumps of body wash on the loofah instead of three."

"And?" She heard the confusion in his tone, but there was no judgment, no condescension, just a desire to understand.

"And it has to be three. I need it to be three. I need to know that I'm in control because when I am nothing bad can happen. I mean, I'm not crazy," she said quickly, looking up to gauge his reaction. "I don't really think that the number of pumps of body wash I use can actually stop anything bad from happening, but I *feel* it. When it's wrong, I feel … this panic inside me. I know it's not right, but there's no way to make it right because it's already done, and I can't take it back, and it feels like it's smothering me, like I want to go back and start my whole life over because it's not right and when it's not right I'm not safe." Juliet shrugged. "I know it sounds weird and I don't expect you to understand."

"I don't have to understand, sweetheart, I just have to know it's important to you." He touched a kiss to her temple.

"That simple?"

"That simple. I can't pretend that I've experienced what you have, so I'll never completely understand what it's like, but I can still empathize, I can still support you, I can still be here and hold you when your feelings are overwhelming you."

She'd really lucked out when she'd met this man. His ability to adapt, to go with the flow, to care about and support others, to try to put a smile on people's faces because he knew that sometimes a moment of joy could change everything, all of that was so much more attractive to her than the muscles and his handsome face. Although those muscles of his were impressive, she thought with a sleepy smile.

"Come here, little cat burglar," he said with an affectionate smile as he scooped her up and set her on his lap.

"Keep telling you I didn't steal anything and I wasn't going to," she said with a smile.

"Eat." He reached over to grab a bowl of M&Ms he'd obviously got out for her for after the shower. "It's not the home-cooked meal I wanted to make for you, but at least it'll get some calories into you."

"Yellow," she said absently as she reached into the bowl. "I always eat the yellow ones first."

"Why?"

"I like to start with the lightest color. Yellow, red, green, blue, brown," she rattled off. "I have to eat them in that order. If I accidentally miss one and I've already moved on to the next color I can't go back."

"Yellow it is," Grayson said, picking a couple out of the bowl and popping them into his mouth.

"Yeah, yellow it is." Juliet rested her head on his shoulder as she ate some candy. She'd never spent much time thinking about the future because she hadn't liked the future her father had planned for her. But sitting here on Grayson's lap, warm and safe, cared about and protected, understood and respected, she realized that this future was one she could enjoy forever.

CHAPTER 5

January 21st

10:23 A.M.

"YOU'RE REALLY TAKING me to a farm?" Juliet asked from the passenger seat.

"I really am," Chaos said, amused by her apparent shock about it. She'd asked him that at least a dozen times since he'd told her after breakfast to dress in something casual and warm and meet him in the car. He'd wanted to take her somewhere fun today, somewhere where she could relax and try to forget what had happened the day before, and this children's farm that allowed city kids to come and experience farm life had seemed like a fun idea.

She was still shaken up about the shooting at the park.

He was still shaken up about the shooting at the park.

This morning though, she seemed to be doing better. He

wasn't surprised she'd ended up breaking down last night in the shower. She'd been so upset that because of her, his team and their families had been in danger, much more upset about that than about her father sending men to shoot at her.

At least that was still their running assumption although the men his team had apprehended had yet to talk.

Today was about fun though, and he'd guessed—correctly—that Juliet had never been to a farm before and thought it would be something she'd enjoy, and that would take her mind off everything she was going through.

"I've always loved animals, but I was never allowed to have a pet. My mom didn't like the mess that goes with them, and my dad said they would be a distraction to all the things I needed to learn if I was going to represent him and attract the kind of husband he wanted for me."

Chaos found himself surprised again that despite their vastly different upbringings, his family hadn't been poor but most of what his parents earned went straight to medical bills for Lizzie, they were still so similar. Juliet wasn't anything like the stuck-up, spoilt, brat she could have turned out to be under her father's watch. Instead she was sweet, down to earth, easy-going if a bit serious, and cared more about others than she did herself. Every minute he spent with her, his opinion and respect for her grew.

He turned the car into the long, tree-lined driveway that would lead to the farm, already thinking that when this mess with her father was resolved he was going to make sure she got herself a pet. "This is where I used to work when I was a kid. The couple who used to own the farm—their son owns it now—used to go to my family's church, and when they mentioned needing some help I volunteered. I knew how hard my parents worked to pay off all the medical bills and I wanted to help contribute, but I couldn't see myself working at McDonald's or something like that, I liked being out in the fresh air, liked working hard, so I thought this would be a good fit for me and it was, I loved it here."

"I can picture you working here," she said, then looked at him with her eyes twinkling with excitement. "What animals are we going to get to see?"

"They have chickens, goats and sheep, cows, pigs, and horses. I thought we could go riding later if you want."

"I *love* riding," she said with a squeal. "I used to do show jumping as a kid, it was pretty much the only thing my father made me do that I actually enjoyed. I always wished that I could spend more time with the horses and take care of them myself, but my father said we had staff to do that. He said it like taking care of the horse would have been beneath me, acted like I should think of it as just a piece of sporting equipment, but the horses were alive, and I would have had fun caring for them, it would have made the bond between us stronger."

"Your father didn't get it because he wasn't like us," he told her as he parked the car in the busy lot. It was another nice winter's day, and there were lots of people out here.

"No, he wasn't. And as bad as I always thought he was, I hate finding out that he was even worse." She shook her head determinedly as though refocusing her mind. "But today isn't about him, today is about us, and having fun. So let's go have some fun."

Impressed with her attitude, he leaned over and gave her a quick kiss. "Let's go introduce you to farm life."

By the time they got out of the car and walked down to the entrance, he could feel that Juliet was relaxing again. Although he knew the owners and they'd told him he was welcome here anytime he wanted, he still paid for admission for the two of them because he knew that running a small business was hard work and that every little bit helped.

"Where to first?" she asked when they were inside.

"What about the chickens? There are usually chicks in there and they're pretty cute."

"Okay," she said excitedly. "What do they do with the chicks when they grow up? Isn't there a limit to how many chickens they can have here?"

"They sell them to other farms, all ones that treat their animals humanely, the Wilkinsons don't want any of their animals going to be kept in tiny cages."

"That's good, no living being should be kept in a cage."

"Agreed," he said as he steered her over to a large barn where he knew the chickens lived. His mind went to Night's sister Abigail, who was abducted a few years back and kept in a cage on a drug cartel's compound in Mexico. She'd been there for over a year before her then two time ex and now husband Spider had stumbled upon her by accident while their team was there rescuing a senator's kidnapped daughters. While she never completely got over that, Abby was doing well now, but still the thought of anyone, human or animal, being imprisoned like that always tightened his heart.

"Oh, they're so cute," Juliet gushed as she tugged her hand free from his and rushed over to a small pen where a dozen chicks were walking around, cheeping and pecking at their food. "Are we allowed to hold them?"

"Sure are," he said, finding the darkness that had been inside him mere moments ago fade away at the sight of Juliet's sweet, open, almost childlike joy at the prospect of holding one of the adorable baby chicks.

With a grin, she reached out to scoop up one of the chicks. It cheeped in surprise, but it immediately settled down when Juliet cupped it in her palm and held it against her stomach. “It's so soft,” she murmured as she stroked its head with one of her fingertips. “And so tiny.”

“Not for long,” he said, picking up another of the chicks. “Soon it will be growing its feathers, losing this soft down, and start trying to fly about, then they’ll be moved over into the pen with the other chickens.”

“It's a shame they can't stay this cute and little forever,” she said as she continued to pet the chick.

“You’re a sucker for a baby animal, huh?” he teased.

“Who isn’t?” she returned. “Look at you, big, tough SEAL cradling a tiny chick in his hands.”

“It's cute,” he said with a laugh.

“Even though I think they’re way cuter like this it would be nice to have chickens and be able to go out in the morning and collect fresh eggs for breakfast.”

“We’ll turn you into a farm girl yet,” he teased.

Juliet smiled back. “I'm not sure about a whole big farm, but some farm animals could be fun. What do you think?”

A flush of pleasure warmed him. Was she asking because she was thinking about their future? “Well, farm animals would be fun, but they’re also a lot of work, especially if you were with someone who was away a lot so not always around to help out.”

The same pleasure he’d felt when she was feeling him out about the future now reflected on her face. “Hmm, I guess that’s true.”

“Fresh eggs are one thing, but you have to try fresh milk.”

“We can milk cows here?” She looked intrigued by the idea.

“Yep, you can milk cows and take the milk home with you.”

“Sounds like fun.”

“Let’s go then.”

They both set their chicks back down with the others, then Chaos took her hand again and led her through the farm to the milking shed. Inside stood a few of the cows the Wilkinsons owned standing in stalls, calming chewing on hay.

"Which one do you want to milk?" he asked.

Juliet studied all three cows like her decision would affect the taste of the milk then finally settled on a pretty brown one with large brown eyes who was watching them with apparent interest. "This one."

"Hi, Bill, we're going to fill two one-pint bottles of milk," he said, waving to the elderly man who had worked at the farm a decade ago when Chaos had also worked here.

Bill nodded and got out two glass bottles. "Here you go, Grayson. Nice to meet you, ma'am," he nodded at Juliet. "This your first time milking a cow?"

"Yep, it's my first time at a farm," Juliet replied.

"You're in good hands with Grayson here then. He's an expert with his hands." Bill winked at them, and Chaos playfully punched him in the arm as Juliet's cheeks reddened.

"You embarrassing my girl, Bill?" he joked.

"No, sir." Bill grinned.

They were both laughing as he guided Juliet over to the cow she'd chosen and pulled up the little wooden stool for her. "Sit here," he directed, then picked up a metal pail and set it under the cow's udder. He pulled up another stool then sat behind her, his arms on either side of hers and he grabbed her hands and guided them to the teats. "Put your hands here, and we're going to squeeze like this." His hands covered hers, and he helped her squeeze, and a squirt of milk shot out and into the pail.

"It's milk." Juliet giggled delightedly. "I mean, I knew milk came from cows but buying it in the supermarket and seeing this, it's just … wow … it's so cool."

"Nature at its finest," he agreed as he continued to help her milk the cow.

"Your friend Bill was right," Juliet said, voice husky. "You are good with your hands."

"Play your cards right, princess, and you'll find out just how good," he whispered in her ear. She shivered against him and pressed back slightly so her back was plastered across his chest.

"I'm good at cards," she whispered back.

"I'll bet you are, princess, and that works in both our favor."

~

2:16 P.M.

HE WAS GETTING bored and annoyed.

Arthur plucked at his jeans, the stiff material felt so uncomfortable, and it threw him back to the past when he'd been dirt poor and forced to wear whatever second-hand clothes his mother could find in the local thrift store. Part of his vow to have more wealth and power than he could imagine in even his wildest dreams had been a determination to never again wear jeans. He spent his days in expensive suits, but he could hardly walk around San Diego looking for his daughter dressed like that.

Especially when his daughter appeared to be slumming it.

Yesterday she'd been at a local park, and today she was at a farm.

A *farm*.

With filthy animals, and she'd been touching them.

Arthur shuddered in revulsion. It was disgusting here, and

his daughter knew that a woman like herself should never be caught dead at a place like this unless she was here for a charity event of some sort. He found himself pleased that she was going to be punished by Dimitri Fedorov for her recent behavior.

If he could get her back home by the end of the day.

He had only hours left to retrieve his daughter and return her to her future husband or he would be the one punished in her place. After his men had finally tracked her to the park the day before, he'd thought it was over, but she was being protected by strong men, skilled men, men who had easily overpowered his men and delivered them into police custody. He had been in the car waiting for his men to bring his daughter to him, but when he saw that they'd been arrested, he had bided his time and followed Juliet when she left with the big, blond man. He'd followed them to a small house, watched as the big man carried her inside, he'd known he wouldn't be able to take the man himself so he was forced to wait for Juliet to be alone.

He was still waiting.

All night he'd sat in his car outside the house, and this morning he had followed them here to this farm. He'd watched as they held baby chicks, milked cows, made cheese, fed lambs and baby goats, gone horse riding, eaten pizza for lunch, and now his daughter and this man she was shacking up with were picking apples. So far the man hadn't wandered far from Juliet's side, and he certainly hadn't allowed her out of his sight. It was obvious that he knew she was in danger and he was well prepared to step in and protect her if that danger got too close.

But the man couldn't be with her every second of every day.

Even if he didn't get her back to the Fedorovs by tonight

and suffered whatever punishment they dished out, he would give Juliet's location to Alexi and Dimitri, and they would come for her. She wasn't escaping her fate that easily.

"Grayson, this tree over here has the biggest, reddest apples I've ever seen. Like *ever*," Juliet said. Arthur knew it was his daughter, was watching her with his own basket in hand from behind the trunk of a nearby tree, but she sounded nothing like the daughter he knew. She sounded lighter, freer, happier, and he didn't like it. Juliet's role was to help him further himself not to go running off with some man who frequented farms.

"Nothing beats eating fresh apples," the man—Grayson apparently—said, indulgent affection in his tone.

"Will we have enough apples to eat some fresh and bake some in a pie?" Juliet asked.

"Sure will."

"Can we bake pie tonight?" Juliet's voice dripped with excited enthusiasm.

"We can do anything you want tonight, princess," Grayson replied in a voice filled with sexual innuendo.

No way did he want this man touching his daughter.

Juliet had been given to Dimitri Fedorov, a rich, powerful Russian mafia prince. She should be at home tending to her fiancé, not gallivanting around with some lowlife who thought the farm was an appropriate location for a date.

"There are some really nice looking ones up high. Can you pick some?" Juliet asked Grayson.

"Sure thing, babe," he replied.

A moment later, Arthur saw the large man climb a ladder and busy himself picking apples. This was as close to a good chance as he was going to get and he intended to take advantage of it.

All he needed to do was draw Juliet just a short distance away from her man.

Moving a couple of trees over, Arthur pretended to fall, grunting as he did and dropping the basket of apples he'd been picking to make sure he didn't look suspicious.

"Are you okay?" Juliet called out, and a moment later, she was walking toward him.

He knew he only had one shot at this and he had to make it count, so he pulled the gun from his waistband and lifted it, pointing it at his daughter. He didn't want to hurt her, wasn't sure he had the stomach for it, but she didn't need to know that. "Don't scream, Juliet, you draw any attention to us and I'll shoot your apple picker, got it?"

Juliet's wide green eyes stared back at him in shock, but she nodded her head. "How did you find me?"

"Tracker implanted between your shoulder blades when you were born," he replied. It would do her well to know that she could never escape him or her destiny. No matter where she went he would find her and so would her new family.

Horror splashed across her face, and she lifted one hand to touch her back. The implant was small, the scar barely noticeable, and it was in a location where she could never remove it on her own. It was there to stay, and she may as well accept it as well as her fate. She wasn't free, she never had been. She had always been a tool for him to use to further his own position in life. The sooner she accepted that and the fact that she belonged to Dimitri Fedorov now, the easier her life would be.

"This doesn't have to be a bad thing, Juliet," he said as he reached for her arm. "Dimitri Fedorov is rich and powerful, as long as you submit to him you'll have everything you could ever dream about."

"The only thing I want is to live my own life," she said.

"He beat me up, Father. At your New Year's party when I said no to sleeping with him he beat me, that's why I ran."

He could see in her eyes that she thought him knowing that Dimitri had hit her would help her cause, but she should know by now that he only cared about himself. "You shouldn't have told him no."

"Shouldn't have told him no?" she echoed incredulously. "Father, he *hit* me because I told him *no*."

"Then you know what not to do next time if you do not like being hit," he replied. Yanking her up close against his body, he pressed the weapon against the small of her back. If they walked like this no one should notice anything was wrong then when they got to his car he'd have her drive so he could keep his weapon trained on her. Once they were somewhere safe he'd tie her up, he didn't trust her not to try to run. He'd drug her too, that way she couldn't do anything stupid, and he could deliver her to the Fedorovs and seal their deal. "Don't try anything stupid, Juliet. I may not want to hurt you, but I will if you leave me no choice."

Her gaze scanned the area. There were families about but no one close enough to overhear them. For a second, he thought she was about to risk it and scream for her man, but apparently she was afraid enough of him that she allowed herself to be held as he started walking her through the farm and back to his car.

It was done.

He had her.

Relief swamped him.

With just hours to spare, he'd managed to find his daughter, get her in his possession, and now all he had to do was drive them both back to his house. Once he had Juliet drugged and restrained, he'd call home, let Alexi and Dimitri know that it was done. After he handed her over to the

Fedorovs, she would no longer be his problem. They were planning to take her straight to Russia where she would be taught her place.

~

2:34 P.M.

How had this perfect date gone bad so quickly?

One second she was with Grayson, and they were picking apples, she was excited to try baking a pie when they got home later, and then the next her father was there and he was holding a gun on her.

All her life she had hated how cold and calculating her father had been. Running her life like she was nothing more than a prop in his game to garner for himself as much money and as much power as he could. She'd hated that he cared so little about her, hated that he forced her and blackmailed her into doing things she didn't want to do, but she'd never truly thought he was evil.

Until now.

Now, as he walked her across the parking lot, his arm tightly around her shoulders, the gun digging painfully into her lower back she realized that he had finally revealed to her his true self.

Juliet could see his car up ahead, knew that once he got her into it, it was all over, she'd never be seen again. Well, that wasn't quite true, she was sure once her father got her back home she'd be sent to Russia with Dimitri Fedorov, and sooner or later she'd be forced to marry him. Photos of their wedding would no doubt be splashed across the society pages, but she herself would be a prisoner of the Russian mafia. She was sure if she played the game, submitted to Dimitri, allowed him to use her as he wanted, she would be treated like a princess, but a princess trapped in a cage. If she refused to submit she wasn't sure what they would do to her, but she knew it would be bad.

Tears burned the backs of her eyes, and she felt icy cold terror grow inside her. Everything that could have been with Grayson, a chance at a real relationship with someone who would love and respect her, had just been snatched away from her.

She wanted so badly to scream for him, she knew he would come, but she couldn't risk him, or anybody else, getting shot.

If you'd asked her a month ago if her father would ever shoot anybody she would have said an emphatic no. There was no way he'd want to risk getting one of his expensive suits dirty, but today … today she wasn't sure what he was capable of.

"When we get to the car, you're going to get into the driver's seat," her father hissed in her ear.

She nodded because what else was there to do?

If she didn't comply he would shoot some innocent person.

But him having her drive gave her some power. Grayson must know by now that she was gone, and she knew for a fact that he would come for her. Maybe he was already following unseen, waiting for the perfect moment to make his move. All she had to do was make the right move at the right time, and she knew exactly what that play was going to be.

Without a word she climbed into the car, her father started the engine, and once they were both buckled in she put the car in reverse.

"When you get to the road, turn right," her father ordered.

She nodded agreeably, but she knew they wouldn't be getting that far. Large trees lined the driveway, and they were the perfect way to end this. If she waited for the road, they'd be going too fast and if she tried to crash the car, she could be seriously hurt or even killed, but here in the driveway, they'd be going slow enough that any injuries sustained would be minor. Crashing the car would hopefully make her father lose his grip on the gun. He wasn't a get his hands dirty kind of guy, and she could tell he had no real idea what he was doing.

Praying her plan worked and that Grayson was out there somewhere ready to come and help, Juliet drove through the parking lot and then turned into the driveway.

It was now or never.

She kept the car steady for the first half and then suddenly without warning she yanked on the wheel.

Her father grunted in surprise, but before he had a chance to do anything they'd hit the tree.

A painful jolt wracked through her body, and pain flared in her chest and stomach as she was thrown against the seatbelt and the airbag deployed making her cheek burn as her face made contact.

But it worked.

The gun fell from her father's hand, landing on the floor beneath him.

Then all of a sudden, the passenger door was yanked open and her father was being dragged out.

Relief swamped her.

Grayson was here.

She heard her father cry out, but a harsh voice shut him down. Suddenly exhausted, Juliet sunk back against her seat as the world around her shimmered slightly out of focus.

Sometime later—she assumed it was all of a minute but it

felt like much longer—her door was eased open and then gentle hands were touching her neck.

"Juliet?" Grayson's worried voice called her name.

She wanted to reply, but she was kind of stuck in no man's land at the moment.

"Hey, princess, can you hear me? Cat burglar?"

The silly nickname made her smile and broke the barrier holding her back. Her eyes opened slowly, and she turned her head to see Grayson crouched in her open doorway. He smiled when he saw her eyes open, but there was still concern in his green eyes. "I didn't steal anything."

"Hey, princess, you okay?"

"I'm okay," she assured him. "Just a little sore. I knew you'd come and save me."

"Looks like you did a pretty good job of saving yourself." There was pride and respect in his eyes and his tone, and her feelings for him grew. Her parents had always treated her like she was one step above completely incompetent and useless, but Grayson didn't and that meant a lot to her.

"I think this one was a team effort," she said. "Where's my father?"

"Tied up, he's not going anywhere."

"Good." Juliet let out a breath she hadn't known she was holding.

Grayson's smile relaxed as she relaxed. "Is your back sore? Your neck?"

"No, mostly just my chest and stomach from the seatbelt."

"Okay then, let's get you out of here." With a gentle touch, he reached around her and unbuckled her seatbelt, then he slipped an arm around her waist and held her against his chest as he eased her out of the car. "I was so scared when I realized you were gone," he whispered as he held his lips against the top of her head.

"I knew you would come after me."

He nodded as he held her tightly against him. "I heard everything your father said to you, but I didn't want to get you shot by moving in too quickly. I better call my team to tell them that you're okay." He started to release her but then tightened his hold again and pulled her closer. "In a minute, I just need to hold you."

Juliet was perfectly okay with that plan because being held by Grayson was exactly what she needed right now. She relaxed against him, allowing his strong, steady arms to soothe her, but nothing was ever going to wipe away the memory of her father holding a gun on her.

Just as quickly as she had started to relax, panic came flooding back.

The tracker her father had implanted was still inside her.

No doubt Dimitri was able to use it to find her just as her father had.

She had to get it out.

She had to.

Had to.

Frantic now, she yanked herself out of Grayson's arms and spun wildly, searching for something she could use to remove the tracker.

"Juliet? What's wrong?" Grayson asked, fear in his voice as he reached for her but she batted his hands away.

He had some sort of Swiss army knife thing on his keys. She'd seen it and asked him about it, she needed it now.

She shoved her hands into his pockets searching for his keys.

"Princess, what's wrong? What's going on?"

She didn't answer as her fingers curled around the keys and she pulled them out. She fumbled to open the tool and find the knife. She was vaguely aware of Grayson watching her, but she was in full-on panic mode now and didn't have it in her to answer.

Managing to open the knife, Juliet shrugged out of her jacket, dropping it on the ground at her feet, but when she reached for the hem of her sweater, Grayson moved to stop her.

"What are you doing? Tell me what's wrong. Did your father hurt you?"

"I have to get it out," she screamed, struggling out of his hold. She yanked the sweater off and moved the blade toward her back.

"Juliet," Grayson sounded horrified and used his much larger body to subdue her, pulling her so her back was pressed against his front, one of his large arms pinning her in place while his other hand circled her wrist preventing her from using the knife. "Tell me what you're doing. Why are you trying to cut yourself?"

The longer that tracker was in her, the more her panic was growing. "I need it out," she sobbed.

"What, honey?"

"A tracker. He put a tracker in me. I need it out, take it out, Grayson, please."

"Okay, honey, okay, calm down for me. We'll get it out, all right? I'll get it out, just calm down."

She struggled to do as he asked but managed to stop fighting against his hold and drag in a couple of deep breaths.

Grayson released her slowly, tentatively, like he didn't quite believe she wasn't going to try to cut herself again. When she didn't, he took the tool from her hand and turned her around. "Where did he say it was?"

"Between my shoulder blades. Get it out, Grayson, please. I need it out right now."

"Okay, baby," he soothed. His fingertips traced the skin

on her back then he paused. “Here it is, you have a tiny scar, barely noticeable if you're not looking for it. Do you want to wait until the ambulance gets here?”

“No,” she shouted.

Grayson chuckled softly. “Okay, princess, I have a first aid kit in my car.” Without giving her a chance to say anything else he scooped her up, bending down to get her sweater and jacket, then carried her back to the parking lot. At his car, he set her in the backseat before retrieving his first aid kit. He turned her so her back was to him, then swiped at her back with an alcohol wipe. “It's going to sting.”

“I don’t care.” All she cared about was getting this thing out of her.

The pain of him slicing open her skin and digging around to find the chip was easily outweighed by the panicked need to get that thing out of her.

“All done,” he said a moment later, touching his lips to the base of her neck.

“You got it?”

“I got it. Let me clean this up and put a bandage on it, then I can hold you.”

That was what she wanted too. She felt him wipe away her blood, then tape a bandage over what she was sure was a relatively small wound. Then his arms were around her, and he was sliding her onto his lap. Juliet buried her face against his chest and clung to him.

CHAPTER 6

January 22nd

12:11 A.M.

Juliet was asleep in the passenger seat by the time they pulled into his garage. The poor thing was exhausted, between her father trying to force her to marry a stranger, her fiancé beating her, spending almost three weeks living on the street, the shooting at the park, and the near abduction, he was pretty sure that she had reached the end of her rope.

Chaos couldn't be more proud of her though.

She had saved herself today. He'd known something was wrong as soon as he'd heard her ask someone if everything was okay. By the time he'd got eyes on her again her father had already had his gun pointed at her, and he hadn't wanted to risk Juliet getting shot. He'd called his team as he followed them, his intent had been to get in his car, tail them, then wait for an opportunity to strike.

In the end, he hadn't needed to do anything, Juliet had incapacitated her father all on her own.

His girl was a tough one.

Rounding the car he opened her door, intending to carry her up to bed, but she woke as he scooped her into his arms.

"We're home?" she asked, blinking sleepily.

"Yeah, princess, we're home," he said, kissing her forehead. He loved that Juliet thought of his house as home, and he was hoping he could persuade her to stay here while she worked on rebuilding her life. He was hoping that now that her father was in prison the Fedorovs might back off, but if they were determined to have Dimitri marry Juliet to get a green card then she could still be in danger.

Closing the car door, he carried her inside and then upstairs. His team had shown up at the farm despite the fact he'd called to tell them the situation was resolved, and he appreciated that they wanted to offer both him and Juliet their full support. They'd hung around while both he and Juliet gave their statements to the cops and answered what felt like a million questions. She had been checked out by paramedics but declined a trip to the emergency room. She'd had something to eat while giving her statement, and now she had to be wiped out and ready for bed.

When he went to set her on his bed, she stopped him. "I need a shower."

"All right, princess, take a shower, or a bath, relax, unwind, call out if you need anything."

He stooped to kiss her forehead, but when he would have turned to leave and give her privacy she grabbed his hand. "Stay. Please."

Even though he knew she wasn't offering him sex, just asking for comfort, he couldn't help but picture him pleasuring every inch of her body while she was naked in the shower, turning the horrors of the day into pleasure. "Sure."

She smiled gratefully up at him, and he took her hand and led her into his bathroom. He wanted her in here tonight, not in the other bathroom down the hall. Chaos turned on the water then stripped out of his clothes, leaving them where they fell. When he turned to see if Juliet needed help undressing, he found her watching him with a hungry expression on her face.

"Juliet," he warned.

"What?" she asked, all innocent as she met his gaze.

"You keep looking at me like that, and you're going to snap my control."

"Good. I want your control to snap, Grayson. I'm ready."

"You've been through a traumatic experience today, you're looking for an outlet, wanting to forget about everything your father did, I don't want this to be something you regret in the morning."

Hurt flashed in her eyes. "I wouldn't regret it. I don't need another man in my life who thinks he knows what's best for me. I know what I want, I want you."

It was the pain in her words that did it. She was right, she was a strong woman who knew her own mind, and she deserved better than another man who thought he could tell her what to do and when to do it. If she said she wanted this and was ready, he should take her at her word.

He closed the space between them, grabbed the hem of her sweater and pulled it over her head, tossing it onto the floor. Then he turned her around and unsnapped her bra, touching his lips to the skin of her back just above where he'd taped the bandage. He continued to kiss his way down her spine as he knelt, reaching around her waist to unsnap her jeans and ease them down her legs.

Her panties came down next, and then he lifted each foot, removing her shoe, sock, and clothing until he had her standing naked before him.

"Gorgeous," he murmured as he ran his appreciative gaze over her body.

Juliet's cheeks heated, but she looked pleased with the compliment. He took her hand to pull her into his large walk-in shower, but she paused, embarrassment had replaced desire, and she looked down at the clothes. "Can we put those in the hamper first?"

"We can do anything you want, princess," he said, trying to hide his amusement because he didn't want to ruin the mood, and it was clear Juliet thought her OCD need to put everything away would do just that. In truth, her quirks only endeared her to him even more.

Quickly, he gathered up their clothes, put them in the hamper, then took their shoes and set them neatly by the door. Then he took this special woman in his arms and guided them both under the hot spray.

Juliet moaned in delight as the hot water hit her muscles and he reached for the body wash. Squirting some of it into his hand, he began to clean every inch of her. He massaged her muscles, working each one until he could feel her turn soft under his ministrations. Only then did he lean her against the tiled wall and kneel before her. He nudged her legs apart then held his nose to the apex of her thighs and breathed in her scent.

"Perfect," he murmured.

"Grayson," she moaned as he touched his lips to the

inside of one thigh and then the other. "Please, more, touch me."

He groaned at her plea and gave them what they both wanted, swiping the tip of his tongue along her.

Her fingers curled into his hair as he took her hard little bud into his mouth and sucked on it before flicking it with his tongue. When he slipped a finger inside her tight heat her legs trembled, and he braced her with his free hand, pressing it to her stomach to hold her in place.

He stroked deep, rotating his hand so his fingers hit that hidden spot inside her that would unravel her world. He kept up his assault with his mouth on her little bundle of nerves, alternating between licking and suckling, as he added another finger, stretching her, preparing her to take him. Not before she exploded first though. Her pleasure came before his own, always would.

Sucking hard, he felt it hit her. Her whole body trembled, her internal muscles clamped around his fingers as she came all over them and his tongue. He continued to work both his hand and his mouth on her, wringing out every last drop of pleasure until he felt her sag, his name falling from her lips in a sated murmur.

She looked exhausted, and he stood, intending to wash her hair then dry her off and tuck her into bed, but she stopped him when she reached out and grasped his painfully hard length.

"You want to go to bed, princess?" he asked.

"No, I want this inside me, now," she said, stroking him firmly as she tried to guide him toward her center.

"You sure?"

"You telling me I don't know what I want?" She cocked an eyebrow at him, daring him to tell her that he knew what was best for her.

"Would never dream of that, princess," he said with a tender smile. "I need a condom first."

"I'm on the pill, always have been, the last thing my father wanted was a baby out of wedlock. I'm clean too."

"So am I."

"Then hurry up and get inside me."

Because he was already balanced right on the edge, he thrust inside her in one move, burying himself in her tight, wet heat. He held still for a moment, giving her body time to adjust, but she began to move restlessly.

"Move," she begged, "make me come again."

"Your wish is my command, princess," he murmured. Chaos lifted her until her legs wrapped around his waist, then planted both his hands on her hips as he thrust into her. "Come for me, baby."

"Need more," she said, her hands on his shoulders as she rotated her hips, her head thrown back, eyes closed.

"Watch me, princess," he ordered.

She complied, watching him with heavy-lidded green eyes as he reached between them with one hand to stimulate her as he continued to thrust into her.

He could feel it coming, knew exactly when it was going to hit her, and he watched raptured as she fell apart again. Spurred on by her pleasure, Chaos found his own release, thrusting into her over and over again as every molecule of his body came alive in a way he'd never experienced before. He felt like someone had lit a fire in him that was raging, spreading, consuming him in a pleasure that was too intense for words.

"You are," Juliet whispered in his ear as he floated back down to earth.

"Am what?"

"Good with your hands."

“Pretty easy to be when I'm touching perfection.” As far as he was concerned there wasn’t a single thing he would change about the woman he was still buried inside, she was already absolutely perfect.

CHAPTER 7

January 23rd

6:39 A.M.

"HMM," Juliet purred as soft lips found hers. "I could get used to waking up like this every morning."

"Can't think of any better way to wake up than by running my hands over this sweet, sexy body of yours. Definitely beats waking up to my teams' snoring."

"Grayson," she laughed, swatting playfully at him, "way to ruin the mood."

"Lucky I know exactly what to do to get your body back in the mood."

It was true, he did. After making love in the shower yesterday morning, they'd both crawled into Grayson's bed, and with his arms wrapped snuggly around her, they'd gone to sleep. She'd slept for twelve hours straight and been pleasantly surprised to wake up to find Grayson still curled around her. They'd spent the day talking and making love, getting to know each other's bodies, and Juliet was finding herself dangerously close to falling for him.

If she was honest with herself she already was.

"Don't you have PT this morning?" she asked, although she tilted her head to the side to give him better access as he kissed her neck.

"I do," he replied, his breath warm against her sensitive skin.

"Then shouldn't you be getting ready to leave?"

"I should."

"So why aren't you?"

"Because I think we have time for a quickie before I leave. Unless you don't want to," he said with a wicked smile as he moved away from her.

"Get back here, mister," she said, grabbing his shoulders and bringing his mouth back to meet hers. They'd already done slow and sweet, they'd taken the time to learn about one another's bodies, what they liked, how they responded. She was definitely not opposed to hard and fast this time around.

"You already wet for me, sweetheart?" Grayson asked as his hand moved down her naked body to dip between her legs.

She was always wet for him.

They only had to be in the same room and all she could think about was touching him, feeling him, joining their bodies together, she wasn't sure she could ever get enough of him or that she would want to. When she was with him she knew she was respected, valued, she wasn't just a commodity to use to further his own interests. He genuinely cared about her and wanted the best for her.

Juliet moaned in delight as he ran a finger through her

folds, teasing that little bundle of nerves that was already swollen with need.

"Grayson, hurry up," she said, shifting restlessly against his hand. He enjoyed teasing her, keeping her right on the edge but not letting her tumble over it. She wasn't really complaining though, she'd never experienced sex like this before, it went so much deeper than anything else she'd had.

"You're so impatient," he said, nipping at her bottom lip.

"Or you're just really, really good at this and I don't want to wait," she said, reaching between them to grasp his length, see how he liked being teased.

"Juliet," he groaned as she gripped him tightly, sliding her hand up and down him, enjoying the way he jerked in her hand.

Claiming her lips in a kiss that felt like heaven, he positioned himself at her entrance and thrust inside her in one smooth move. Having him inside her made her feel complete like the piece of herself that she'd always felt was missing but never known where to look to find was suddenly right there.

They'd developed their rhythm yesterday, and as he moved, Juliet met him thrust for thrust. It didn't take long until the world around her began to shimmer and sparkle like the whole universe wanted to celebrate with them.

Her release hit her like a firecracker sparking all her nerve endings and making them glimmer like glitter. She cried out her pleasure into Grayson's mouth as she felt him thrust faster, harder, until his body went still, taught, and she knew that he had found that same peak.

By the time he lifted his head to look down at her, her fingers were already stroking along the smooth skin of his back. He had a tattoo back there, it was magnificent. She'd never really been into tattoos before, never thought they were hot or sexy, but on Grayson it made her want to run her tongue all over it. In fact she had indeed done that yesterday. It was a large five-point star, and she knew that each point represented a member of his family. Beneath it were the words risus sit optima medicina, it was Latin for laughter is the best medicine. She thought it suited him perfectly and loved how enthusiastically he embraced life.

"I wish you didn't have to go," she said without thinking, then quickly straightened. "I mean, I understand you have to, I know what your job is, I know how important it is to you, how big a part of your life it is, I'd never hold it against you, I hope you know that."

His large hands lifted to frame her face, his thumbs brushing across her skin in the softest of caresses. "I know that, Juliet. I think you're a woman strong enough to handle SEAL life. It won't be easy, there will be times I'll have to leave right in the middle of something important, times when I won't be there for you when you need me. I'll miss special occasions, birthdays, and Christmases, and I won't be able to tell you where I was or what I was doing. But you would know that when I'm with you, you have all of me, and that when I'm not with you I'm thinking about you and wishing I was."

She smiled and leaned over to touch her lips lightly to his. "And I would know that, so you wouldn't have to walk around feeling guilty like you were letting me down. I would be proud of you, and I would cherish every second that we would have together. And when you weren't here I'd have your SEAL family to support me." They hadn't known each other long, and it was too soon to claim that they loved one another, but Juliet knew she felt a connection to Grayson, and she wanted to see if it could grow into love.

"I guess I'm lucky it was my house you decided to break

into that night, aren't I, cat burglar?" he teased, his green eyes dancing with humor and affection.

"You're lucky I didn't steal anything." She huffed good-naturedly, lightly shoving at his shoulders so she could climb out of bed. "Are you going to be home for lunch?"

"Hopefully a late lunch." He followed after her as she headed into the bathroom. "Are you going to be okay here on your own?"

It was sweet that he was so worried about her, and although she was definitely still freaked out about what had happened with her father he was in prison now, she was relieved that she hadn't heard anything from the man he was trying to force her to marry. Hopefully the Fedorovs wouldn't want to get mixed up with the daughter of a man who had been charged with multiple felonies and kept their distance. She was okay though. "I'll be fine. Your friends' wives are all going to be over here soon anyway."

"Who?" he asked, standing behind her, hands on her shoulders, his gaze meeting hers in the mirror.

"*Our* friends," she corrected. It was odd to have a group of friends she was actually looking forward to hanging out with. There wasn't a single friend from her life back in Orange County that she had even thought about calling since she'd left home. "Grayson, do you think I could go back home soon to get some of my things?"

"I think that once we hear from my contact and make sure the Fedorovs are in Russia that we can go and get your things, and you can get your car and start using your bank accounts and everything again."

Since she was still holding his gaze, she saw the question he didn't ask with words flitter through his eyes.

He was worried that once she had access to her money and house and things again that she would leave.

But she didn't want to.

She was happy here with him.

Juliet turned in his hold and wrapped her arms around his waist. "Grayson, would it be okay if I continued to stay here with you, even if it is safe for me to start letting people know where I am?"

His hold on her tightened, and he held her pressed firmly against his chest. "I would love it if you continued to stay here with me, but I also understand if you need space. You've never had a chance to live your life on your own terms, and I'd never hold you back, Juliet. Ever. If you need time to go and find yourself then you know I'll be here waiting for you when you're ready."

Her heart melted. A month ago she would have agreed with him, she would have said that all she wanted was space and the freedom to get away, to be able to do whatever she wanted, not to have anyone to answer to.

But things had changed.

She had already found herself.

Right here, in the home of this Navy SEAL with a huge heart and big smile.

~

11:22 A.M.

PT WAS ALWAYS GRUELING on his body, not that Chaos ever minded, he's always enjoyed pushing his body to its physical limits, but today he barely even noticed. He'd skipped it yesterday not wanting to leave Juliet alone so soon after what she'd been through, and he'd loved every second of the time they'd shared.

It wasn't just the sex, hot and steamy though it had been, it was holding her naked body against his as they talked about everything. He'd shared more with her about how hard it had been growing up with a critically ill sibling, and she'd shared more about her life with parents who didn't care about her at all. She'd told him more about her OCD and also her dreams for her future, and he had never in his life felt a connection to another human being like he had with Juliet.

She seemed to understand what life would be like marrying a SEAL, and he believed that she was strong enough to cope with the demands it would put on her. She was strong and tough and didn't give up even when she was afraid, she was sweet as well and not afraid to be vulnerable with him. She was everything he had ever hoped for in a partner, and he was thrilled that she wanted to stay here with him even once she was out of danger.

Everything was going perfectly, and he couldn't remember a time in his life when he'd been happier.

"What?" he asked, aware as he stood to set the weights he'd been using back on the shelf that his team was staring at him.

"I wasn't aware it was possible for you to look any happier, but Juliet seems to have proved that wrong," Fox said with a grin.

"I'm always happy, you guys know that," he said, rolling his eyes.

"Happy, yes, but this is otherworld level of happiness," Spider said.

"You're exaggerating."

"He's not," Night said.

"I don't even look that happy in a bar surrounded by dozens of beautiful women," King joked.

Chaos studied his friend for a moment. If he and Juliet

worked out then King would be the only one on their team left who wasn't married or involved. He wished that his friend would open himself up to the idea of meeting one woman and falling in love, but knowing how King had grown up and the example his parents had set for him, he thought it was unlikely. While the rest of them were married with kids, King would probably still be hanging out in bars, picking up women, spending the night with them then never seeing them again.

"Things with you and Juliet getting serious?" Spider asked.

"Yeah, they are. I know we just met, and I'm not saying I'm in love with her yet or anything, but there's definitely something between us and we both want to see where it goes," he explained. He liked being able to keep things pressure free while at the same time know that they were both committed to seeing where this thing with them went. It sounded contradictory, if you were committed things were hardly pressure free, but that was exactly how it felt. He and Juliet were on the same page, there was just no pressure to get to the ending in any sort of timeframe, they got there when they got there. They had the whole rest of their lives ahead of them.

"That's great, man." Night slapped him on the back. "I'm happy for you. And Lavender thinks Juliet is great, even more so since she offered to help organize all of Anastasia's toys. Since you," he said, pointing at Spider, "and Abby are adding another baby to the family we decided we better keep up and start trying for another as well."

"Abby will be thrilled, she loved having a pregnancy buddy last time," Spider said. "You and Claire better hurry up and get reproducing," he said to Shark, who looked back at him in horror.

Shark was a huge man, intimidating and usually silent unless he was with his fiancée, and then it was like he changed into a different person. "I don't think I'm ready for the stress of having two people to worry about."

Just like Claire hadn't yet fully recovered from her ordeal in Afghanistan four months ago, Shark hadn't either. He'd blamed himself for her abduction and subsequent rape and torture, and he didn't like to let Claire out of his sight.

"It's not going to be long till Claire will start getting baby fever, and we all know Shark is a sucker when it comes to her, whatever Claire wants Claire gets," Fox teased.

Shark just glowered, but his face softened. He did indeed do whatever made his fiancée happy. "Maybe after we're married," he grunted.

"Who's ready to start taking bets on how long it takes Chaos to propose to Juliet?" King asked, a huge grin on his face.

"Dude," Chaos said, shaking his head at his friend. "I only just met her."

"You want to waste time like that idiot?" King asked, waving a hand at Spider. "Took him three tries with Abby to get it right. Or you could mess up like that one," he pointed to Night, "he sent the woman who was pregnant with his child running into the arms of someone who was insane."

"That is not a true representation of what happened," Night grumbled.

"It kinda is, dude." Chaos laughed.

"I got it right in the end," Night said. "And I'm in on placing bets. I say Chaos doesn't last a month before he proposes."

"I call by the end of the month," King said.

"I think Juliet is going to keep him waiting before she's

ready for a proposal, I'm going for Valentine's Day," Spider said.

"Chaos is a romantic at heart, but not cheesy, I think he'll forgo Valentine's Day because everyone proposes then, it's too artificial. I think he's going to propose on the first day of spring. Spring is all about new beginnings after all," Fox said.

"Shark?" King asked, typing away on his phone entering the bets.

Shark cocked his head, appeared to be giving the question a lot of thought. "When's Juliet's birthday?"

"March 10th," he replied.

"March 10th," Shark said to King.

"So, what does the winner get?" Spider asked. "And it can't be money, we have another baby coming and Abby got mad the last time I bet and lost money we could have used on something for the house or RJ."

"Losers have to complete whatever dare winner wants," King said with a grin.

The others groaned but all agreed, and Chaos rolled his eyes at them but couldn't not smile. They'd placed bets on when all of them would propose to their women, and he was kind of excited that it was his turn, not that he'd decided when or where he would propose, he'd have to wait and see how things developed.

His phone rang and he snatched it up, pleased to see Eagle's name on the screen. "It's Eagle," he told the others, then answered and put the phone on speaker so they could all hear. "Hey, man, everyone is here. What do you have? Are the Fedorovs in Russia?" He was hoping so for Juliet's sake. She deserved to live her life free and clear, on her own terms, without being afraid.

"They are," Eagle replied.

That should have made him smile, but there was something in his friend's tone that said bad news was coming. "But?"

"Arthur York's house was trashed sometime after he was arrested, all valuables, mostly jewelry but also some paintings, were taken, and his wife was murdered, slashed to pieces, looks like someone did it with a lot of anger," Eagle told him.

His gut clenched, Juliet had already lost her father, now she'd lost her mother as well. He knew that she had mixed feelings about them, especially given how they'd basically sold her to the Russian mafia, but they were still her parents, and the loss of her mother would still hurt her.

"Can we narrow down a timeline?" he asked.

"Best guess is late on the twenty-first. Staff left as usual at nine and everything was okay. There were orders for no one to come in on the twenty-second. According to the staff this was unusual, they worked every day. Body was found this morning. Although we have a window of more than twenty-four hours the alarm was disarmed around ten on the twenty-first and never reset. We're assuming that's when the killer came in," Eagle explained.

"The Fedorovs?" he asked.

"They were on a plane back to Russia at the time. Not that that discounts them, they wouldn't have done it themselves, but they could have paid someone to," Eagle said. "I had word put out that if anything popped up with the Yorks that I was to be notified and this only just came in about an hour ago. Do you want to be the one to notify Juliet? I can tell the cops to hold off, let it come from you if you think that would be best, or if you think she'd rather hear it from a stranger I'll tell them to go ahead and make the call."

That was an easy one. It had to come from him. Juliet deserved to hear it from someone who cared about her, someone who would break the news gently and comfort her afterward, not from strangers doing their job.

"I'll do it."

1:03 P.M.

JULIET KEPT SNEAKING glances at the baby in her arms. She'd never really been around babies before. She was an only child, she didn't have any cousins as her mother was also an only child and her father wasn't close with his family. The few friends she did have weren't married and didn't have kids, so before she'd met Grayson and his friends she'd never even held a baby.

Now she was sitting at the table in Grayson's kitchen with Evie and Fox's six-month-old son Sullivan snuggled in her arms and she couldn't take her eyes off him. She was trying to pay attention to the conversation, Abby and Lavender were putting their toddlers down for their naps in the portable cribs they'd brought with them, through in the living room, but Evie and Claire were talking away. She really should be listening, it was rude not to, but this little guy was so cute with his dark lashes fanned out over his soft little cheeks, all snuggled up in his blanket and a lion onesie that had the cutest hood ever, making the baby too cute for words.

"You look good with a baby in your arms."

She glanced up to find Evie and Claire staring at her. They both had smiles on their faces and didn't look angry at her, still she smiled sheepishly. "Sorry I was distracted."

"Yeah, with that little guy," Claire said. "I said, you look good with a baby in your arms. You ever thought about having kids?"

"Not really. I mean, I knew my father wanted me to have a son, he was always disappointed that I was a girl, in his mind, that made me unfit to take over his business. So the plan was for him to marry me off and for me to get pregnant almost right away with a son. I don't think the plan was for me to do much of the raising of him though. He would have had a nanny, and I would have been nothing more than the woman who held him for photo ops."

"I'm sorry, it sucks to have a family that doesn't care about you," Claire said, reaching out to touch her shoulder. Something in the other woman's voice told her that Claire knew exactly what that was like.

"What about now though?" Evie asked. "Now that you're free of your father and you're with Grayson, you think you might want one of these?" She ran the back of a finger over her son's chubby cheek.

"Yeah," she said slowly. "I think that I see babies in my future. Not yet, I'm not ready, and this thing with Grayson is new, but yeah, maybe in a couple of years I'd love to have kids, raise them the way I wish my parents had raised me."

"That's what I plan to do," Claire said.

"Me too," Evie added, and it was clear she too hadn't had a great relationship with her parents.

It helped to know that there were others who might not have lived the same life she had, but had felt that same sense of isolation and loneliness. It made her feel like they understood, that she wasn't alone. "I guess even bad parents can teach you lessons, what not to do."

"Definitely," Claire said.

"Totally," Evie added.

She heard the front door open and she couldn't not smile.

Grayson was home, and even though they could hardly make out in front of their friends who were staying for lunch, she could at least kiss him hello, maybe hold his hand, sit close enough beside him at the table that their legs touched.

Her smile faded away when he and his team joined them in the kitchen.

Grayson wasn't smiling.

In fact he looked tense.

Something had happened.

Was it her father?

Had he somehow managed to buy his way out of jail?

"What's wrong?" she asked, standing on shaky legs and passing the baby off to his mother.

"We have to go, fairy," Fox said, reaching for his wife and son.

Shark too went to Claire and snapped a lead onto Goldilocks' collar. "Come on, sweetheart."

"No one is staying?" she asked. If they were leaving to give her and Grayson space then whatever he had to tell her was bad.

Really bad.

"What is it? What's wrong?" she demanded.

"Call if you need us," King said, shooting her a sympathetic glance before clapping Grayson on the back.

He nodded his thanks and seconds later they were standing alone in the kitchen. Part of her wanted to go to him, wrap her arms around him, lead him upstairs, make love to him, pretend he didn't have something awful to tell her. The other part of her wanted to pause this second in time so they didn't have to talk.

The decision was taken out of her hands because Grayson crossed the kitchen to take her hand. He led her through to the living room and eased her onto the couch. Instead of sitting beside her, he crouched in front of her, his hands resting on her knees.

"I'm sorry, Juliet," he said, his green eyes filled with pain.

"What? Why? Is it my dad? Was he killed in jail or something?"

"No, honey, it's not your dad, it's your mom."

"My mom?" she echoed. As far as she knew her mom was home at her parents' house in Orange County. Unless the Fedorovs had been angry that her father hadn't produced her and as a punishment to her father had killed his wife. "What happened to her?"

"It looks like someone broke into your parents' house. They ransacked the place and killed your mom. I'm so sorry."

He moved to embrace her but she fended him off.

Her mom was dead?

Murdered?

By someone who broke into the house.

Was it a random home invasion, the Russian mafia, or was her father mixed up in something else she didn't know about?

"Wh-who?" she asked.

"I don't know, honey. Is there anyone you can think of who might want to hurt your mom? Or your dad?"

Juliet shook her head. "Well, I mean, I guess the Fedorovs if they were angry with my dad for not bringing me back to Dimitri. But I don't think they'd kill my mom over it. Although I don't really know much about the Russian mafia so maybe they would. Maybe it was just random, a home invasion or something?" She looked up at him with hopeful eyes, but the look on Grayson's face squashed that hope.

"The alarm was disarmed, so whoever did it either knew the code, or it was someone your mom knew and trusted and let in," he told her. "Is there anything in the house you think they might have been looking for?"

"I don't know, I don't think so, but I was a girl, a disappointment to my father, he didn't include me in anything he did. I might have worked for him but I was just another employee, his head designer yes, but in name only. If he was into something else he wouldn't have told me. He didn't even tell me that he had promised me to a Russian mafia prince," she finished bitterly. "My mom had to be in on it, she had to know who the Fedorovs were and she didn't care. Part of me hates her, Grayson, really hates her. She's supposed to be my mom but she never acted like it, she never told me she loved me, never cared about me at all, but …"

"But she's your mom and you still love her, and now she's gone." He moved to sit beside her and enfolded her into his warm embrace.

As soon as his arms closed around her she broke.

Part of her truly did hate her mother—her father too—but at the end of the day, they were still her parents, and despite their betrayals her mother didn't deserve to be killed in her own home.

Her tears came in a torrent and she curled her fingers into Grayson's shirt, pressing her face against his neck as he rocked her gently and whispered soothingly in her ear. She couldn't make out the words through her sobs, but she didn't care, they weren't important. All that was important was that he was here and he was holding her.

Juliet had no idea of how long she lay in Grayson's arms crying, but eventually her tears dried up leaving her feeling shaky and unsettled. "I need to drive over there."

"No, honey," he said, stroking her hair. "Not today. Tomorrow I'll take you there and you can talk to the cops, check the house to see if you can find anything else that's missing, see your mom's body if you want, but today you're going to stay here and let me take care of you."

Take care of her.

When was the last time someone had taken care of her?

Nannies when she was sick when she was a kid, but that wasn't the same, they hadn't cared about anything other than meeting her physical needs.

Grayson cared.

He'd tend to her heart as well as her body, and the thought of that made her start crying all over again.

CHAPTER 8

January 24th

9:47 A.M.

JULIET WAS quiet in the car beside him, but she had her fingers curled around his, and she was holding on tightly enough that Chaos was worried about his fingers going numb.

Not really.

She wasn't strong enough, but he was worried about how she was handling the news about her mother. It was another blow that she didn't need when she was already dealing with so much, but he knew she was strong enough to get through this like she'd been strong enough to handle everything else life had thrown at her.

Still he worried about her.

She'd been walking around in a fog since he'd broken the news to her yesterday afternoon. They'd curled up on the couch together for most of the afternoon watching movies, but he was pretty sure she couldn't tell him what movies they'd actually watched. He'd had to force her to eat dinner, and while he'd wanted to tuck her into bed when night came, she'd begged him to make love to her and he couldn't say no. Afterward he wrapped her in his arms and held her for hours after she had eventually drifted into a restless sleep.

This morning she'd been on edge, anxious to make the ninety-minute drive to her parents' house, and they'd ended up leaving earlier than he'd intended. Not that it mattered, they may as well get this over and done with. Juliet needed the closure of seeing her mother's body, and they needed to talk with the local cops, see what they were thinking.

Eagle had promised to look into it as well, and since he ran the most respected private security company in the country, Chaos hoped that the cops would share everything they had with him. If they didn't, he had no doubt that Eagle would have his computer whiz of a sister Raven take a peek at the investigation.

For now, his focus was on Juliet, she was his number one priority, and the first thing he needed to know was whether or not she was in danger.

"You want to stop and get something to eat?" he asked.

"Not hungry."

"You said that yesterday," he reminded her. "You hardly ate any lunch or dinner, and you barely touched your breakfast this morning."

"I'm not hungry, Grayson," she snapped angrily, then immediately her face fell in remorse. "I'm sorry. I'm so sorry. I shouldn't have yelled at you, I didn't mean to, I just … I don't even know, I just want to get this done. I want to know who killed my mom and if they're going to go after me or my dad next. Do you think it could have been the Fedorovs?"

They'd already gone over all of this yesterday, but he knew she'd been in shock then and might not remember what they discussed, or she just needed to hear it again. Whatever the case, he'd tell her as many times as she needed to hear it. "We're not sure, princess. It could have been the Fedorov's way of punishing your father for not delivering you to them by taking his wife." Chaos hesitated, there was a reason that both Eagle and Chaos and his team weren't sure that was the case, but he wasn't sure that Juliet needed to hear it.

"What?" his intuitive girl asked. "You're holding something back, I can tell. Whatever it is I can handle it, Grayson. I need to know, the not knowing is worse than anything you could say to me."

Still he hesitated, some things you couldn't unhear or unlearn, and this was one of them. Still, Juliet was strong, and she knew her own mind. If she said that it was worse not knowing then he would take her at her word, she deserved not to be underestimated ever again. "The Fedorovs are well known for taking a pound of flesh from those that they want to teach a lesson to. Your mother had been stabbed dozens of times, but they hadn't removed a pound of flesh. Plus the Fedorovs were on a plane back to Russia when we think your mom was killed."

Juliet stared at him, her face paper pale. Then she lifted a hand to cover her mouth. "Pull over," she instructed.

They'd left the highway behind and were now on a relatively quiet road as they made their way to the exclusive area she had grown up in. Chaos veered over to the side of the road and as soon as he did, Juliet threw her door open, staggered out, and dropped to her knees, throwing up what little he'd managed to get her to eat.

Bringing a bottle of water with him, he rounded the car and crouched beside her, stroking her back as she continued to dry wretch. When she was done, he handed her the uncapped bottle. “Here, wash your mouth out and then drink some water,” he said softly.

She did as he said, rinsing her mouth then gulping down a few mouthfuls. “They really do that?” she asked shakily.

“Yeah, princess, they do.”

“And my dad knew that?”

“I'm guessing he did.”

“And he was still going to sell me to them?”

“I know it sucks, honey, and I can't give you an answer that you’ll like, or one that makes sense because a father doing that to his daughter doesn’t make sense to me, but yeah, he obviously knew who he was getting into bed with and he just didn’t care.” Chaos didn’t want to bash her father to her face, but he also wasn’t going to pretend the man was a good one because he wasn’t, and Chaos would love to get him alone for a few minutes to give him a taste of what his daughter was going to get as the wife of a Russian mafia prince.

“I hate him,” she said, tears brimming in her eyes.

Pulling her to her feet, Chaos enfolded her in his arms, rocking her as they stood at the side of the road. His heart broke for her. He knew that not everyone had parents like his, knew that parents abused their kids in all ways, shapes, and forms, but to sell your own daughter to the mafia, knowing she would be beaten, raped, and tortured as she was taught her place was a special kind of cold.

“I know you do, honey. If it was the Fedorovs who killed your mom, then I promise you we will make them pay, and if it was someone else, we’ll find out and make sure that they get the book thrown at them. I promise you.” He needed her to believe that, needed her to know that she wasn’t on her own, he was here, he would do anything she needed, he’d find a way to bring her some measure of peace. "What do you need from me, sweetheart? What can I do for you?"

Juliet tilted her head up and gave him a watery smile. "You're already doing it. You're holding me."

It was such a simple thing, and yet something her parents had deprived her of. When she'd been a child who needed to be shown love and affection, they'd instead isolated her and used her OCD to control and manipulate her. She wasn't used to having someone there to hold her when she needed them, and while he was happy to do it for her it broke his heart that she'd never had the simple comfort of a hug before she fled her family.

"All right, princess, that I can do." Usually he'd make a joke, try to lighten the mood, but right now he couldn't find it in him to find anything even vaguely humorous. So he just stood there and held her, smoothing a hand down the length of her spine and touching kisses to her temple.

A couple of minutes later, he felt her pull herself together and she gently pulled back. "Thank you, I'm ready to go now. I'm glad you told me what the Fedorovs do, I need to know what I'd be up against if the worst happened and they somehow get to me."

While he hated that she thought that was a possibility—mainly because there *was* a chance that they would come for her—he was so proud of her for trying to approach this rationally and with as much logic as she could muster. In the end it just might save her life.

"You're welcome." He tipped her face up so he could kiss her on the lips, and then he guided her back into the car, clicking her seatbelt into place and then pressing the bottle of water back into her hands. "Drink some more and we'll stop someplace soon to get something to eat. I know you're not hungry," he added before she could protest, "but regardless, your body needs fuel, and one thing you learn in the SEALs is that it's important to take care of your body's needs whether you feel like it or not. It could end up being a matter of life or death. Besides, I told you I was here to take care of you, and making sure you're holding up and keeping up your strength is a part of that."

Juliet nodded and brought the bottle to her lips as he straightened and turned around, closing her door. Chaos took only another step before something slammed into his chest, pain exploded inside him, and the world spiraled into a black vortex of nothingness.

His last thought was that he had failed the woman he was falling for and left her alone and vulnerable to whoever had just shot him.

~

11:13 A.M.

JULIET SPRANG AWAKE ON A SCREAM.

Grayson.

He'd been shot.

She remembered the loud crack of the gunshot, then there had been men running toward her, pulling her from the car. Something sharp had pierced her skin and then the world had gone all fuzzy, eventually fading away into nothingness.

Abduction.

It had been a planned abduction. Someone must have been following her and Grayson, taken advantage of the fact that they'd pulled over to the side of the road, then taken him out when he was distracted by her. With Grayson down she'd been a sitting duck, easy prey for whoever wanted to kidnap her.

Now Grayson was gone, and she was …

For the first time it occurred to her to see where she was. Grayson had died trying to protect her, she owed it to him to do everything she could to survive.

It was dark wherever she was, and whatever she'd been put on was hard and uncomfortable. Her hands weren't bound, and she wasn't sure if that was a good thing because it meant she had a chance at fighting off whoever came for her, or a bad thing because her abductors knew that her chances of escape were zero.

Still, she wasn't going to waste the freedom the use of her hands afforded because she had no idea who had taken her or why, but she didn't need details to know that right now freedom was a rare commodity and one that wasn't likely to last. Pressing her hands against the floor, she ran her fingers across it.

Wood.

It felt like wood.

A little rough to the touch but smooth in some places, and she could even feel a few knots. Juliet continued to trace along the floor with her fingertips until she reached something that went up. A wall. She continued her exploration wincing when a splinter stabbed into her palm, until she found the top of the wall. As she suspected there was a roof. Well not really a roof—she was in a box.

A large wooden box.

She stretched out her legs until they touched one end of the box then tried to lie down. She quickly found out that she couldn't quite stretch out the whole way. The box was probably around five feet in length, so her five-foot-three frame wouldn't be able to lie flat. She stretched her arms above her head and was able to get them almost straight, so not enough room to sit up, and when she moved her arms out straight from her sides, she found she could only get them about halfway to straight.

She was trapped.

In a wooden box.

Panic settled in her stomach, it tasted foul and made her nauseous, but she fought against the urge to throw up. No way she could handle being in here and having to smell and touch her own vomit.

Her torso began to rock slightly, a keening wail that took her a moment to realize was coming from herself began to fall from her lips.

Trapped.

Abducted.

Alone.

For a second she hated Grayson for showing her what it was like to have someone by her side, holding her hand, supporting her, and caring about her. If she'd never met him, she would have been so much better equipped to deal with this. All her life she had been used to dealing with things on her own and then in had come Grayson with his infectious smile and big heart and he'd changed everything.

He'd changed her.

Now the idea of going through this alone was so overwhelming that it smothered her.

Her fingers clawed at her face trying to dislodge the sickening feeling, but there was nothing there to remove because the panic was inside of her. In the end, all she achieved was a raging headache from her frantic tossing of her head.

Following on the heels of fear was horror.

Had she really just wished—even for one second—that she had never met Grayson?

Had she allowed the word hate to even enter her mind in conjunction with the man who had grown to mean so much to her?

Self-loathing had tears streaming down her cheeks. The tears seemed to sink inside her, filling up her stomach and her lungs until she felt like she was being drowned alive. Drowned in her own sorrow, her own regret, her own disgust.

She didn't hate Grayson, she was very close to loving him.

And she didn't regret a single second that she'd spent with him. So what if it had made her go soft? She'd needed a touch of softness in her life. Even if she had known what was going to happen, she wouldn't have traded a moment she spent in his arms, in his home, or in his bed. He'd taught her what it was like to really live, opened up a whole new world to her, and for that, she would be eternally grateful.

Because of him, she knew what it was like to feel cherished, special, wanted. She'd experienced a gentle touch, a warm heart, steamy kisses, and tender lovemaking. She'd experienced the good in the world.

She'd thought she could have that for a lifetime.

It had been so close.

Right within her grasp.

Until it hadn't any more.

Now Grayson was dead and she had been kidnapped. His body would be found, and she thought his team would come looking for her. She didn't think they would blame her for their friend's death, they weren't those kinds of people, and they knew that she meant a lot to Grayson. She thought they would come looking for her, but she wasn't positive.

Maybe no one was coming.

Maybe no one cared enough.

No.

No.

Her new friends cared, they'd come, she just had to keep believing that.

Voices had her head snapping to the side. Someone was coming.

All of a sudden light glowed through a small hole in the wooden box directly above her face, and Juliet propped herself up so she could peer through it.

From what she could see, the box she was being kept in was one of many large wooden boxes stacked around her. Were there other women in them? Was she not the only one who had been kidnapped?

That made no sense.

Why would someone follow her and Grayson, kill him and abduct her, and then have also abducted other women too?

She'd thought this had something to do with the Fedorovs, or her father, or her mother's death, or maybe all three, but she didn't really know anything about her kidnappers or their reasons for taking her.

The voices got louder, but they weren't speaking English, they were speaking … maybe Portuguese?

Why would Portuguese people be abducting her?

Her head ached from trying to figure out what was happening to her.

The men, she heard at least four different voices, were laughing and talking, and she could hear them moving about, she guessed loading the boxes onto something. Was she being taken to Portugal? How would Grayson's team ever find her there?

Panic was taking hold again, and when the box she was in suddenly started moving she couldn't help but scream.

The men laughed, and while she couldn't understand the words they were saying she knew that tone.

They were talking about having sex with her.

Were they human traffickers?

But didn't they usually snatch people off the streets? It felt more like she had been targeted, so what did they want with her?

Juliet was jolted around inside the box, hitting the sides more than once as she was carried. Then pain shot through her as her box was dumped down and she hit the bottom of it hard, her head smacking the side hard enough that she saw stars.

More boxes must have been piled in around her, and a moment later the darkness was back.

This time it felt blacker.

More ominous.

She wasn't getting out of this box, she wasn't getting away from these men, and she was sure that she wasn't going to survive whatever they were planning on doing to her. She was also sure that they didn't intend for her to have a quick death. They'd taken her for a reason, even if she didn't yet know what that reason was, and if someone went to all this trouble to grab another person they weren't going to kill them quickly.

Juliet lay there, panting, crying quietly, her hands pressed to the top of the box as she tapped each finger one at a time in an attempt to calm herself.

"One, two, three, four, five, six, seven, eight, nine, ten," she whispered, repeating it over and over like a mantra.

Until a loud noise startled her.

An engine.

She was on a plane.

They were taking her out of the country, to Portugal or

somewhere else, it hardly mattered where. What mattered was that she was gone and while she hoped Grayson's team wouldn't give up on her, she had to acknowledge that they would have no idea where to look for her.

~

6:36 P.M.

As he woke slowly, Chaos was aware that something was wrong, he just couldn't figure out what it was.

Something had happened.

Something bad.

Something that had him feeling like he'd been kicked in the chest.

He just wished he knew what that something was.

The room had that awful antiseptic smell that reminded him of a hospital, and he could hear something beeping incessantly behind him. Add both of those things to the pain in his chest and Chaos knew he was in a hospital.

His eyes opened slowly, his eyelids feeling sticky as well as heavy, and immediately saw his entire team lounging around. Fox was in a chair, Shark leaning against the wall, while Spider, Night, and King were all sitting on the floor, their backs propped against the walls. They were talking in hushed voices, and it took a moment for them to realize that he was awake.

"Hey, man, how're you feeling?" Fox asked, leaning forward to prop his elbows on his knees.

"What happened?" he asked, annoyed when his voice came out a weak croak.

"Got yourself shot," King said with a smirk. It was a team

custom that if you got yourself shot you had to buy everyone dinner at their favorite bar as soon as you got out of the hospital, or if they were on a mission as soon as they got back home.

Chaos groaned, no wonder he felt like there was a rock sitting on his chest. Still it could have been worse, he was obviously all right, awake, alert, talking, couldn't have been too bad. "Through and through?" he asked.

"Yeah, you were lucky, went through just under your left armpit but missed all the major arteries. You lost a lot of blood, but no surgery needed. You'll be out of commission for a few days at least though," Spider explained.

More like he'd give himself twenty-four hours then start working out again, no way he was hanging around for days, or even a week or two, he'd go crazy if he had to sit still that long. Something was niggling at him though, he didn't think that he'd gotten shot on a mission, hospitals were kind of generic so it was hard to tell if they were in the US or somewhere else. But why would he have gotten shot at home?

A training exercise somehow gone wrong?

No.

That didn't feel right.

Then it clicked.

"Where's Juliet?" he demanded. He'd been taking her to Orange Country to go to her parents' house, then speak with the cops about her mother's murder. They'd stopped at the side of the road because Juliet had needed to throw up when he told her what the Fedorov family was known to do to anyone they wanted to teach a lesson to.

That was the last thing he remembered.

Had she been shot too?

If she was here in the hospital somewhere then one of his

team should be guarding her. Why were they all hanging around in his room?

"Why aren't one of you with her?" he growled.

Their exchanged looks did little to calm the storm of fear raging inside him.

"What's the last thing you remember?" Night asked.

"Juliet and I stopped at the side of the road on our way to her parents' house. I'd just put her back in the car and was turning around when there was a blinding pain in my chest, and then I blacked out."

"It was lucky you were turning right as they shot you, saved your life," Spider said.

"Was Juliet shot too?" he asked. "Is she here? None of you answered. Why aren't one of you in her room? I don't want her alone."

None of them offered a comment, and the fear inside him grew until it far outweighed the pain. If they weren't going to answer him then he'd go and look for her himself. Chaos sat up and threw the blankets off him, he was reaching to remove the IV when Fox stopped him.

"Fine," his team leader said, raking his hands through his dark hair. "Juliet isn't here."

Relief would have washed over him, but he already knew he wasn't going to like the reason why Juliet wasn't here in the hospital. Still he wasn't quite ready to release the death grip he had on denial just yet. "Is she with the cops talking to them about what happened to her mother? Did she go back to my place to rest?" He might not have known Juliet for long, but he knew with a certainty he felt down to his very bones that there was no way she wouldn't be here, sitting beside his hospital bed, unless she couldn't be.

"She's not with the cops and she's not at your place," Night replied.

He didn't want to say the word, it tasted foul in his mouth, but he had to know. "Dead?"

"No," Spider said quickly.

"At least we don't think so," King added.

"No body," Fox explained when he saw the obvious confusion on Chaos' face. "You were the only one there when cops arrived on the scene."

"A kidnapping," he said grimly. "We thought it was a possibility that the Fedorovs would still come after Juliet even with her father in prison, but I didn't think they'd kidnap her in broad daylight. The road we were on wasn't a highway or anything, but it was hardly some small, secluded country road, there would have been other people about."

"There were," King nodded.

"They shot at another six vehicles. No one else was seriously injured, they shot only to disable the cars," Spider told him.

"So there are witnesses." That was better than he could have hoped for. Witnesses meant that they had a chance at finding Juliet and that was all that mattered to him. This thing between them was real, and it was big and special, there was no way he was letting anyone take her from him now.

"Yes," Fox agreed.

"They saw Juliet getting kidnapped?"

"They did." Night nodded. "Reports are that four men dressed in black with ski masks covering their faces pulled in behind you in a white van. They shot you, grabbed Juliet, and drove off. She wasn't fighting them as they put her in the van, but there was none of her blood in your car."

"They drugged her," he said.

"That's the assumption," Spider agreed.

"Witnesses said the kidnappers weren't speaking English," King told him.

"Russian?" Chaos asked. They'd wondered if the Russians had killed Juliet's mother and trashed the house, but there was no way for sure to know that yet. If it was someone else, he had no idea how they would track Juliet down before she was hurt. Or killed.

"No, witnesses were asked to listen to a range of languages and it seems like the kidnappers might have been speaking Portuguese," Fox explained.

Portuguese?

Had Juliet been taken to Portugal?

That made no sense at all.

"I don't understand," he said, scrubbing his hands across his face and sinking back against the bed.

"We know someone who might though," King said.

"Who?" he asked.

"Arthur York," King replied. "If anyone would know who trashed his house, killed his wife, and then kidnapped his daughter, it's him."

"He was refusing to cooperate," Chaos reminded him.

"He was, but that was then, now that his daughter is gone he might change his tune," Spider suggested.

"I don't think so, he doesn't care about Juliet beyond how he can use her to further himself. Now that he knows he's facing years in prison there's nothing Juliet can offer him," Chaos said, feeling frighteningly close to losing it. Juliet was gone, drugged, taken who knows where. She could be tortured or killed, and he had no idea how he would find her.

"Self-preservation," Shark said, speaking for the first time as he pushed away from the wall and crossed to the bed. "Arthur York is all about self-preservation, so we offer him a deal, a reduced sentence in exchange for everything he knows, but only if we find Juliet alive and unharmed."

"It might work," he said with cautious optimism. "And

it's not like we have any other options anyway. We need to speak with Arthur."

"I'll see if we can set something up for tomorrow," Fox promised.

He didn't want to wait that long, but it was dark out, and he was sure Arthur wouldn't talk without his lawyer present. It would probably be tomorrow before they could set it up even if they tried to make a time tonight. "I want to go home," he said, sitting up again.

"No," Fox said firmly. "You were shot, you lost a lot of blood, your body needs rest. You spend the night here and we'll leave in the morning to go back to San Diego. Nothing you could do at home tonight anyway, so you may as well stay here."

Chaos didn't like it, but his friend was right. He needed his strength back if he was going to find Juliet, and that was all that was important to him. He would find her. He had to, he couldn't accept the possibility that she was already gone from his life for good. That left him feeling like there was a huge gaping wound in his soul that was too big to be stitched closed.

"We'll find her," Shark said vehemently. It wasn't long ago that he'd been desperate to get back the woman he was falling for, and those wounds were still fresh for both Shark and Claire.

He nodded, his friend had gotten a happy ending, he prayed he and Juliet were that lucky, but he had a bad feeling that there was a lot more going on here than they knew, and that Juliet might already be too far out of their reach to get back.

CHAPTER 9

January 25th

8:56 A.M.

HER HEAD FELT like someone had filled it with cotton candy.

It felt sticky, fluffy, like it didn't quite know how to work properly.

Juliet groaned groggily and reached up to rub her temples, hoping that she could wipe away whatever was wrong with her.

It didn't help.

But the movement did wake her up a little and with returned consciousness came a sudden awareness of her situation.

Her eyes snapped open and she bolted upright on the bed.

Bed.

She was no longer in that awful wooden box, now she

was in a room, a bedroom. It was light outside, she could see blue sky through the curtainless window. The room had a bed, a dresser, and a desk with a chair. All the furniture was simple, all made from wood, it wasn't painted or polished, it looked like the kind of thing you might have expected to see in a home from two hundred years ago.

Her gaze settled on the door.

She was alone in the room, and her mind was filled with only one thing.

Escape.

Juliet stood on shaky legs and fought off a rush of dizziness that would have had her toppling over if she hadn't flung out a hand to brace herself against the bedhead.

She had to get to the door.

If she could get through it she could get out of here.

Wherever here was.

The last thing she remembered was the plane landing, the wooden box she was in being moved, and then opened. A man had been there, but before she had a chance to react in any way, he'd jammed a syringe into her arm and drugged her. Once she was unconscious she must have been brought here, but she still had no idea where she was or why she'd been kidnapped.

When her head stopped spinning enough that she could walk she hurried to the door, grabbing the handle and yanking on it.

Nothing happened.

Locked.

She was locked in.

Before panic could take hold she stumbled to the window. If she couldn't get out the door then she'd escape her room this way.

"No," she screamed in frustration when she saw there

were bars on the outside. Big thick metal bars, there was no way she could get through them.

She was trapped.

Again.

"No, no, no," she screamed, curling her fingers into her hair as she spun in a circle taking in her new prison.

What did these people want with her?

Why had they gone to so much trouble to get her here?

That they intended to keep her—at least for a while—was plain, but she had no idea why and that made her feel so out of control.

Juliet dragged in huge lungfuls of air, attempting to slow her breathing but it didn't work. She might be out of that awful box but she was still trapped, her prison was just a little larger this time.

What was she going to do?

Helplessness knocked her to her knees and she fell to the floor, curling up in a ball and rocking herself. Fear ate at her, tearing her apart piece by piece as she realized she was probably never walking out of this room alive.

A sound outside her room made her head snap up. Was somebody coming?

Her door swung open, and a large man dressed in an expensive-looking black suit stood there sneering at her. Afraid, she skittered backward on her bottom until she was pressed up against the wall. He didn't need to do anything but stand there looking all menacing to have her half wishing they'd just killed her instead of abducting her.

"Stand," he said in heavily accented English.

He was huge, well over six feet tall, closer to seven, with dark skin, eyes that looked like two black orbs, and hair cut short so it was nothing more than black fuzz across the top of his head. She didn't want to stand, but she also didn't want to cower in front of him. She had a feeling he would take advantage of any weakness, and she wanted him to know that he couldn't break her. She was strong, and she would survive this.

She had to.

It was the only way to honor Grayson's memory.

Juliet stood, standing straight before him, meeting his gaze.

He seemed surprised that she wasn't cowering at his feet, but his tone was mocking when he spoke. "Welcome to Angola, Ms. York."

He knew her name.

Her abduction hadn't been random. Juliet had never really thought it had been but hearing it confirmed was still terrifying.

She still had no idea why she'd been brought to Angola though.

"Angola?"

"In Africa," the man replied.

"I know where Angola is. I just … I don't … why did you bring me here? Who are you? And what do you want with me?" Despite her best efforts her voice wavered a little, but she did manage to maintain eye contact.

The man threw back his head and laughed. "Your father, he did not keep you informed of his business dealings."

"No, he didn't," she agreed. "I was just the head designer, all I did was design jewelry, nothing else."

"And do you know where those jewels and diamonds came from?"

"No. Well my father bought them straight from diamond miners in Africa, he didn't like to waste money and he thought using a broker was a cost he could forgo, so he dealt directly with …" Juliet trailed off as she realized that she was currently in Africa, and that this guy was talking about her father, didn't take a genius to figure out this was who her father had bought diamonds from.

"With me." The man grinned. "Only your father, he didn't like to pay his bills."

"Okay," she said slowly. She had no idea what that had to do with her.

"He owes us a large sum of money. He has been given many chances to pay up and yet he does not. We grow weary waiting so we have decided to take payment in another form."

Juliet gulped. "Another form?"

"You, Ms. York," the man said.

"Me?" she squeaked. What exactly did that mean?

"You will work here. You will cook and clean for the men who work here, and cook for the miners. You will also be available to service my men," he said with a dark smile as he leaned in close, his hot breath against her ear made her shudder. "You are a beautiful woman, Ms. York, and the men here have not seen a pretty woman in a long time. I am sure your services will be greatly appreciated."

"Y-you use slaves to w-work the m-mines," she said. Her entire body trembled as she struggled to stand her ground instead of shrinking away from this man. "You sell black market diamonds."

"I sell high-quality diamonds to people who prefer to do business without a third party sticking their nose into that which doesn't concern them. Your father was a man who appreciated a good deal, he liked to drive a hard bargain, both of those things I could appreciate. But when he took millions of dollars worth of diamonds and paid only half of what he owed me, I'm sure you can understand why I needed to find a way to rectify that."

"I'm not worth millions of dollars," she said, staring at him in open-mouthed shock.

The man laughed like he found her hilarious. "No of course not, dear. But between you, the shedding of his wife's blood, and the diamonds and precious stones we were able to find from his personal stash, I think we can call it breaking even."

The break-in at her parents' house, it had been these men. They'd killed her mother, obviously tossed the house to look for any jewels her father kept there, then they'd come after her, killing Grayson to get to her. Now they wanted to keep her here as a live in maid and sex slave. It all sounded so insane that if she wasn't standing here, this man close enough to wrap one of his massive hands around her throat, she wouldn't believe it.

"Do not get any ideas about trying to escape, Ms. York. You will be kept locked in your room overnight. During the day there are three dozen guards patrolling the grounds, and we are many miles from the nearest town. You are not leaving this property, and if you have any trouble following orders there will be consequences. We are not unkind, you will be fed and clothed, and you have your own room. We could have housed you with the slaves but we have decided to show you kindness since you are not responsible for your father's bad choices. Do not make us regret that decision, Ms. York."

He made it sound like she ought to be grateful to these men. He said that she was not responsible for her father's choices, yet they had abducted her to pay for his debts. She was trapped here, helpless, and completely at the mercy of men who were making no pretense at hiding what they planned to do to her.

~

3:09 P.M.

"YOU SHOULD HAVE STAYED at home, rested so you can heal, we could have handled this," Fox said as they waited in an interview room at the prison.

"Yeah, of course, because that's exactly what you would have done if Evie was missing," Chaos said with a roll of his eyes. He'd been a good little camper, stayed in the hospital overnight, allowed Fox to drive him back to San Diego, even took a nap while they waited to speak with Arthur York, but there was no way he was sitting this one out. Juliet was gone, he hadn't protected her or kept her safe like he promised, so he was going to do whatever was necessary to get her back alive. His entire team was here with him, there was nothing more intimidating than a team of six SEALs crammed into a small interrogation room, and Chaos intended to use every tool they could to get Arthur talking.

If it wasn't already too late.

Since they had no idea who had taken her or why, he had no idea what her chances of survival were because he didn't know what they wanted from her.

Arthur York was their only chance at getting the answers they needed, and he was going to make sure the man told them what they needed to know. He didn't care how he had to do it, and he didn't care about the consequences of getting it done. Right now, he had a single focus and that was getting Juliet back. Nothing else mattered.

"I wasn't shot when Evie was in danger," Fox said, a spark of fear in his brown eyes as he no doubt recalled the hours where Evie was in the hands of a cartel boss.

"Shark was still recovering from being in a helicopter crash when he went looking for Claire, *and* he'd been shot,"

Chaos said, a little belligerently but they were trying to shut him out and he needed to be involved. Didn't matter that he would have attempted to do the same thing if their positions had been reversed, he *needed* to do this. He had never in his life felt fear like this, it was strangling him, and the lack of answers was only making it worse.

"Claire needed me," Shark said simply.

"And now Juliet needs me," he shot back.

"Fine," Fox relented. "But don't let things get out of hand. We're not here to beat answers out of him."

Chaos shrugged. "That depends on how cooperative he wants to be. My only concern is finding Juliet."

"We get that, man, we really do," Spider told him, and Chaos knew that they did. With the exception of King, all the other guys on his team had lived through the women they loved being in danger.

"Just remember you won't do Juliet any good if you get yourself locked up," Night reminded him.

He nodded, he would remember that, but he'd gladly sacrifice his freedom if it meant they were able to save Juliet.

The door to the interrogation room opened, and two guards led a shackled Arthur York into the room. For a man accustomed to the finest things in life, being kept in a cell, dressed in a hideous orange jumpsuit, and forced to follow orders, prison had to be Hell on earth.

It filled him with grim satisfaction to know that Arthur would suffer while he paid for what he'd done to his own daughter.

Not wanting to waste a single second of time, as soon as Arthur was secured to the table, Chaos asked, "Do you know who took her?"

"Took who?" Arthur asked. There were dark circles under his brown eyes, and it was clear the events of the last few days had taken a toll on him. Arthur knew about his wife's death, but he had refused to give any explanation as to who he thought had killed her.

That wasn't flying this time.

Arthur would tell them what they needed to know.

"Juliet. She's missing," Chaos replied.

Surprise flitted through Arthur's eyes for a moment, but then he simply shrugged.

"We know that you're in bed with the Russian mafia," Chaos informed him. "We know that you blackmailed Juliet into becoming engaged to Dimitri Fedorov. Do you know that he beat her? That he tried to rape her? That's why she ran. Now someone has killed your wife, trashed your house, and taken your daughter. Who did it?"

Arthur shot him a mutinous glare and pressed his lips together.

"That's not an option," he said. "You *will* be talking to us."

"You going to beat me up if I don't?" Arthur sneered. "I can't believe *you're* the man my daughter is shacking up with," he muttered.

"Well believe it, and believe that you're going to help me find her. I get that you don't care about her and I'm not going to sit here and try to make you care. She's always been nothing but a tool to you, something for you to use to further your own interests. Well, that's what I'm offering you now, a chance to use your daughter to further your own interests." They'd spoken with the DA and got the okay to offer Arthur York a deal, information that resulted in the safe return of Juliet and his charges would be reduced meaning he'd do less prison time. As much as Chaos hated the idea of this man not being punished to the full extent of the law, he deserved it for everything he'd put Juliet through, if it came down to the amount of time Arthur was punished and the amount of time Juliet suffered it was an easy choice to make.

The older man didn't say anything, but he did arch a brow and Chaos knew that they'd sparked his interest. Arthur York was nothing if not self-serving.

"We'll save you from having to ask how," Chaos said. "You tell us who you think would abduct your daughter, and if we find her alive your charges will be reduced, you'll get out of prison earlier."

"I'm pleading not guilty to all charges," Arthur said.

Chaos scoffed. "Dozens of people saw you hold a gun on your daughter and attempt to abduct her, you're not getting off on those charges, it's already a done deal. Right now your best option is to use Juliet like you always have and pray we get to her in time."

For a long moment the man studied them, the wheels in his head obviously spinning as he tried to figure out if this was his best play. He must have decided that it was because he nodded slowly.

"Did the Fedorovs take Juliet?" he asked. Given that witnesses heard Portuguese-speaking people commit the abduction, he wasn't sure the Russians were involved, but maybe they had paid someone to do the job, keeping their hands clean.

"How was Juliet taken?" Arthur asked.

"We were stopped at the side of the road, they shot me and took her. Witnesses heard the abductors speaking Portuguese," Chaos replied.

Arthur's eyes widened in shock, it was obvious that meant something to him.

"What do you know?" he demanded.

"Portuguese, it must have been the Angolans," Arthur replied.

"Angolans?" Chaos echoed.

Arthur hesitated.

"You don't talk, you get the book thrown at you," Chaos reminded him.

"I bought diamonds from a mine in Angola," Arthur said. "I was having some business troubles, and I couldn't pay them everything I owed them."

"That's why you went to the Fedorovs, they offered you a deal, they'd pay off your debts to the Angolans, and you give them Juliet so Dimitri can get his green card," Chaos said.

Arthur nodded. "Only I didn't use all the money to pay off the Angolans, I only ever paid for half of those diamonds. They must have come to collect, they killed my wife, stole whatever valuables they could take with them, and then they took Juliet."

"They took her as payment for your debts," Chaos growled, a deep-seated protective rage rolling through him. He'd never felt this level of fury in his life, it was all-consuming, his vision turned red and his muscles trembled. Juliet was suffering once again because of the man who had given her life. "You did this to her. All you've done her whole life is use her, hurt her, and now she's been taken to Angola because of you. When I find her, if a single hair on her head is hurt, then you will suffer. So this is what you're going to do. You're going to tell us everything you know about the Angolans, every deal you've ever made with them, locations of their mines, number of men involved, bank accounts, everything you have on them you give to us. And then you sit here and pray that I find Juliet and that she's okay because if she's not, you're going to regret the day you ever decided to use her for your own personal gains. Never forget one thing, Mr. York, I have the power to destroy you, and nothing would give me greater pleasure than doing it."

CHAPTER 10

January 26th

6:12 A.M.

THEY WERE ALWAYS WATCHING HER.

Always.

Ever since the man—whose name she didn't know but who in her head she thought of as the giant—had come into her room and told her why she was here, someone had had their eyes on her.

Their disgusting, lust-filled eyes.

They wanted to touch her. Juliet wasn't quite sure why they hadn't yet, not that she was complaining, she wanted to put that horror off for as long as possible. It was coming though, she knew that. If Grayson's team didn't find her first, then these men would rape her. They had her all to themselves. They'd shown her around this place, around the house where she would work, cooking and cleaning and pleasuring the men. They'd shown her around the property too, the cages outdoors where they kept the slaves who worked in the mines, the guards who patrolled day and night. The mines were close, within walking distance and the slaves were escorted there each day and then escorted back. There were a few vehicles but she had yet to find out where they kept the keys. As far as she could see there was nothing but trees and mountains and open landscape around them. She wasn't going to walk her way out of here.

Trapped.

She was still trapped.

She'd been told that breakfast must be prepared by five in the morning, so she'd gotten up at four to find a man lounging in her doorway, his shoulder propped up against the doorframe, his arms crossed over his chest, his eyes roaming lewdly over her body. At least he hadn't followed her into the bathroom down the hall that she was to share with the men. She'd showered, twisted her hair into a braid, then put on one of the white linen dresses that filled her dresser. They'd taken her clothes, her underwear too, and all they'd given her to wear were the dresses.

No underwear.

She assumed that was because they wanted easy access to her whenever they pleased.

Juliet shuddered at the thought.

Her father might have been a horrible human being, but at least he'd never put his hands on her. She'd always had a roof over her head, food to eat, and any physical item she'd asked for. She'd never been afraid for her physical safety before Dimitri, she'd only ever feared for her emotional and psychological health in her father's house.

But here she knew what it was to fear for your life.

Here, where she was surrounded by men who made no secret of their leering or what they would do to her.

Instructions had been left on what to cook for the slaves and once she'd prepared the food some of the men had taken it out to them. The food for the men who lived in the house was different, nicer, and since she hadn't been sure which option she was supposed to eat, she'd refrained from eating at all. Her stomach couldn't take anything right now anyway. It was a constant twisted ball of anxiety, and she found herself jumping at every little sound.

With everyone fed, she'd filled the kitchen sink with hot soapy water and washed each dish. The noise of the slaves being walked to the mines at six a.m. sharp had caught her attention, and she'd drifted to the window to watch as the dirty and emaciated men and women had trudged along. They were connected by heavy chains, linking the metal cuffs around their ankles to each other, making escape impossible. A dozen guards followed along with them, laughing and chatting, mocking the slaves, taking what looked like great pleasure in poking them when they stumbled, repeatedly knocking them back down before roughly pulling them to their feet and ordering them on.

The men who worked here were cold, malicious, vicious men who enjoyed the suffering of others and she was theirs now. As much as she was used to the idea of being used by another, her father had been doing it since she was born, she'd always had some independence, however small. She'd gone to boarding school, attended the extra-curricular activities they planned for her, she saw other people and had a few friends. As an adult, she had her own place and was allowed to have some choices over how she spent her time.

But not here.

Here she was quickly coming to learn what it meant to

belong to someone. She had no rights here, no one cared about what she wanted, she was here to serve in whatever way she was told or she would be hurt and eventually killed.

The thought filled her with a deep grief. She may be alive, but she was already living on borrowed time. The Angolans may have taken her as payment for her father's debts but they wouldn't keep her forever.

A hand brushing against her shoulder made her scream, and she dropped the dish in her hand, sending it shattering on the floor at her feet.

She whipped around to see one of the men standing behind her. This one was much shorter than The Giant, maybe only a couple of inches taller than her, but it was obvious he worked out, probably wanting to make up in bulk what he lacked in height.

"You will be punished for breaking that," he drawled, reaching out to brush his knuckles across her cheek.

Juliet didn't think about whether it was a wise decision or not, she just flinched away from his touch. It revolted her, sickened her, made her want to scream, and sob, and rage at the unfairness of what was happening to her.

It wasn't her fault.

She hadn't done anything wrong.

She had nothing to do with her father not paying these men what he owed them.

Yet despite that here she was, at these men's mercy, paying for her father's sins.

"You think you can pull away from me?" He sneered angrily. "Come here."

Resisting was stupid. She needed to do whatever it took to keep herself alive. When Grayson's team came for her, she wanted to still be here. She wanted to go home but wasn't sure how she would face them knowing she'd gotten their teammate and friend killed.

Moving to go around the shattered shards of china, the man stopped her with an out held hand.

"No," he said, giving her an evil smile, "walk through the mess you made, you broke the dish you should be punished."

So he was one of those.

Someone who was aroused by pain.

Biting on her bottom lip so she didn't cry out as the sharp china cut into her bare feet, Juliet walked across the broken dish to the man who she knew was about to give her first taste of just how awful her life here was going to be.

"I like seeing your blood," he said, staring at the floor, a vacant look on his face now as though tossed into a euphoric state by the sight of her blood. "Kneel on it," he ordered. When she took a moment too long to comply, he grabbed her shoulders and shoved her down.

The shards sliced through her knees and she knew blood would be smeared all over the floor by the time he had done whatever it was he planned to do to her.

"I think this gives the term blood diamond a new meaning, yes?" he asked with that sick smile on his face as he ran his fingers down her braid. When he reached the string she'd used to hold it in place, he ripped it away and untangled her hair so he could run his fingers through it.

Since she was sure anything she said was only going to make things worse, Juliet just knelt there, trying to ignore the pain in her knees as she tried to steel herself for what was coming next.

"You have very pretty eyes," he said. One of his hands remained in her hair while the other traced the skin under her eyes. "I will enjoy looking into them while you suck me off."

Her eyes widened.

He wanted her to perform oral sex on him?

She'd never done that before, and she certainly didn't want to do it now.

But of course what she wanted didn't matter here.

The man unzipped his jeans and shoved them halfway down his thighs, then freed himself from his underwear.

He was already hard.

His hand curled tightly into her hair and yanked her head back, then his other hand cupped her chin, his thumb on one of her cheeks, his fingers on the other, he pressed hard until her mouth opened.

Tears leaked from her eyes as she met his cold, hard gaze, she knew her tears would further turn him on, but she couldn't stop them. He was about to steal something from her, a piece of herself, one that she would never be able to get back.

~

12:25 P.M.

"COME ON," Chaos snapped irritably as they carried their gear into the small cabin they'd rented. The place had only one bedroom and the living space looked impossibly cramped as the twelve SEALs filled the room.

Not only was his team here in Angola to rescue Juliet, but another team had come with them. From the intel they'd received, the men Arthur York had dealt with were known to be involved in human trafficking, using the people they bought or abducted as slaves to work the mines. Slaves didn't need to be paid, meaning all the money they received from their black market diamonds could be used on themselves.

While they didn't know for sure what the point of taking Juliet was beyond the fact they considered her to be payment for Arthur's debts, Chaos had a pretty good idea what they had intended to use her for.

What else would they use her for?

She was here to service the men, a live in sex slave, one who was trapped and helpless, completely at their mercy.

These men had had her for over forty-eight hours now, even taking traveling time out of that, and the time that she would have been unconscious from whatever they drugged her with, that was plenty of time for her to have been violated.

Nausea churned in his gut.

The thought of those men touching Juliet made him ill.

"We're working this as fast as we can," Matthew "Wolf" Steel assured him as the leader of the other team set down the equipment he'd carried in from the truck.

Chaos knew they were. He knew that everyone else here in the room with him was every bit as invested in finding Juliet as he was. Well *almost* as invested. They might not care about her in the same way that he did, but every single one of them, with the lone exception of King, had all gone through an ordeal with the women they loved. They knew what he was going through from experience, and he knew they would work this as hard as if it was their wives in Juliet's place, but none of that soothed the beast of terror that was living inside him.

"Try to hold it together, man," Christopher "Abe" Powers said, giving him a sympathetic slap on the back.

"I am trying," he muttered.

"We know what this is like, we get it," Hunter "Cookie" Knox assured him. "You know we're going to do whatever it takes to get your girl back."

He knew they would.

Just like he knew there was no guarantee they would even if they all gave this everything they had.

They'd pulled together this operation quickly, much quicker than they usually did when they were sent on a mission, but they didn't have the luxury of time. Juliet couldn't wait, and thankfully between John "Tex" Keegan and Eagle and his company Prey Security, they'd been able to gather enough intel to come out here with a mere twenty-four hours to plan everything. So far things had fallen into place. They had this cabin which was just ten klicks from the compound where the mines were. They had a few drones on them which they would send up to get the lay of the land, so they knew what they were facing when they stormed the place. Besides Juliet, they believed almost two hundred human trafficking victims were being held there, and from what they knew, there were a few dozen guards who patrolled the compound.

Between the two SEAL teams, they could easily take the guards.

"You're staying here," Fox informed him, then added, "no arguments. You know you're not up to this, and the last thing Juliet needs is for us to find her and get her out but to lose you in the process."

"I'm not staying here while you guys go and find her," Chaos growled. If Fox thought that then he was insane. This was the woman he cared about they were here to rescue, he wasn't hanging back. He wanted to be the one to save her, he wanted to be the first thing she saw when help came. He wanted to be her hero.

He was a SEAL, a protector, it was who he was not just what he did, and he had already failed Juliet once, he needed to rectify that.

"It's not up for discussion," Fox said firmly, and the look on Wolf's face said that he supported Fox's decision.

"You can run comms from here, man the drones," Wolf said.

"I need to be there for her," he ground out. They were so close to her, it was already taking all of his willpower to remain here in the cabin instead of throwing on his gear, grabbing his weapon, and going to get his girl. No way could he handle waiting here.

"Yeah, you do," Sam "Mozart" Reed said softly. "That's exactly what she needs from you, she needs you to be here. We don't know what they did to her, we don't know what she's gone through, but we know that she's going to need you. You slept the entire flight here. You can't move without favoring your good side, you're still in pain, still weak from blood loss. You make a fuss, insist on going in with us, you'll be a liability. That means our attention is going to be divided between finding Juliet and covering you. When our attention is divided that's when things can go wrong. You want to risk Juliet's life because you want to be the one to save her? Isn't the important thing that we get her out alive and in one piece?"

Chaos deflated like a balloon, sinking onto the lumpy couch and dropping his head into his hands.

He hated that they were right.

He wasn't at one hundred percent, not even close. He should probably still be in the hospital not traveling halfway around the world and storming a secure compound with two hundred victims including one who had burrowed into his heart.

"I hate that you're right," he said.

"I know," Kason "Benny" Sawyer said sympathetically. When Benny had first gotten together with his now-wife

Jessyka, they'd both ended up kidnapped by her ex and Benny had been helpless, tied to a tree, while Jessyka had saved him. He understood what it felt like to know the woman in your life needed you but not be able to help her.

"We know from Arthur York that the slaves work twelve-hour shifts in the mines, and are then brought back to the outdoor cages where they're kept," Spider said, distaste evident in his tone. His wife Abigail had been kept in a cage for fourteen months, so anytime they saw something similar it was rough on him.

"That means that after seven when the slaves are caged and have been fed, the number of men on patrol decreases," Faulkner "Dude" Cooper said. "My guess would be by ten everyone is basically drunk and busy either with the slaves or any other guests." Dude shot him an apologetic look like he hadn't already figured out what Juliet's fate would be.

"The timing is perfect to hit them now," Mozart said, "Paxton Pedro is the owner of the mines, and he's hardly ever present. He comes maybe once or twice a year, so this is like hitting three birds with one stone. We take down one of the world's biggest dealers in black market diamonds, we rescue two hundred trafficking victims, and we get Chaos' girl back."

Paxton Pedro was a huge man, six-foot-nine inches of solid muscle, with eyes that were said to be as dead as the Devil's. Because he mostly stayed in the shadows despite numerous attempts from different countries, and pretty much every agency known to man, so far he had managed to evade capture. As much as it would be good to bring down such a notorious trafficker and rescue so many victims, all Chaos cared about was getting Juliet back in his arms where she belonged.

"Getting Chaos' girl back is definitely top of that list. I

can't stand seeing our resident ray of sunshine all gloomy like this," Wolf said.

"Amen to that," King echoed.

"I'm trying, I've … I've never felt this way before," he admitted. "I was able to keep my family smiling when we thought my sister was dying, I was able to make her laugh even when she was in pain, I've always been able to hold onto my sense of humor, but now … it's like it's just gone. I couldn't summon a joke if my life depended on it. I just … I need Juliet. I *need* her. I can't explain it."

"You don't need to, brother," Cookie said. The empathy and understanding on his face was echoed on the faces of each of the other men in the room. "We've all been where you are, we've all gone through it, and that's why we're going to do whatever it takes to get your girl back to you."

That's what he needed. He needed Juliet back, he needed to touch her, hold her, and kiss her. He needed her to know how much she meant to him. He needed her because she was his future, and without her, he didn't know what he'd do.

10:10 P.M.

THIS WAS the first time she'd been alone, and Juliet didn't want to waste it.

No way was she hanging around here hoping someone came for her.

No way.

She couldn't stay and assume that Grayson's team would come. She was sure they would look for her, and that they would come if they could, but they'd be looking into the

Fedorovs as her abductors, not the Angolans. Their only chance at knowing where she had been taken was if her father decided to do the right thing for the first time in his life and tell them that he had been in debt to black-market diamond dealers.

But her father wouldn't.

He didn't care what happened to her.

And even if the cops did talk to him, and he was feeling generous enough to be forthcoming with information, surely he too would think that it was the Russians who had kidnapped her.

She was on her own.

Today, when she'd been down on her knees on the kitchen floor, forced to do things she wasn't ready to process yet, she'd come to a decision.

She would take her chances out there rather than stay here and wait for them to use her as they pleased.

It was going to get worse.

They'd told her that.

Someone called Mr. Pedro was in charge here, and he was to be the first to take her. Apparently, he wasn't here very often, but he had a thing for women with green eyes and had decided to coincide his visit with her arrival. Juliet thought back to the huge man in the expensive suit who had been the one to explain to her why she was here. Was he Mr. Pedro? He had an air of authority about him that said he was used to giving orders and being obeyed.

Well, she wasn't going to hang around to obey his orders.

It was late, dark out, she'd seen the slaves put back in their cells around six, and once they'd been fed, and she'd cleaned the kitchen, she had eaten a little of the leftover food herself and then hurried back to her room. Thankfully nobody had followed, and she could hear the men laughing and talking downstairs, it sounded like they were drunk and she knew she wasn't going to get a better chance at escaping.

When they were finished drinking, she knew what they were going to do for entertainment.

Her.

She had to leave now. She'd go to the kitchen, pack some food and bottled water into the little backpack she had made out of one of the dresses, and then she was sneaking out of here. Juliet wished she had something darker to wear, the white dress would be like waving a beacon in the dark alerting anyone looking to her presence, so she would have to be really careful.

Carefully, she peeked out into the hallway. When she saw it was empty she crept slowly out of her room. It was at the end of the hall, and she wasn't sure if anybody else was up here. She would have to walk past six rooms to make it to the stairs, and any one of them could have someone inside.

Holding her breath, afraid to even breathe, she tiptoed one excruciatingly slow step at a time toward the stairs.

Relief had her sagging against the wall when she made it.

One part of her plan to escape down and now she was on to the next. This would be harder and riskier. She knew the men were down there, she could hear them, and any one of them could decide to head into the kitchen to get a snack. Thankfully she had spent a large portion of the day reorganizing the kitchen, it had given her something to do and kept her hidden away from most of the men, and now she knew exactly what she would take and where it was. Hopefully, she could be down the stairs, through to the kitchen, and out the back door before anyone even thought to go looking for her.

Time seemed to move so slowly, her heart hammered in her chest, and it was an effort to keep her breathing even and quiet, but eventually she was stepping into the quiet, dark kitchen.

Juliet let out a breath of relief. Her whole body trembled from the stress, and she knew she was nowhere even close to out of the woods yet. She still had to get out of the house, then off the compound, and then find a town or something where she could call for help.

One thing at a time, she reminded herself before she could talk herself into losing it. This plan was only going to work if she could keep it together.

Quickly, she grabbed as many water bottles, and as much packaged food as she thought she could physically carry and tied it into her makeshift backpack. She was just settling it onto her back when she heard something.

Footsteps.

Someone was coming.

Frantically she scanned the room searching for a hiding spot. The pantry was no good because no doubt the person was coming to get a snack. She'd be a sitting duck if she tried to hide under the table. Even drunk the men would be sure to see her there. That really only left hiding behind the door and hoping that whoever was coming didn't close it. If they found her now she was going to be in for a world of trouble. It was plain to see that she was trying to escape and she would be punished for that. And worse, they'd keep a closer eye on her in the future. She could take the punishment but not losing what could be her only chance at running.

She'd just pressed herself against the wall behind the door when the lights flicked on. Thankfully because she'd just rearranged the entire pantry no one would be able to tell that there was food missing, so this man should be able to just get whatever he'd come in here for and leave.

She hoped.

She prayed with everything that she had.

Juliet could hear him stumbling about, obviously drunk, a crash said he had knocked over something in the pantry, and she could hear him mutter under his breath in Portuguese. The tap turned on, ran for a bit, then turned off. She stood perfectly still, all it took was one wrong move and she'd send the door bumping forward, alerting him to her presence.

She counted to five in her head.

Over and over again.

One, two, three, four, five.

One, two, three, four, five.

Finally the light flicked off, and she listened to his footsteps retreat down the hall.

Tears of relief burned her eyes, but she didn't have time to fall apart, she still had a long way to go before she was out of here. Even then she wouldn't really be safe. She was going to have to walk—barefoot—for miles through the trees and over the mountains, and as soon as they realized she was gone they'd come looking for her. While she'd be walking they'd have cars, maybe even helicopters too, finding her would be easier for them than evading them would be for her.

Slipping back down the hall, she headed out the back door. She'd chosen this door because it was furthest from the living rooms, and while the side door opened onto the open area where the cages of slaves were, the back door opened onto empty garden. Hopefully there should be fewer guards here so no one would see her fleeing the house. There was a fence surrounding the property, it was wire, and topped with coils of barbed wire, but she was hoping that even if she couldn't climb it she could perhaps dig under it to escape, or if she was really lucky, she'd find a hole to just climb through.

At least the men here were cocky enough to think they

had everything under control. They kept the slaves exhausted enough that they didn't have the energy to mount an escape attempt, and they thought the fact that they were armed gave them an edge. Which it did, but their arrogance also worked to her advantage.

Tentatively, she stepped outside. This seemed too easy, so far everything had gone just as she'd hoped. All she had to do now was get away from the windows and into the gardens where she would be better hidden.

With a last look around her, Juliet took off at a run. She didn't slow when she reached the cover of the trees, now that she could move quickly she felt a driving need to keep going. She wasn't sure how far it was to the fence, but she knew the quicker she got there and the more distance she put between herself and her kidnappers the safer she would be.

Luck was definitely on her side tonight.

At least that's what she thought until arms suddenly closed around her, hauling her up off her feet and pinning her against a body so much larger than her own.

Juliet lost it.

Let all the fear and terror and grief that had been slowly building inside her since she woke up in that wooden box break free. She thrashed like a cornered animal, swinging her arms as best she could with them partially trapped by the arm of the man holding her, and she kicked with her legs. She must have connected with something because the man grunted and loosened his hold.

Taking advantage, she spun around and rammed her knee up into his groin then when his hands automatically flew there, she turned and ran.

She didn't get far.

Again she was grabbed and lifted off her feet only this time her arms were pulled behind her back, her wrists secured with zip ties. A gag was placed over her mouth and then she was hoisted over a shoulder and carried away.

Away from her freedom, away from safety, away from her one chance at escape.

Defeated, Juliet slumped against her captor and began to cry.

~

10:34 P.M.

"GOT a female figure running from the house."

Chaos straightened as he heard Benny's voice come through the comms. "Juliet?"

"Looks like it," Benny confirmed.

His brave—and oh so very stupid—girl was trying to escape on her own. He couldn't be more proud of her for being strong enough to try to save herself, but he was also furious. There was no way she could get to safety herself. The villages around the mines were all owned by Mr. Pedro, no one there was going to help her. They would send her right back to the very house she'd just fled.

Fear for what could have happened to her pulsed through him mingling with relief that they'd got to her in time. Until he could see her and touch her the relief wasn't enough to tamper down his fear.

"Got her," Benny announced a moment later.

"Take her back to the cabin," Wolf said, "the rest of us can handle this."

"Hurry," Chaos said. He was dangerously close to the end of his rope.

“Not long now and you’ll have her in your arms,” Benny promised.

The not long turned out to be thirty excruciating minutes.

Before Benny had even stopped driving, Chaos was moving toward the car. “What the hell, man?” he asked when he saw that Juliet was sitting gagged and restrained in the passenger seat of the car. Her eyes were wild and unfocused, and although she was buckled in, she had pulled her knees to her chest and was shaking badly.

“She was freaked out, I was worried she was going to hurt herself. I didn’t want her screaming and alerting everyone to our presence so I had to put on the cuffs and gag her. They’re loose, not tight enough to hurt her, barely enough to keep her hands together, if she wanted she could get free. She’s zoned out, Chaos, I told her who I was, that she was safe, but she’s not hearing me. I thought I would uncuff her at the car, but she was still in shock, and I was concerned she might try to throw herself out of the car. I didn’t want to hurt her, Chaos, or upset her, but the priority was getting her out alive,” Benny explained.

As much as the sight of Juliet restrained made him see red, Chaos had to agree with Benny’s thinking. The priority *had* been getting her out alive.

Yanking open her door, he crouched beside her, slid the gag off, then reached behind her and cut the zip ties away, then he pulled her into his arms. In that moment his entire being settled. She was here, he was holding her, she was back where she belonged.

Pulling back enough to frame her face with his hands, he stroked her cheekbones with his thumbs then leaned in and kissed her forehead.

“It's okay, baby,” he murmured, “you’re safe now.”

Juliet blinked slowly, like she was walking out of a thick

fog, her brow furrowed in confusion. “Grayson? But … you're … dead …”

“No, princess, I'm not dead. I'm right here.” Hating that she’d spent the last couple of days believing he was dead, he leaned forward and kissed her forehead again. The need to pick her up, feel her weight in his arms, clutch her close, and not let go, was overwhelming, but first he had to make sure she knew she was safe.

“But how …?” she trailed off, looking around, her eyes growing wide when she saw Benny sitting beside her. Immediately she began to panic, thrashing in his grip. “He kidnapped me.”

“No, honey, he was trying to rescue you. The only reason he put the cuffs on was because he was worried you were going to hurt yourself and he didn’t want to risk accidentally hurting you. He’s a friend of mine, his name is Benny, he’s a SEAL too, and his team came with mine to find you and rescue the other people being held there.”

“Nice to meet you, ma’am,” Benny said, shooting Juliet a reassuring smile.

A faint blush stained Juliet’s cheeks. “I'm sorry, I thought you were one of them. I kneed you in the groin.”

Benny just laughed and waved off Juliet’s apology. “No need to apologize, you did what you had to do to save yourself. I tried to tell you who I was, but you were in shock.”

“You kneed him in the groin?” Chaos snickered, hoping to soothe Juliet with a little humor, an ability that seemed to have returned now he had her back. “Once I tell the guys that they’re never going to let him live it down.”

“Sorry,” Juliet said again, but the smallest of smiles touched her lips.

Benny smiled kindly at her. “A small price to pay. I'm sorry I scared you, it wasn’t my intention, but I had to get you out of there as quickly and quietly as possible so the men didn't know our teams were there."

Juliet responded by throwing her arms around Benny's neck and kissing him on the cheek. "Thank you."

"No thanks needed," Benny assured her.

When Juliet turned back to Chaos there was shock on her face again. "You were shot, I thought you were dead." This time she threw her arms around him, pressing her face against his neck as she began to cry.

"I'm sorry I didn't keep you safe." He squeezed her tighter, burying his face in her hair and thanking God he'd gotten her back alive.

"Not your fault. How did you find me?"

"Your dad accepted a deal, we get you back alive, and the charges against him are reduced."

"I wasn't sure you'd be able to find me, and I couldn't stay there, I was going to run, I know I might not have made it but I had to try."

She shuddered in his arms and the tone of her voice told him that something awful had happened to her in that house. "Come on, princess, let's get you inside."

Carefully, he lifted her into his arms, trying to hide his wince as Juliet's additional weight pulled on his wound. Of course she noticed. "How badly are you hurt? Put me down, you shouldn't be carrying me. You shouldn't even be here. Why didn't you stay home so you could heal?"

"Would you rather I wasn't here right now?" he asked as he carried her inside the cabin.

"N-no." She shuddered again. "I'm so glad you're here. I thought I was never going to see you again."

"I know the feeling." His own body shuddered as he realized how close he had come to losing her. When he'd set her down on the couch, he pulled up the coffee table so he could sit in front of her. "How badly are you hurt?"

"I'm not really, not much, just my feet. I dropped a dish, and … I … uh … stepped on some of the pieces." She wouldn't meet his eye when she said that, it was obvious she was holding something back—something she didn't want him to know. The problem was, if he was going to help her deal with this, he had to know what had happened to her.

"I'll grab a first aid kit," Benny said, giving them some time alone.

"Anywhere else, princess?" he asked, brushing his knuckles across her cheek before tucking a lock of her tangled hair behind her ear.

"Umm … my knees are cut up too."

"From the broken dish?"

Juliet gave a shaky nod.

"You have some bruises here." His fingers traced lightly over faint bruises on her cheeks. They were older than thirty minutes which meant they weren't from Benny.

She shrugged but wouldn't look at him.

Keeping his voice gentle when all he wanted to do was grab a weapon, jump in the car and drive to the mines to exact revenge on the men who had hurt her was difficult, but he did it because Juliet needed to feel safe to talk. "Honey, you know what my job is so you know I've seen a lot."

Another shrug. "I'm sure you've seen worse."

"Not a competition, princess, bad stuff is bad stuff. Let me see your feet." Circling her ankle with his hand, he lifted her foot, freezing when the dress she was wearing shifted, and he saw that she wasn't wearing any underwear. Quickly he reached for her hands, checking them for cuts, but they were clean. He let out a breath of release as he realized that she probably hadn't been raped anally or taken from behind.

Didn't mean she hadn't been raped though.

Benny set the first aid kit beside him as well as a dish filled with warm water and a cloth.

"You know you can tell me anything," he said as he picked up her other foot, set both in his lap, and began to clean them. One of the wounds looked deep but wouldn't need stitches, the others were shallower but still painful. Knowing that she had been prepared to try to walk to safety in bare, cut feet filled him with pride, she was something else.

Juliet gave a hesitant nod.

"Nothing you tell me can make me think anything bad of you. If you had to do things so they didn't kill you then you made the right choice," he assured her as he set her feet down and turned his attention to her knees. They were more badly damaged than her feet, and as he gently probed the half dozen or so cuts he found that there were still some shards left inside. Unfortunately, he could think of only one reason why she would have been kneeling in shards of china and have bruises on her cheeks, but he needed Juliet to trust him enough to tell him what they'd done to her. It was the only way he'd be able to help her through the fallout from this ordeal.

CHAPTER 11

January 27th

12:00 A.M.

SHE DIDN'T WANT to tell him.

If Juliet had her way, he would never know what those men had done to her.

It was humiliating and embarrassing enough as it was without him knowing that she had been down on her knees, forced to perform oral sex on a dozen men while the others watched and taunted her.

How did she explain that to him?

How would he see her when she did?

It was all well and good for him to say that he had seen all sorts of things in his job, that there was nothing she could say that would turn him off, but thinking that and then hearing her tell him what she'd done was different.

Would he really not think badly of her if he knew she had just knelt there and done what they told her to without fighting back?

"You know, Juliet, that whatever you did while you were there was the right thing to do because it kept you alive until we could come for you," Benny said, and she looked over at him. He was handsome, with short dark hair and chocolatey brown eyes, and since she'd only just met him, she felt like he had less reason to lie to her than Grayson did. Grayson might pretend that whatever she told him was okay because he didn't want to hurt her, but Benny would be honest with her.

Her gaze swung to Grayson's and he nodded at her. "Benny is right, you have nothing to be ashamed about."

Only really she did.

And she burned with shame.

Grayson picked up some tweezers and began to remove the shards of china from her knees she hadn't had a chance to tend to earlier. She'd cleaned out what was in her feet since she needed to walk but hadn't wanted to waste time on her knees.

"I bet you're starving, Juliet. How about I cook us some dinner?" Benny suggested.

"Say yes," Grayson gave her a wide smile. "Benny is a great cook, but don't ask him to let you help, he refuses to cook with anyone, well, anyone except his wife."

"Jessyka doesn't get in my way," Benny shot back with a grin.

Their easy banter helped soothe her a little, maybe she should just do it, say it, and get it done. She was pretty sure it would come out at some point anyway and she'd rather Grayson hear it from her so she could explain, defend herself. Fixing her eyes on Grayson's large hands tenderly cleaning up her knees she blurted out, "They made me suck their … you know."

Grayson's hands froze.

A tremble rippled through them.

Juliet chanced a glance at his face and saw it set into a hard mask.

So unlike the Grayson she had been falling for back at home.

This Grayson made her want to shrink away from the fury that pulsed through him as clearly as blood dribbled from her wounds.

She was pulling herself away from him when he suddenly stood, scooped her up, and sat with her on his lap. His arms were like metal bands wrapped around, and he was rocking her, his lips pressed to her temple, kissing her over and over again.

"I'm sorry, princess." His voice was tortured, and his hold on her tightened until it was almost crushing, and yet nothing would make her ask him to lighten it.

"Why are you sorry?"

"Because I didn't protect you. I promised you that I would keep you safe, that no one would hurt you again, but you were taken and assaulted. I failed you."

"No!" The word burst out of her, a vehement protest against his words, and she moved in his arms until she was straddling his thighs, her hands curled into his shirt. "No, I thought you died because of me, I was devastated that I'd never get to see you again. I never blamed you, not even once."

"I let you down."

"No. Never," she contradicted. "You could never let me down. You're here, with two SEAL teams, when you should be in a hospital. You are the best man I've ever met, and there is no way you could let me down, it's just not possible."

Grayson's green eyes lightened like she had taken away a heavy weight that had been slowly crushing him. "You know what you are?" When she shook her head, he continued, "You're the strongest woman I've ever met. Benny is right, you did what you had to do to stay alive, and that is never anything to be ashamed of. I hate that you went through that, I hate that they hurt you that way, I wish with everything that I have that I could take it back, make it go away, but I can't. What I can do is be right here, beside you, holding your hand. I'm here, Juliet, don't shut me out. Please."

Part of her wanted to insist that he push her away, agree with her when she said that she was ashamed of what she'd done despite his take on things, she felt dirty and he should too, but she couldn't do it. She needed him. She needed this. "Hold me," she murmured, leaning forward so she was lying across his chest.

"Always, princess." His arms closed around her again as he held her close. His arms were warm and strong, and she could feel strength emanating off him. This was what she needed to deal with what had happened to her, and she was glad she'd told him even if there was lingering embarrassment.

She began to feel sleepy, with all the drugs she'd been given and living in constant fear over the last forty-eight hours, on top of the stress of the last few weeks, she suddenly couldn't keep her eyes open. Grayson stroking the length of her spine soothed her, and her eyes fluttered closed as she relaxed into him.

The sound of whispered voices had her snapping awake in a panic.

The men.

They were back.

She hadn't escaped.

She must have fallen asleep in her room before she could make a run for it, and now the men had come for her.

Juliet bolted upright and scrambled off the bed, backing herself into a corner. She wasn't going to make this easy for them. If they wanted her, she was going to fight them every step of the way.

A figure loomed in front of her, and she screamed and lashed out.

"It's okay, honey, it's only me, you were dreaming. You hear me, cat burglar? It's just Grayson."

Cat burglar.

The two words pierced the fog of fear she was engulfed in, no one else would ever call her something so silly. Grayson. It was just Grayson.

Fighting back a sob, she wrapped her arms around his waist, burrowing into his warmth as she suddenly felt ice cold.

"It's okay, shh, it's okay, princess," Grayson soothed as he scooped her up and carried her back to the bed.

"You shouldn't be carrying me, you're hurt," she whispered as she began to shake, unable to get warm.

"Not hurt enough that I can't hold you."

He laid her down on the bed, then slid in beside her, pulling her so she was draped across his good side then covering them both with the blankets.

It wasn't enough to warm her. "I can't stop shaking."

"Shock, princess, it will pass. Your body hasn't quite caught up to the fact that you're safe now."

"I'm not sure my brain has either," she said.

"It's going to take time, princess, but you have time."

"I didn't think I did, I thought what we had was over before it even really began."

"I did too," he admitted, and she felt his lips touch her forehead. He held them there for a long moment before he gently grasped her chin and tilted her face up. His eyes met hers and she saw the question in them. He didn't want to kiss her if it was going to spark bad memories, but nothing about kissing Grayson was bad.

When she nodded, his lips met hers, and she felt the heavy weight of fear that had been covering her ever since she woke up in that wooden box start to lift. Grayson wasn't dead, and he'd found her, come for her, and now he was here holding her and kissing her and everything finally felt like it was righting itself.

She might have been tempted to take things further, make love to Grayson, but she wasn't sure if Benny was still here in the cabin, and even though they were in a bedroom she was sure he would be able to hear everything, and she wasn't ready for any more humiliation. Still, she might have risked it had Grayson not ended the kiss and settled her against him again.

"Sleep now, princess. I just want to hold you in my arms."

A small smile curled her lips up. Being held by Grayson sounded like heaven. Everything she had wished for when she thought he was dead and gone forever, was now a reality. Despite everything that had happened, Juliet knew she was one lucky woman, Grayson was alive, she was alive, and they were here together.

What more could she ask for?

~

2:40 A.M.

. . .

JULIET SHIFTED RESTLESSLY AGAIN. Despite her obvious exhaustion, she was having difficulty staying asleep.

When she'd first fallen asleep, he'd held her for a bit before he finished cleaning her knees. A couple of the cuts had to be glued, and he'd added antibiotic cream and bandaged her knees when he was done. He'd removed the dress her captors had given her and replaced it with one of his t-shirts and a pair of his sweatpants.

The sight of her dressed in his clothes had gripped him tight and still hadn't let him go. She looked like she belonged in his life, and as far as he was concerned, she was there to stay. Chaos hoped that Juliet felt the same way, and he was pretty sure that she did. Although she had been reluctant to tell him what had happened to her, she had trusted him enough to open up, and that trust meant everything to him.

It meant that they still had a chance.

A future.

That once he got her back home, they could start the rest of their lives. He wanted to take her out on more dates, take her back to his place at the end and make love to her, make his home feel like her home, and he wanted to help her start the business she wanted. He wanted them to spend as much time together as they could, he wanted to know every single thing there was to know about her.

"Can't sleep, princess?" he asked when Juliet began to toss and turn again.

"No. Every time I drift off I have nightmares." She was currently lying with her cheek pillowed on his chest and one of her legs hooked over his. Her hand rested on his stomach, and her fingers began to trace circles against his bare skin.

"Princess, you might want to stop doing that," he warned, her touch that close to the part of him he would love nothing more than to bury deep inside her, imprint himself on her body and her soul, was only going to lead to one thing.

"What if I don't want to?" she asked, propping her chin on his chest.

"I want to too, princess, but the guys could come back at any time." He also wasn't sure that after being assaulted she was quite ready to do that yet, and besides, there was no rush. When they made love next he wanted to be able to take his time, enjoy touching and tasting every inch of her delectable body.

"Is Benny still out there?"

"No, he left just after you had your first nightmare. He did leave us something to eat though if you're feeling hungry."

"Actually, yeah, I am a little hungry."

"Then you're going to love what Benny made. When we rented the cabin we asked to have it stocked with food, and Benny made arroz da Ilha, it's rice with fish, and it smells amazing."

"Sounds good."

"You sure? I know you said you were a picky eater."

"I love fish, and rice, so long as it doesn't have too many vegetables or anything mixed through it."

"It doesn't. I told Benny that you didn't like food mixed together and he said he'd just do the rice and fish."

"Then it sounds perfect."

"Good." He gave her cheek a quick kiss, then helped her out of bed. Since her knees were bandaged and had to be sore, he gathered her into his arms and carried her to the kitchen table, setting her on one of the chairs. As soon as his team and Wolf's finished up and got back here they'd be packing up and flying back Stateside, but until then he was going to take care of Juliet, feed her, give her a shower, and then they'd go back to bed and hopefully she'd get the sleep she needed.

In the kitchen, he dished them both up plates of food, it had cooled down but wasn't completely cold so he didn't bother heating it in the microwave.

"Wow, this is *really* good," Juliet said when she took a bite. "Now I feel extra bad for kneeing Benny in the groin."

Chaos laughed. "Nah, he doesn't care, not the first time any of us have been hit on a mission."

"Yeah, but I was the person you were here to rescue, wasn't very grateful of me."

"Also not the first time a victim in shock and in fight for their life mode has lashed out and gotten a hit into one of us. Benny will gladly take the guys ribbing because it means you're alive and mostly unhurt, and that we successfully saved you. That's all that was important to any of us."

"I don't know how to thank you all," she said, her fork fiddling with her food.

"You don't have to." Not only was this their job, but Juliet was important to him, and he knew all of his friends would have done anything to rescue her just like when the women they loved had been in trouble, he'd been prepared to do whatever it took to get them back alive.

"I feel like I do."

"Then you live your life to the fullest, make all your dreams come true, that's how you thank us," he told her, reaching out to cover her hand with his.

"That I can do." She smiled at him, and just like that, he felt the light that had vanished from his world when he woke to learn Juliet had been abducted return.

Despite his vow to himself to not push Juliet for anything she wasn't ready for, to simply take care of her and make sure she knew that he was here for her, Chaos stood, rounded the table, and placed his hands on her hips. He lifted her easily, barely noticing the twinge in his chest as he walked to the counter and set her down. Letting his fingers linger on her sides, he stepped between her knees and brushed his lips across hers.

"Tell me to stop if you don't want this," he said softly.

"I want it so much it hurts," she whispered back. "I want to feel you, I want to feel alive, I want to feel safe, and I want to feel special. That's how *you* make me feel, Grayson. You. Only you. I don't feel unwanted when I'm with you, and I don't feel weird, I just feel like I belong. I like that feeling."

"You are special, princess, and wanted. When I hold you I feel complete. You do that for me, honey, you complete me." As he kissed her again his hands slipped beneath the t-shirt, trailing across her soft skin. Chaos took his time, enjoying the feel of her lips on his and the way she shifted restlessly as he moved his hands higher. When he finally palmed one of her breasts she moaned into his mouth. "You like that, honey?"

"Yes. More," she murmured, arching her back to try to encourage him to do more than simply touch her breast.

"The guys could come back at any second," he reminded her, although he himself was beyond caring at this point.

"Don't care," she replied. "Touch me, Grayson, give me all of you."

"You have all of me," he promised as he took her nipple between his thumb and forefinger and tugged gently.

"Mmm," she moaned, tipping her head back, her eyes falling closed. The more pleasure he brought her, the more he wanted to give her.

"Bedroom I think," Chaos said as he picked her up again.

"I don't care where we go as long as you keep touching me like that."

"I'll have to remember that, my little exhibitionist cat burglar," he said with a laugh as he headed for the bedroom.

"Keep telling you I didn't steal anything," she reminded him.

Chaos was laughing, his attention on Juliet when he realized he'd made a mistake.

By then it was too late.

All he could do was angle his body toward the threat he sensed a moment before the shot rang out.

Pain seared through his thigh and he stumbled.

As he fell, Chaos rotated his body so he took the brunt of the fall.

He cursed his own stupidity not having his weapon on him, but he'd thought they were safe here at the cabin.

Despite the pain in his leg and chest, he was staggering to his feet as someone came toward them.

Before he could react, something slammed into the back of his head and he went back down onto his knees.

"Grayson!" Juliet screamed.

His vision was hazy, but he could see someone grab her.

She fought against her captor, and all he could think about was getting to her.

Another blow to the back of his head had the world fading away.

The last thing he heard was Juliet crying out for him, and his last thought was that once again he had failed to keep her safe.

~

3:53 A.M.

. . .

About time.

Dimitri Fedorov smiled as he watched the SUV pull up to his private plane.

Money certainly had its advantages. The more of it you had, the easier it was to get anything that you wanted. It had been his experience that everyone had a price, all you had to do to get your way was figure out what each person's price was.

Fear, too, was a great motivator, but it alone wasn't enough to sway everyone.

There were some—strange people as far as he was concerned—who didn't seem to respond to fear. It was like their principles meant more to them than the threat of harm. As far as he was concerned that was insanity, but to each their own. Money on the other hand, the promises of a better life it brought with it, often proved to be a much better tool in negotiation. Everyone had debts, dreams, and the ability to wipe the slate clean and make the future anything you wanted it to be was usually more effective.

If it wasn't for his money, he wouldn't have been able to track down his fiancée and reclaim her.

One of his men stepped out of the black SUV, walked to the back door, and opened it, then reached inside and pulled out Juliet York.

The woman was beautiful. There was an innocence about her that made him eager to get her home to Russia. He was going to enjoy breaking this one, molding her into his own creation. The perfect mafia bride. She would learn that her place was to look beautiful on his arm at social engagements, keep him satisfied in the bedroom, and keep herself occupied and out of the way when she wasn't needed. She was not to question anything, not to offer an opinion, not to insert herself into business that wasn't any of her concern. Her only role in life was to serve him, her husband, nothing more and nothing less.

In time she would learn.

They all did.

And with this gorgeous green-eyed beauty on his arm, he would be the envy of the entire Russian mafia scene.

As soon as they were officially married he would begin proceedings to get his green card, then he and his father would be able to live and work free and clear in America. Their business would grow, money would continue to come pouring in, and they would be one step closer to their goal which was to build the Fedorov organization into a global phenomenon.

It all started with Juliet York-soon-to-be-Fedorov.

Her limp body was carried up and into the plane and deposited on one of the plush leather seats.

"Remove those awful clothes," he said, curling up his nose in distaste at the black t-shirt and sweatpants that she was wearing. They were obviously a man's clothes, and no woman of his would be wearing clothing belonging to another man.

Dimitri didn't share women.

Well, correction, he didn't share his women with other men, he had no problem sharing another man's woman.

Juliet was his woman now, his soon-to-be wife, not just one of the whores he used for fun, she belonged to him, and no other man would ever lay a hand on her.

Egor, the head of his personal security detail, the one who had brought him Juliet and removed the threat of the American SEAL, stood and with quick, impersonal movements removed the woman's clothing. She had no underwear underneath the clothing, but Dimitri made no move to give an order for her to be dressed. He liked the sight of her unconscious and bare before him.

She had lost weight since their first meeting last Christmas, no doubt because she had been hiding out on the streets. She would lose more before she learned that from here on out he would control her every move.

It was a learning process, but he hoped that Juliet would be a quick study, after all, she was used to living her life under another's controlling influence. Her father had been running her life for her since the moment she was born, so the transition should go smoothly. Not that he minded if it didn't, using a firm hand to teach Juliet her place would be a pleasurable experience.

"Sir, we're ready for take-off," the captain's voice announced over the PA system.

"Buckle her in, Egor," Dimitri ordered as he poured himself a drink before taking his seat beside his fiancée.

Minutes later they were cruising above Angola on their way back to Russia. They'd land at the family's private airfield, and then he'd bring Juliet home. She wouldn't leave the Fedorov estate until he was confident that she knew the rules, that she would follow all expectations without exception. Once she had been molded into the wife he wanted, then she would be allowed some measure of freedom.

Although it hadn't been the plan, having her father out of the picture worked in his favor. With Arthur in prison, and his wife deceased, Juliet would take over the business, well he as her soon-to-be husband would take it over in her place. Besides, he already owned half of it. It was only natural for him to take control.

Meeting Arthur York was a stroke of pure luck. The man wasn't the only one who dealt with Mr. Pedro and while there on a business trip one time, he and his father had run into Arthur. As soon as he learned the other man was in debt to the diamond dealer the perfect opportunity to build connections in America presented itself. He and his father had offered Arthur a deal, they would pay off his debts to Mr. Pedro in exchange for half his company and his beautiful daughter's hand in marriage.

The man had jumped at the opportunity.

Little did he know Arthur had held back part of the money. For what reason Dimitri didn't know or care, he had gotten what he wanted out of Arthur. If he had known the Angolans would go after Juliet he would have pre-empted them, but the SEALs had proved themselves useful by disposing of the diamond dealers, saving him the trouble of having to do it himself. It also afforded him the opportunity of taking over the mines himself. An intriguing possibility and one that he would look into once he got his fiancée settled.

They had several hours of flying ahead of them, and while there was business he should be attending to, his gaze landed on his fiancée. Even with the loss of weight Juliet had long, lean limbs, her alabaster skin was soft and supple, her brown locks were dirty, but he knew from their previous encounter that they were silky and smooth when clean. Her eyes were definitely her best feature, her breasts were a little small for his liking, but they were still pert, and her figure could do with a little filling out. He loved a sexy hourglass figure. All in all, she would make an exceptional wife and he couldn't wait to claim her.

He reached out and ran a fingertip across the slope of one pert breast. She didn't stir and his fingertip traced around her nipple, watching as it automatically pebbled at the feather-light touch.

So she was one of those women with a sensitive body.

That pleased him. There were dozens of things he would enjoy doing to a body this responsive.

Pleasure rippled through him at the thought, but he withdrew his hand. Juliet must first learn her place in the world her father had sold her into, not until then would he touch her again. Her life from here on out didn't have to be an unpleasant one. She would be richer than she could imagine, she could have anything she asked for, people would cower in her presence because of her last name, and she would be free to travel the world by his side. All she had to do was accept her fate.

Accept it and embrace it.

He had been born into the Fedorov name, but she had been chosen to receive it, and it was a gift she should treasure.

As her husband he was in control, and there were certain things he expected, obedience, a willingness to please, children when the time was right. He had the power to make her life one filled with nothing but pleasure or one filled with nothing but suffering.

It would be Juliet's choice. Obey and reap the rewards, or be stubborn and refuse to play the game and suffer the consequences.

"Cover her with a blanket," he ordered as he stood to refill his whisky glass. Soon he would take his bride home, they would be married almost immediately, and then he was free to begin creating the perfect wife. Next would become the perfect heir, and one day soon his family would be unstoppable. They would rule not just Russia but the world.

And it all started with the unconscious green-eyed brunette sitting before him.

~

8:47 P.M.

JULIET GROANED as she woke up.

Drugged.

Again.

The sticky, foggy feeling meant that once again someone had drugged her unconscious. She was getting sick of people using her, plucking her up from one place and taking her somewhere else just for their own purposes.

She was literally sick as well.

With a pained moan as movement made her head begin to ache, Juliet rolled sideways and began to dry retch.

Tears stung her eyes as she wrapped her arms around her bare stomach and sunk back down. She was freezing cold, which wasn't a surprise since she was naked, sick to her stomach, with a raging headache, and yet she knew curling up in a ball and sobbing wasn't something she could afford to do. Once again she had to figure out who had taken her and why.

Which started with remembering what had happened.

She remembered being with Grayson at some tiny little cabin near the mines in Angola. She'd had trouble sleeping, then they'd gone to the kitchen to get something to eat. She remembered him kissing her, his hands soft and gentle against the sensitive skin on her stomach and breasts. She remembered him picking her up to carry her into the bedroom, then gunshots and blood.

Grayson had been hurt again because of her.

Hurt. Not killed.

She couldn't believe he was dead. Last time he had lived, and she couldn't allow herself to think that this time he hadn't survived. If she let herself think that there was no Grayson to go back to then she really had no reason to survive, no reason to fight.

So she had to decide now.

Keep hope alive and do everything she could to survive until someone came for her or she found a way out, or give up now and accept her fate.

Despite her exhaustion and the lingering effect of the drugs, determination gave her strength. She wasn't giving up. No way. She wanted to live, she wanted the chance to explore her relationship with Grayson and do anything she wanted with her life, free from the controlling influences of others.

Nothing was going to make her give up.

Grayson and Benny's words returned to her mind. They'd told her whatever she'd done to survive with the Angolans had been the right thing because it meant she was alive, the same was true now. She had to do anything it took to make sure her captors had no reason to kill her. She knew that Grayson would come, and if he couldn't, he would send his team in his place.

Blinking away the last of the blurriness in her eyes from the drugs, Juliet took in her surroundings.

It looked like she was in a dungeon.

An actual dungeon.

The kind of place you usually saw in movies but that she didn't think actually existed.

The walls and floor were stone, large, gray stones that looked like they had been here for hundreds of years. They were cold to the touch and hard as, well, stone, and there was nothing in her cell that would give her any relief from them. In fact the only thing in her cell at all was a hole in the floor in one corner that she guessed was supposed to pass for a toilet. There was no window to her cell, and the stone walls went right to the ceiling, but the front wall of the small room was made of metal bars and a narrow door.

Pushing to her feet, Juliet winced when her injured knees took her weight, but she hardly had time to worry about the minor injury right now, so she ignored it and hobbled to the bars. Outside them was a passageway, the floor the same stones as her cell. Across from where she was standing was another room identical to hers, and when she twisted her head to look left and right she saw more cells lining the passageway as far as she could see.

There was no light in her room, but bulbs hung from the passageway ceiling, giving the whole dungeon a creepy feel.

Sinking down to sit on her bottom, resting against the metal bars, Juliet wondered who had taken her and where she was now. Had some of the Angolans escaped and come back for her? She supposed it was a possibility, or it could be the Russians. She didn't know enough about the family to determine whether or not they were likely to give up on her. Or it could be some other group her father had cheated that she didn't know anything about.

Juliet wasn't sure how long she sat there, her teeth chattering, body trembling, but the next thing she knew she heard the sounds of footsteps and quiet voices.

Someone was coming.

Seemed like she would be getting her answers soon enough.

"Good evening, darling," Dimitri Fedorov greeted her as he strolled toward her. He was dressed like he always was in an expensive suit, wearing too much cologne, with his thick dark hair perfectly combed into place. If you didn't know that he was an evil psychopath, you'd probably think he was quite handsome, and he took care of himself, his body was toned and muscled but nothing compared to Grayson and his team.

For some reason, Juliet didn't feel the fear she thought she would when she came face to face with her latest abductor.

Instead of cowering or crying, instead of begging and pleading for her life, all she felt was a rage unlike anything she had ever experienced.

As a kid she'd loved cartoons, always thought it was funny when people were angry how they drew them turning red and heating up, with steam coming out of their ears, but that was exactly how she felt right now.

Juliet was furious.

Her blood heated and she was sure her face had reddened, and she glared at Dimitri. She was so sick of people trying to run her life, if it wasn't her father it was the Angolans who thought they could take her as payment for her father's debts, and now it was Dimitri thinking she had to honor a deal her father had made. But she wasn't just some object for other people to use, she was a person, a human being with her own wants and needs. And what she wanted was to go home to Grayson so they could start their lives together.

"You don't look pleased to see me, darling," Dimitri mocked. "Or is it the accommodations? Not up to your usual five-star standards?"

She knew the dig was supposed to upset her, but to be honest, while yeah she enjoyed staying at a luxury hotel, she would be just as happy going camping and sleeping in a tent.

"You will be marrying me, Juliet, and you are going to learn how to play the part of my wife to perfection. You will be kept here until you learn what being a mafia bride is about. You will not be given clothing, or blankets, and bedding, you will be fed broth and water. You want to earn privileges then you need to learn your place. Each time you show me that you're learning what is expected of you then you can receive a reward of my choice. Better food, clothing, blankets, a bed, and once I'm confident in your ability not to embarrass me and be the perfect wife, then you will be given a room upstairs, and once I know for sure that you are as committed to this life as I am you will be allowed to leave the house."

So basically what he was saying was that he wanted to train her as though she were a dog.

That did nothing to improve her mood.

With a glower that felt like there were sparks leaping from her eyes, Juliet tossed her head and stalked to the back of her cell. She knew she shouldn't be antagonizing her captor, Grayson had told her what the Fedorovs were capable of, and she already knew Dimitri had a violent temper. It had been his assault and attempted rape that sent her running onto the streets in the first place. But right now, Juliet just didn't have it in her to care.

She had reached the end of her rope, only apparently there wasn't hopelessness and despair, there was simply anger.

"Attitude like that isn't going to win you any favor, Juliet," Dimitri snapped, obviously irritated that she wasn't cowering at his feet. "Have you forgotten who you are marrying? I am a powerful man, one who is used to getting his way, one who doesn't take kindly to insubordination."

"Then I foresee our marriage is going to be a rocky one," she snapped back. Grayson had taught her that not all men were controlling jerks, some were strong, kind, compassionate, they lifted you up rather than beating you down. They encouraged you to find yourself rather than cower to someone else's vision for your life. There was no way she was ever going back to the woman she'd been before because for the first time in forever Juliet actually respected herself, and there was nothing Dimitri could do to change that.

She wasn't going to submit to him.

She wasn’t going to be his version of the perfect mafia wife.

She wasn’t going to let him own her soul.

She would play the game, stay alive, wait for Grayson and his team to find her, or an opportunity to escape.

Learning to respect herself was something she wasn’t prepared to compromise. It was a gift she hadn't known she needed but would be forever grateful to Grayson for giving her.

CHAPTER 12

January 28th

4:13 A.M.

HIS HEAD WAS POUNDING.

The kind of vicious throbbing that even half-conscious he knew was the result of a concussion.

Chaos groaned, knowing this wasn't going to be pleasant but cracked his eyes open anyway. A head injury always meant only one thing. Something was wrong.

His last memories were hazy, but if something was wrong it had to do with Juliet.

That he knew for certain.

When his eyes, still open just to slits, adjusted to the muted light Chaos saw that he was in a hospital, and just like last time his team were strewn about the room watching over him. Only this time Wolf's team were here too, the eleven big men took up almost the entire cramped space, but he knew any attempts he made at telling them they didn't have to hang around would be pointless.

"You awake, man?" Fox asked softly.

"Yeah." His voice came out with more of a croak than he would have liked, but at least he was awake and functional. "Juliet?"

"What do you remember?" Wolf asked.

"The cabin, eating, I was kissing Juliet, then I got shot. Again." He had allowed his guard to go down. He'd kept track of what was going on at the mine through his comms, knew that the two SEAL teams had Mr. Pedro and the men who worked for him contained, and had believed that the threat to Juliet was over.

A mistake.

One he prayed she wasn't going to pay for with her life.

"Just a graze," Cookie informed him, "the real problem is the head injuries."

"How long have I been out?" he asked.

"Around twenty-four hours. You've been in and out but not awake enough for us to get anything out of you about what happened," Spider told him.

"Juliet is gone?" he asked, although he phrased it as a question he already knew the answer.

"Yes," Abe confirmed.

"But you already know how tough she is," Benny reminded him. "I beat you to the punch and already told the guys about how she scored a direct hit of the crown jewels," he teased with an encouraging smile. "A girl who can get herself out of a dangerous situation knows how to stay alive until we find her."

Chaos didn't doubt that. The problem was what would be the cost of her survival. She'd already endured so much, and he hated the thought of her suffering all over again, especially because he had let her down.

Again.

Guilt thrummed a steady beat inside his skull alongside the pain. As much as it urged him to give into it, he knew he didn't have that luxury right now. Juliet was counting on him and if there was one thing he was vowing here and now it was that he would never ever let her down again.

"Do you remember anything about who attacked you?" Dude asked.

He tried to recall the memories, but they were fuzzy, bathed in a light of disconnect that didn't allow him to recall them clearly. Frustrated at his own body he let out a growl. "Nothing definitive. I just remember a feeling someone was there but it was too late. I remember pain and Juliet screaming my name. That's it." This wasn't his first concussion, and he knew that those memories were probably gone for good, the blow to his head wiping them away as though they'd never happened. Trying to force himself to recall something that no longer existed inside his brain was a waste of his time, and yet he didn't know how else to figure out what had happened to Juliet.

"The easy answer is the Fedorovs," Night said slowly.

"We thought it was them last time and were wrong though," Mozart reminded him.

"Eagle is looking into them, but we should keep our options open," King said.

"Where are we?" Chaos asked. Hospitals were pretty generic, and since he hadn't seen any of the staff he hadn't been able to hear what language they spoke. It was disconcerting enough to lose some of his memories, and knowing that Juliet was once again in danger, he at least wanted the grounding of knowing what country they were in.

"We're back Stateside," Fox told him. "When we couldn't get a response from you, Spider and Night went back to the cabin to check on things. As soon as they found you unconscious and Juliet gone the rest of us handed things over to the cops, got you stabilized, and flew back here."

"And when we find Juliet?" he asked. SEALs didn't travel the world working on personal crusades. But this was Juliet, and there was no way he was leaving her wherever she'd been taken. If it came down to a choice between his job and rescuing her, he knew which option he would choose.

The guys exchanged glances. "If," Fox started slowly, "we get something concrete to say that Fedorov has her then we might get the green light to go in after her. Fedorov is wanted by pretty much every government in the world, but any time someone even gets close to nailing him the evidence always disappears. Statements get retracted, or witnesses can't be found, this time though we have Juliet. I'm guessing that Dimitri is banking on the fact that she'll play the loyal, dutiful wife and refuse to admit she's a kidnap victim, but somehow I can't see your girl going along with that."

"No way in Hell," Chaos agreed vehemently. He knew Juliet and the last thing she was going to do was ever allow another person to control her.

"If we don't get the okay for the mission, Eagle said he'll get a few of his guys together and go in after her," Fox added.

As much as he wanted to go in for Juliet himself, in the end, all that mattered was that she be rescued, so if he had to take a back seat and allow Eagle and his team to get her out then he'd do it. He wouldn't like it, but he'd do it.

"Speak of the devil," Shark said, pulling his phone from his pocket.

"What is the world coming to when *Shark* is the only one

who answers his phone?" Eagle grumbled when Shark put the phone on speaker.

"What do you have?" Chaos demanded before Eagle could get sidetracked. His headache was improving with each passing minute and his need to get up and start doing something to rescue Juliet was growing.

"Took Raven a while to find anything but she managed to hack into video surveillance footage from every airfield in Angola, and she found something. Give that woman a computer and an internet connection, and I don't think there's anything she can't do. Don't tell her I said that though, her ego is big enough as it is."

Despite his words, Chaos knew that Eagle thought of the world of his sister Raven, as well as the rest of his siblings who all co-owned Prey Security. "What did Raven find?"

"Your guy Dimitri Fedorov, on a private plane in a small airfield about two hours from the cabin where they kidnapped her. A black SUV drove up, and someone carried what looked like an unconscious woman onto the plane. Raven was able to track the plane back to Russia to a tiny, privately owned airfield."

"So we know where she is?" Hope flooded through him. If they knew Juliet's location then all they had to do was go and get her and bring her home where she belonged. She had a family here now, people who cared about her, not just him but his team and their wives as well. She could finally live the life she'd always wanted for herself, free of her father's control, but none of that mattered if they didn't get to her in time.

"We know her approximate location," Eagle replied.

"But it shouldn't be hard to track down. The airfield has to be close to the Fedorov place, and we know that their estate is large, all we need to do is check out the area and we'll know where she is," Chaos said.

"Agreed. Raven will keep working on an exact location, but for the time being at least, you guys can see about setting up a mission to go in after her. I have a few of my guys lined up if you need our help, so keep me updated."

"Thanks, man, for everything you've done for me and Juliet," Chaos said.

"Pfft," Eagle made a dismissive noise. "We have each other's backs, you know that, no thanks needed. Call if you need anything. Go get your girl, Chaos."

That was exactly what he planned on doing.

Juliet had a fire inside her he wasn't even sure she'd known about until the day Dimitri Fedorov put his hands on her. But she'd discovered that side of herself. She'd fought for herself, fought to break free of her father's hold, and he knew there was no way she was going to give up no matter what Dimitri threw at her.

There was no way he was giving up on her either.

9:06 A.M.

A SCREAM PIERCED the previously quiet dungeon.

Juliet jolted from her doze and stumbled to her feet. They hadn't fed her since she'd been brought here, and she'd barely eaten since the Angolans took her, actually the last good meal she'd had was breakfast the day she learned of her mother's death, and that was … well, she'd lost track of time, but that had to be four or five days ago at least. The lack of food, coupled with all the drugs she'd been given and the fact that she'd been living hopped up on adrenalin had all taken a toll on her body. She was feeling weak and shaky, but the scream roused her enough that she managed to make it to the bars of her cell and curl her fingers around them.

Pressing her face as much through the bars as she could, she looked to the left and then the right, trying to see who had screamed. She had wondered if she wasn't alone down here, what was the point of having so many cells if you didn't plan to have at least a few of them occupied, but she'd been too afraid to call out and ask if she had company.

Another scream cut through the air and Juliet jerked.

That was a scream of intense pain.

Of agony.

A heavy dose of hopelessness was mixed in with it.

And undiluted terror.

"H-hello?" she called out tentatively. If someone was suffering she wanted to do what she could to help them.

There was no reply.

Juliet stood there, clutching the bars to keep herself on her feet, waiting for whoever screamed to say something.

Maybe they were unconscious now?

Had passed out from the pain perhaps? That made sense. Only what had been the cause of the person's pain? Maybe their cell had more things in it than Juliet's? Maybe they had tripped on the uneven stone floor and fallen, broken a wrist, or even a knee.

Another scream tore through the dungeon.

If the person had fallen and hurt themselves then why did they keep screaming?

Maybe they were trying to move? Put a broken bone back in place?

Why did that feel so unlikely?

It could happen.

That could be the reason.

"Hello?" she called out again. "Who are you? Are you okay?"

She waited tensely but no one answered her.

What was going on here?

Her brain was trying to tell her but Juliet was shutting it down. She knew she didn't want to know what was going on in another cell. She knew that whatever was happening was going to make her current situation seem horrifyingly real.

She was doing her best, clinging to hope and her determination not to allow Dimitri Fedorov to destroy her. She wanted to fight her way through this, come out the other side alive and maybe even a stronger person than she'd been before. She'd learned not to be a doormat, she'd found her strength, and she had finally found a way to completely embrace her OCD without being embarrassed by it.

No way was she going to die now.

And certainly not here in some dark, dank dungeon.

Nor was she going to allow another man to control her, Dimitri could try, he might even get her to comply with some of his demands, but he would never own her.

He couldn't.

Her heart already belonged to a certain tall, blond, green-eyed navy SEAL who loved to make people laugh, and as such her life and her soul, she had nothing for Dimitri to take from her.

A howl of agony that sounded barely human echoed through the dungeon and this time she couldn't cling to denial. Juliet was horribly afraid she knew the exact cause of the other prisoner's pain.

"Please, tell me what's wrong," she cried. The screams were freaking her out, and she was trying really hard to hold it together.

Someone laughed.

Actually laughed.

If she hadn't known better, she might have thought it was someone just trying to freak her out, playing a trick on her, but no one could fake the agony she'd heard.

Footsteps clicked against the stone floor, and then a huge man appeared. He was wearing a black shirt, sleeves rolled up to his elbows, and a pair of dark-colored jeans, he was grinning at her, but it wasn't a nice smile.

"You wish to join in?" he asked in heavily accented English, then he threw his head back and laughed. His dark hair was long, brushing the top of his collar, and his dark eyes glittered with a cold, hard emptiness she hadn't seen before. This man didn't feel emotions like normal people did, she could tell with just one look at his expression. He took pleasure in hurting others, probably got off on it.

He was the cause of the screams.

He'd been torturing someone else who was being held prisoner by the Fedorovs.

Torture.

The thought made her sick.

"You want I make you bleed." The man stepped closer, and Juliet scampered back, crossing her cell and pressing her back against the far wall, putting as much distance between them as possible. Since she had nothing to cover her naked body but her hands, she crossed one arm over her chest and placed her other hand above the apex of her thighs. For the first time she was glad of the metal bars that prevented him from getting to her.

Unless he had keys.

She began to tremble.

"I get boss and see if time for you to play," the man said,

aiming his vicious snarl in her direction, but he didn't open the door to her cell, and she thanked her lucky stars.

Her momentary reprieve didn't last long.

Her so-called fiancé appeared beside the giant, and her tremors turned to full body shakes. She might have decided not to allow this man to break her, but that didn't mean she wasn't afraid of him. Dimitri had been the catalyst for her running. When he had cornered her at her father's New Year's Eve party and tried to have sex with her, beating her when she wouldn't comply, she had realized that one moment that would define the course of her life.

Stay and that was all she would ever be, the beaten down, abused, brainwashed wife of a violent monster.

Run and finally be free to be in charge of her own life.

She had chosen to be free and in a weird way she had Dimitri to thank for that, but she was pretty sure telling him that would only further anger him.

"Good morning, bride." Dimitri gave her that smile she was sure charmed anyone who was too busy looking at his body and not his eyes.

"Bride?"

"That's right." Dimitri's smile grew wider. "I see no reason to wait to make things official between us. You've already done enough damage with your little running act. Do you know how much damage control I had to do to cover for you? Everyone knew that we were to marry on the first of the year. When I had to return here with no wife, everyone wanted to know why. I didn't appreciate having to lie for you, *darling*." He sneered.

They had been supposed to marry the day after the party?

Her father hadn't told her that.

If she hadn't run when she did, she would already be married to Dimitri and she would never have met Grayson.

"You have a lot to be punished for, darling, and I'm sure Michail is anxious to get started, he does so love the sight of blood. But I cannot have my bride sporting cuts and bruises on her wedding day. Tonight you will be branded with the Fedorov family crest, and then we will be wed in a small ceremony in the chapel on the estate. Forget about the American SEAL, Juliet, you will never see him again. This time there will be no running, by midnight tonight you will be marked as mine, the marriage will be legal, and it will be over. No one is coming for you, you belong to me now, don't fight it. You can have a good life here, the wife of one of the most powerful men in the country. You can have the best of everything, and if you submit to my will I will treat you like a queen. Don't be stupid, Juliet, Michail here loves any opportunity to cause pain, but you won't have to suffer if you learn what is expected of you. You are a smart woman, don't play this stupidly. Make the right choice, you submitted to your father for so many years surely it can't be that hard to submit to your husband. Get some rest, darling, you have a big night ahead of you."

With a final wink, Dimitri disappeared. Michail too gave her a leering onceover before heading back the way he'd come no doubt to continue torturing whatever poor soul had found themselves imprisoned here.

Tears leaked from her eyes and she scrunched them closed. She was trying to be strong, she really was, but in just a few hours Dimitri was going to brand her flesh with his mark and then marry her. This wasn't like the Angolans' house, there was no way she was escaping this room, there was no way to stop the wedding, or what Dimitri would do to her on their wedding night.

She wanted to survive this.

She wanted to go home to Grayson.

She wanted to live the rest of her life to the fullest.

But she was afraid that this was already a done deal.

~

8:24 P.M.

"I SEE movement in the northeast quadrant of the estate."

Chaos bristled when he heard Dude's voice through the comms.

Once they'd located the Fedorov family's large estate, hidden deep in the woods, miles from any of the nearby towns, they had all spent hours studying the layout. He knew what was in the northeast quadrant and he didn't like it.

"Isn't that where the chapel is located?" King asked.

"Yes," Chaos replied, resisting the urge to grind his teeth. If there was activity around the chapel then he knew what that meant. "Dimitri is planning on marrying her tonight. Given that she ran on him last time he no doubt wants to make it official, give himself a legal claim on her just in case something goes wrong and he loses her. Harder for her to make a claim of kidnapping if she married the guy."

No way was he allowing that man to make Juliet his wife.

Even if the marriage could be easily challenged, his injuries would help prove she hadn't left of her own free will and they had footage of her being carried unconscious onto the plane—although knowing Dimitri, he would probably have some lie to explain that all away—it was a complication Juliet didn't need as she dealt with the aftermath of all of this.

"There are more guards than we were hoping," Wolf said.

"We're not pulling back," Chaos growled. No way was he

walking away now, not when they were this close to getting Juliet back.

"Wasn't suggesting that we did, brother," Wolf calmly replied. "Was just thinking it was lucky that Eagle sent us a few of his men to help."

Between the two SEAL teams and the half dozen men who worked for Eagle at Prey, they had eighteen highly trained special forces or former special forces men here in Russia, more than enough to combat whoever the Fedorovs had working for them. Not that this would be as easy as breaching the mine in Angola. Those men had relied more on their weapons and brute force to intimidate already vulnerable people, people who were mostly human trafficking victims, then they kept them weak from lack of food and proper sanitary conditions, and always chained up, and you didn't have to have a lot of training to maintain the upper hand. Whoever Alexi Fedorov hired would no doubt be former Russian special forces, chosen because they possessed a mean streak and a propensity to get the job done without emotion and without questioning anything.

Still, Chaos was confident that they had the ability to breach the estate, find Juliet, and get her out of there. They had the element of surprise on their hands, the Fedorovs were arrogant, they believed they were superior, that no one would ever catch them, and it was that exact cockiness that gave Chaos and the others the ability to do just that.

"Everyone in position?" Fox asked.

Once everyone had confirmed that they were, they received the signal to breach.

It was cold tonight, thankfully there was heavy cloud cover and just a few snowflakes in the air. With their night vision goggles, they would be able to see everything, but hopefully the Fedorov guards wouldn't see a need for NVGs since they weren't expecting any problems. The guards wouldn't know they were there until it was too late.

He and Benny were teamed together. While the other two-man teams would work on eliminating the guards, they would be searching for Juliet.

The large house—which looked more like the sort of castle you would find in a Disney princess movie—was quiet, only a couple of the windows showed any light. There were so many of them it would take a while to search each one, he wanted—needed—Juliet in his arms now.

Still, the only way to get her back was to do this calmly and methodically, the same way he would on any other mission. Not that this could be in any way deemed any other mission, not when the woman who was very quickly claiming his heart was in danger.

Somehow he managed to hold it together—the gunshot wounds in his chest and leg and the concussion long since forgotten—and before he knew it they were entering the castle through the back door. They were in a kitchen, and two young women startled, freezing in the middle of assembling what looked like it was supposed to be a wedding feast.

Not wanting to kill the women who were no doubt victims themselves, he and Benny gagged and restrained them, once they had everyone else contained they would interview the women, and if they were innocent victims they would see they were returned to their families.

Moving on from the kitchen they cleared each room with excruciating slowness. They found another four young women decorating a large dining room and contained them the same way they had the others.

Still no sign of Juliet though.

She was here somewhere.

The activity around the chapel, coupled with what they'd

seen in the house confirmed that someone was planning a wedding here. The only logical assumption was that Dimitri had Juliet in his sights.

If it hadn't been for Raven Oswald and her ability to get any information from any computer in the world, they wouldn't have found the plane Juliet had been on and wouldn't be here right now. By the time they had managed to find the estate some other way it would have been too late. Dimitri would have already forced Juliet to marry him, done any number of other things to her.

They rounded another corner in the far too opulent mansion and came face to face with a startled Alexi Fedorov.

The head of the renowned crime family recovered from his shock quickly and gave them what Chaos was sure was supposed to be a menacing smile. Too bad for the older man that Chaos had dealt with people who were a lot more terrifying than him. Alexi Fedorov was nearing seventy, he was a short and thin man who looked every one of his years and more. The only lingering remnant of his youth was a still full head of thick dark hair and dark brown eyes that seemed to cut through you like a knife.

"You are my daughter-in-law's American soldiers, yes?" Alexi asked.

"SEALs," Chaos corrected.

Alexi waved a hand like none of it mattered. For a man who had two American special forces men standing in his home he seemed unconcerned. There was that arrogance again, and it was going to get him killed. "You are here too late."

"I don't think so," Chaos said. "The wedding hasn't taken place yet, and even if it had it wouldn't have stopped us taking her back. Juliet is a person, a good person, one who deserves—who has the right—to live her life the way she wants, she's not a tool for you to use to further your own agenda."

The old Russian just scoffed. "When you are a powerful man like myself you can do anything you want."

"Not this time."

At that, Alexi threw back his head and laughed. "There is no way you and your friend here are leaving this place alive."

This time it was Chaos who gave a sharp, humorless laugh. Taking a step forward, he let every ounce of the deep, violent rage that had been festering inside him since the moment he found out that people were playing with Juliet's life like it meant nothing shoot from his eyes. "No," he said coldly, "you are the one who won't be leaving this place alive."

For a moment fear sparked in Alexi's eyes as he obviously realized that for two men to have breached his secluded property, they couldn't have done it alone.

"Where is she, Mr. Fedorov?" he demanded.

"She is learning what is expected of her as my son's wife," Alexi said smugly, regaining some of his composure.

"If you think this is working out in your favor then you are delusional. It's over, Alexi, everything, you can choose prison or death, personally, I hope you choose death because I know it will be easier for Juliet to deal with this if you're no longer alive, but the decision is yours."

Chaos knew the exact moment when Alexi Fedorov made his choice.

The man would rather die in his own house and forgo the humiliation in the crime world of being caught on his own turf. In the Fedorov's world it was better to die than to be humiliated. And Alexi was currently facing the worst kind of humiliation that existed for a man like himself.

Alexi reached a hand under the jacket of his expensive dove gray suit and pulled out a gun.

Chaos took the shot before the old man had a chance to aim.

Dead.

One of the men who had conspired to use Juliet like she was nothing, to control her life for their own personal gain, was dead, but the rage inside him only grew. Juliet was still here somewhere, no doubt with Dimitri, and he had no idea what they'd done to her. She had been in the Fedorov's company for over thirty-six hours now, anything could have happened to her, and the not knowing was killing him.

It was time to go find his girl.

~

9:09 P.M.

EVEN THOUGH SHE knew it wasn't going to do any good, Juliet pressed herself into the corner of her cell when Dimitri produced a key and unlocked the door.

While being trapped in here had given her a sense of claustrophobia and hopelessness as there was nothing she could do to help herself, at least it had offered some measure of safety. No one could touch her, she knew what to expect, and she didn't have to worry about being raped or tortured. In there she was alone, but not anymore.

Now Dimitri was walking toward her, and the scary man he'd called Michail was with him. Michail carried an iron bar with him and wheeled in a small portable fire pit, already stacked with wood.

Her eyes locked on the iron bar, the branding iron, and

terror rippled through her. If Grayson and his team found her, they could undo a marriage, get it annulled or declared invalid since she'd been kidnapped, but the brand would last forever. The scar on her skin would be a constant reminder of this whole horrific ordeal, something she would have to carry around with her for the rest of her life.

She shied away from Dimitri when he came toward her and it made him laugh.

"Not so cocky now that there isn't a wall of metal bars between us, darling," he said.

The endearment sent a spear of anger through her. He had no right to pretend there was anything sweet or caring or loving between them. He might be able to force her to marry him, he might be able to keep her prisoner here while he tried to use torture to gain her compliance, but that was it. She would be his wife in name only. "Don't call me darling," she snapped.

Her outburst seemed to amuse him further, and he laughed again as he reached out for her. Juliet wasn't going to go easily, he could marry her today as planned, he could dress her up in a pretty dress for his photos, but she was going to make sure that he didn't look picture perfect for his ceremony.

Thrashing in his grip when he wrapped a large hand around her bicep, she wasn't trying to get away—there was no way she could escape the two men—her goal was just to mark Dimitri the same way he was about to mark her. Aiming for his face, she scratched her fingernails down his cheek, satisfied by his grunt of pain, she knew she'd caused the damage she wanted.

Dimitri backhanded her. The force of the blow sent her slamming into the wall and then sinking down to the floor. Pain bloomed in her cheek and the length of her side where she'd made contact with the stone, but it was worth it. More than worth it, now today when he took her to the wedding chapel all dressed up like she was a real bride and not a prisoner, she would have something to focus on while she listened to the minister. She had hurt him, she wasn't completely powerless here, she might not be able to find a way to escape, but she could still fight Dimitri every step of the way.

He glared down at her, and she gave him a smug smile when she saw the red streaks on his face. "You will pay for that, *darling*," he snarled. Looking over his shoulder at Michail he ordered, "Start the fire and get the branding iron heating." Anger and satisfaction sparked in his eyes when he turned back to her. "Your little game won't change anything."

"Sure it will, now at our wedding everyone is going to ask you why you have scratches on your cheek and who caused them."

"No one would dare to ask me that."

Juliet shrugged. "Whether they ask it or not you know they're going to be thinking it. Just like they're going to think that it was me. Given that we didn't marry when you told everyone we would, and that you couldn't produce me for almost a month, they're going to wonder what's going on between us. That you can't control your own bride is going to make you look bad, and you're all about your image."

His hand curled around her neck, and he dragged her back to her feet, shoving her up against the wall. "You *will* learn to submit to me. You think you're so strong because you survived a day in the cell, but you're wrong, this was nothing. Once you're branded you will be taken upstairs, bathed, and dressed for the wedding. You will behave at the ceremony because if you don't I'll send people after those SEALs of yours. As I hear some of them have small children. Unless you want to be responsible for their deaths, you will play the part of bride to perfection. After dinner, I will take you to my bedroom where you will learn every single one of my sexual preferences. Then you will be brought back down here to spend the night and every other night after that until the will to defy has been beaten out of you. You will be my wife, and you will learn to play that role perfectly, if you think otherwise you are merely naïve. How is the branding iron heating, Michail?"

Michail had built a fire with ease and was now holding the branding iron in the flame's heat. The end of the iron was turning red, and Juliet prepared herself for the coming pain. It started with the brand but it didn't end there, she had no intention of submitting to Dimitri no matter what he did to her, so pain was about to become her new best friend.

"It's going to hurt, darling, but not nearly as bad as what I'll do to you tonight after the wedding dinner," Dimitri said.

"Ready," Michail said as he held up the glowing iron.

"Wonderful, want a kiss for luck, darling?"

Juliet pressed her lips together and glowered at him. The man was disgusting, he thought money and power made him something special, but in reality, he was just a common criminal who enjoyed inflicting pain and taunting those weaker than himself.

"Lesson number one, darling, your body no longer belongs to you, it is mine, and I will do with it whatever I choose." With that, Dimitri crushed his mouth to hers, the kiss almost bruising in its force. When he was done he spun her around so her back was flush against his front, he had one arm across her chest, just below her neck, and his other crossed just beneath her breasts. One of his hands circled one of her breasts as Michail stepped toward them and she realized that was where he intended to brand her.

Although she knew it was futile, she couldn't help but struggle as she felt the heat of the iron as it came close to her skin.

She braced herself as best as she could for the coming onslaught but was totally unprepared for the quiet pop and sudden spray of something wet against her bare skin.

The branding iron clattered to the floor, and Juliet blinked in surprise as two men dressed in fatigues appeared in the doorway of her cell. They were both wearing paint on their faces, but she didn't have to be able to see his features to know the one on the right was Grayson.

"It's over, Dimitri, your men are all either dead or captured. Your father is dead too. He chose death over prison, you don't have to make the same choice. Let Juliet go and get down on your knees," Grayson ordered

He wasn't going to do it.

Juliet could feel the anger vibrating through his body.

Dimitri was too proud to go to prison. He'd lived his entire life with more money than he could spend in ten life-times and more power than any man should ever have. There was no way he was losing both and being confined to a prison cell.

The arm that had been wrapped beneath her breasts moved, and for a moment, she thought that she was wrong, that Dimitri in fact valued life above all else, but then he gave an almost maniacal laugh.

"You can kill me, but I'm taking her with me."

"Juliet, get down," Grayson screamed.

She was throwing herself to the ground when a bang echoed through the room and pain exploded in her lower back.

A second bang quickly followed, and she heard someone hit the ground a split second after she did.

She hoped it was Dimitri and not Grayson or whoever had been with him.

She wanted to lift her head to check but it suddenly felt heavy. Her entire body felt like it had been encased in concrete, and she hurt so badly.

"Juliet, princess, talk to me," Grayson ordered as he dropped to his knees beside her.

Good.

He was alive.

Relief made her lightheaded.

"Juliet?" Grayson repeated, fear evident in his voice as he touched his fingers to her neck.

She didn't want him to be afraid anymore.

All she'd done since she'd entered his life was cause him fear and worry, and yet he kept coming back for more.

Was that what love was?

Coming after someone no matter how many times they left?

A smile touched her lips at the thought that he might love her. Was it too much to hope for?

"Come on, cat burglar, talk to me," Grayson demanded.

A small laugh rumbled through her chest. "Didn't," she paused as a painful cough hacked from her lungs, "steal anything."

"There's my girl." The relief in his voice was evident, and she was glad her words had soothed him. The pain she'd suffered was a small price to pay to take away even an ounce of his fear. "I'm sorry, princess, I'm going to have to roll you over, I need to see if there's an exit wound. It's going to hurt," he added.

"Already hurts."

"I know, honey, I'm so sorry."

"Not your fault," she reminded him.

He didn't answer, his large hands closed around her shoulder and hip, and he turned her very gently. His careful actions did nothing to ease the growing agony that was consuming her, and she cried out before she even thought that addressing her pain out loud was going to hurt Grayson.

Her eyes must have been open because she caught his wince as his gaze moved from her face to her stomach. From the tight way he pressed his lips together and the worried crinkle in his brow, she knew that it was bad. Possibly even life-threatening.

"I'm so sorry," he murmured again as his eyes returned to her face and he eased her back down.

Juliet shook her head, winced at the pain, then said, "No, don't apologize, you came for me."

"Princess, there is nowhere in this world that you could go where I wouldn't follow you." One of his hands stroked her tangled hair, and then he leaned down and touched his lips to her forehead.

Someone dropped down on her other side, but Juliet couldn't take her eyes off Grayson. She watched as he took bandages and pressed them to the wound in her stomach. It hurt less this time when he rolled her onto her side to do the same with the wound on her back.

Her pain was fading, but along with it the rest of the world faded too.

She was cold.

Almost numb.

Everything around her but Grayson's face was blurry, in contrast it stood out in high definition.

He was talking to someone, but she wasn't sure who.

A blanket was draped over her naked body.

Someone took her arm and started an IV.

Through it all she just locked her gaze on Grayson. If she

was going to die then she wanted his face to be the last thing she saw.

"You hold on, okay, princess," Grayson said, taking her face between his hands. His hands were red, stained with her blood, and she hated that this would be his last memory of her.

"Sorry," she whispered.

Breathing was starting to become a challenge.

She wasn't sure she could keep her eyes open much longer.

"Don't give up on me, princess, don't you dare even think about it. You hold on, okay? You fight this. Keep breathing and trust me to get you to help."

"Do trust you," she murmured.

"I know, baby."

He touched his forehead to hers and feathered his lips across hers in the softest kiss imaginable. Yet somehow that one kiss of all the ones they had shared was her favorite. She felt everything he felt for her in that brief, simple touch, and it settled her. She might be going to die, but she would die knowing what it felt like to be loved, and for someone who had been deprived of that for a lifetime it was a precious gift she would cherish in these last moments.

"Don't give up on me, princess, please. Fight for me. Keep breathing, keep your eyes open, stay with me. Please, sweetheart."

He was begging, and she so badly wanted to give him what he needed, but she wasn't sure that she could.

Exhaustion was weighing heavily upon her. She no longer felt the pain and wasn't sure if it was because of whatever drugs she was being given or because she was mere moments away from death. All she felt now was peace. She was going to die in the arms of the man she loved, she wouldn't be alone.

"Hold me," she murmured so softly she wasn't sure anyone heard her, but then she felt his arms come around her as someone helped maneuver her carefully onto Grayson's lap.

"I'm here, princess, I have you," he said. One of his hands stroked her side, the other cradled her head against his chest.

As the world faded further away a soft, peaceful light settled around her, Grayson's love circled her just like his arms did, and there was a smile on her lips as she disappeared into the light.

CHAPTER 13

January 29th

3:35 A.M.

HE'D HAD ENOUGH of waiting.

If he had to sit here for another minute without news he was going to lose his mind.

Chaos stood and paced once again around the surgical waiting room. The last few hours had been a blur. They'd flown Juliet on a helo to Germany, lost her twice on the way, and as soon as they'd reached the hospital, she'd been whisked away and rushed into surgery.

Watching her heart stop beating had been the most terrifying moment of his life.

Having her code in front of him had reminded him of everything they hadn't gotten to share yet. They'd had only a couple of dates, not nearly enough, they'd only made love a handful of times, not nearly enough, they hadn't told each other they were in love, hadn't married or had kids, hadn't been able to grow old side by side. It wouldn't be fair to lose her when they'd only just found each other.

But life didn't always play fair.

Sinking back into his seat, he looked around at the packed waiting room. All the guys were here with him, silently offering their support. It had been three hours since Juliet had been taken in for surgery but they hadn't left. No one had even gone to the bathroom, they were all right beside him waiting for news.

Their support meant everything to him, and he knew that if the worst happened and Juliet didn't make it they would be there for him as he dealt with the loss, but he was praying with everything he had that wouldn't be the case.

An exhausted-looking woman in surgical scrubs walked through the door and Chaos was out of his chair and rushing toward her before he even thought.

The woman took in the room filled with large men dressed in fatigues and asked, "Juliet York's … group?"

"I'm her fiancé," he lied. There was no way he was not getting the information on her condition, besides, she didn't have any other family. Her father was in prison, her mother was dead, she had no siblings, he and his family were hers now.

The doctor nodded. Although she didn't look convinced that he and Juliet were engaged, the understanding in her eyes told him she was going to give him the update anyway. "She coded on the table, and we had to give her several transfusions, but she made it through, she's in the ICU. The bullet did a bit of damage, but we repaired everything and barring any infections or unforeseen complications, she should make a full recovery. We're going to keep her here for the next few days, but when she's strong enough to travel you can take her back home."

"Can I see her?" He didn't care how long Juliet had to stay here, he'd be staying right here with her. What he needed now was to see with his own two eyes that she was still alive. The last time he'd seen her she'd been naked, soaked in blood, with a tube down her throat to breathe for her, she'd looked as close to death as anyone he'd ever seen, and he needed the reassurance of being able to see her and touch her.

"Of course you can, but for now just you," the doctor replied, glancing at the dozen men standing behind him.

"Go see your girl, we'll be right here," Fox told him.

"You guys should go check into a hotel, shower, get something to eat, sleep," he said. They'd stayed with him through the waiting, but now that they knew Juliet was okay they didn't have to hang around anymore.

Wolf just rolled his eyes. "We're staying."

The others all nodded, and Chaos was smiling as he followed the doctor to ICU. It was nice to have a whole bunch of friends he considered family to support him, and he was glad that Juliet too had that support system she'd been missing all her life. Never again would she feel alone in the world, never again would she doubt that anyone cared about her. From here on out, she was going to know what it was like to have people in her circle who cared about her just for her, and not for what they could use her for.

When they walked into Juliet's ICU room he couldn't help but wince. He'd seen people in ICU before, guys he served with, friends, some who hadn't made it, but nothing could prepare him for seeing the woman he loved so still and lifeless looking. She was as white as the sheets she was laid on, a tube looped across her face helping to deliver oxygen to her lungs, she had an IV in one arm, and there were other tubes and wires attached to her body.

"You can sit with her, talk to her, hopefully she'll wake up soon."

The doctor left him alone, and Chaos crossed the room and pulled up the only chair so it was right beside the bed. He reached out and lightly brushed his fingertips across her face before cupping her cheek in his hand.

"I'm here, Juliet, I'm sitting right here beside you waiting for you to wake up."

Picking up her hand he cradled it in his, needing the contact to reassure himself that she was alive and going to be okay.

The doctor's idea of soon and his differed greatly. In the end it took Juliet's exhausted body close to four hours to emerge from sleep. After the first hour, he'd gone looking for a doctor or nurse, concerned that something was wrong because she hadn't woken up. After reassurances that everything she'd been through had taken a toll on her mind and her body, and that Juliet would wake up when she was ready, he'd resumed sitting beside her, talking to her about the future they'd have and waiting.

And waiting.

And waiting.

Until finally her lashes fluttered against her pale cheeks, and the hand he held in his gave the faintest of squeezes.

"Juliet? Hey, princess, can you hear me?"

She gave a tiny nod, barely discernible. If he hadn't been looking for a response he would probably have missed it.

"Wake up for me, princess, let me see those pretty green eyes of yours."

A small smile tugged up the corners of her lips, and he

couldn't resist leaning down and touching his lips to hers in a soft kiss.

"Come on, cat burglar, you've been sleeping long enough now," he teased.

Juliet's tongue darted out and wet her bottom lip, and then she rasped, "Didn't steal anything, wasn't going to, get that through your thick head."

Chaos laughed, the weight of worry lifting from his shoulders. "There's my girl."

Her smile grew and her eyes opened slowly, then she was looking up at him, and everything was right again in his world.

"How are you feeling, honey?" he asked, smoothing her hair and lacing their fingers together.

"Tired," she replied.

"Sleeping Beauty didn't get enough sleep, huh?" he teased. After everything she'd gone through the last few days and the weeks preceding them, it was no wonder her body had hit a brick wall. "You can close your eyes, go back to sleep," he told her, now that she'd woken, spoken to him, and he knew for sure that she was going to be okay, he could finally stop worrying. "You don't want to overdo things, you lost a lot of blood, coded three times, your body needs rest to start healing."

"Three times?"

"Three times," he echoed. The terror he'd felt as they'd lost her pulse threatened to come back, but he shoved it away, not wanting to upset Juliet.

"You were scared." Dismay covered her features, and she lifted their joined hands and kissed the back of his. "I'm sorry."

"Don't be sorry, you fought, you came back to me."

"Had to. I love you."

Of all the ways he'd ever imagined hearing those words come for the first time from the lips of the woman he loved this was never one of them, and yet it felt perfect. He'd known she was special the night he'd found her seeking shelter from the storm in his house, and while he'd only known her for a few weeks it felt like forever.

"I love you too, princess, so much. I can't wait to take you home, look after you while you heal, help you make all your dreams a reality."

"You already made my dreams a reality. You love me, nobody has ever loved me before," Juliet said, as tears trailed slowly down her cheeks.

"Never again will you lack for people in your life who love you. My parents and sisters are going to adore you. My team and their wives already do. You're going to have an extended family who would go to the ends of the earth for you."

"You already have. You came for me in Angola, you came for me in Russia, and I never doubted for a second that you would. I love you, Grayson, always."

"I'm always going to be there for you, princess. Even when we fight you'll know that I love you, that nothing could or would ever make me leave your side."

CHAPTER 14

February 2nd

4:51 P.M.

"HOW ARE YOU FEELING?"

Juliet fought the urge to roll her eyes. That had to be the thousandth time Grayson had asked her that today, add in all the times he'd asked her in the four days she'd spent in hospital and they had to be nearing a million.

As much as she wanted to roll her eyes the repeated question also made her want to smile. No one had ever bothered asking her that before because nobody had ever really cared, but now having a man who cared so much that he kept asking her over and over again made her feel like her heart was swelling to bursting with all the love in it.

And Grayson didn't just care about her, he *loved* her.

Her.

Juliet York.

Grayson "Chaos" Simpson, a big, strong, Navy SEAL with a body most women dreamed about loved her, quiet, awkward, slightly odd Juliet York.

The very idea of it still shocked her, but in a good way, and she was so glad to be out of the hospital and back in the USA so now their lives together could really begin. There was no power-hungry Russian mobster out to marry her to get a green card, and there were no black market diamond dealers wanting to steal her as payment for her father's debts. There was nothing left standing in the way of her and Grayson getting their happily ever after.

"If you don't answer me in the next three seconds I'm heading straight to the nearest hospital," Grayson warned, sparing a look her way.

The borderline panic on his face made her giggle, but then she sobered. She knew how rough the last week had been for him. He'd been shot twice, hit over the head, had to go running to two countries searching for her, watched her die three times, then sat beside her bed in Germany for four days straight. He had every reason to worry, and she shouldn't have gotten lost in her own head and not answered him immediately.

Reaching over, she rested her hand on his thigh. "I'm fine, Grayson, just tired and a little sore." The first twenty-four hours after surgery basically all she'd done was sleep. Over the next three days, her strength had started returning, and she spent more time awake and talking to Grayson and the guys, but today the flight home had wiped what little strength she had accumulated, and now she was actually looking forward to getting back into a bed.

Taking one hand off the steering wheel, he covered hers. "Only another five minutes and we'll be home."

"Home," she said with a happy sigh.

"You sure you want to stay with me? I mean, after you're healed, if you want I'll help you find your own place."

"You don't want me to stay with you?" As far as she was concerned, Grayson's house was her home, it was the only place that had ever felt like a home and not just a house, but if he wanted space while they dated, she could always move somewhere else.

"Princess, I don't even want to let you out of my sight let alone have you live in a whole different house, I just don't want to be selfish."

"You are the least selfish person I've ever met," she told him, curling her fingers around his and squeezing. "And good, because the last thing I want is to be anywhere you aren't." Although it was something she would have to get used to because Grayson's job meant he could be called away at any time. She wouldn't know where he was going or what he was doing while he was there, and she'd know that every minute he was away from her he was in danger. He could be gone for days, weeks, or even months, and when he returned, he'd give her no information on his time away. But it would be worth it, all the sacrifices of being with a SEAL would be more than worth it to share her life with this man she admired as much as she loved.

"You know for the next three weeks at least I'm all yours, my team won't be called out," Grayson reminded her, this time the one to squeeze her hand reassuringly.

"I know." And she was so grateful to know that at least while she recovered from the gunshot wound that had nearly ended her life, she would have Grayson by her side.

"Having second thoughts on this whole date a SEAL thing?"

"Never," she answered honestly. "I know it will be hard,

but I don't care, I want to be with you, I don't even want to imagine my life without you in it. You'll be careful, won't you? When you have to leave me."

"Always. I will always do everything I can to come home to you," he promised.

"I love you."

"Love you too." He lifted their joint hands and kissed the back of hers before settling them on his thigh again. "Here we go," he announced as he pulled into his driveway.

Juliet let out a breath she hadn't known she'd been holding. She'd missed this little house. She might not have spent long staying there but those days—and nights—had been the best of her life, and she was so glad to be back here.

"Wait for me to come round and get you," Grayson ordered once he'd parked in the garage.

This time she did roll her eyes. He was being so overprotective, doting on her, barely letting her do anything on her own, and it was as annoying as it was sweet. To humor him, she stayed in her seat and waited for him to round the car and open her door. When he scooped her up into his arms she didn't protest. What would be the point? Wasn't this exactly where she longed to be anyway?

He carried her inside and paused in the living room. "You want to sit on the couch for a bit or go straight to bed?"

"Bed," she answered without hesitation. She was tired and hurting, and she couldn't wait to snuggle down into sheets and blankets that smelled like Grayson.

Upstairs, he set her on her feet only long enough to strip off her clothes and dress her in one of his old sweatshirts. Then he pulled back the covers, propped up some pillows, and gently set her down. He disappeared for a moment, returning with a glass of water and some pills. She swallowed them before patting the bed beside her.

"Come sit with me."

"You should be sleeping," he said.

"I don't want to sleep, I want to sit here in your arms."

Grayson gave her a tender smile before slipping off his shoes and socks, removing his shirt, then rounding the bed.

"Ah, clothes," she said with an embarrassed smile as she pointed at the clothes he had intended to leave discarded on the floor. No way would she be able to think of anything else if he left them there.

He chuckled, but the smile he shot her was full of affection as he picked up the clothes. "I'm going to have to get used to living like a neat freak, aren't I?"

"Yep."

He put the clothes in the hamper in the bathroom, then joined her in the bed. Mindful of her wounds, he lifted her carefully, set her on his lap, and then covered them with the blankets.

Juliet gave a content sigh. "This is perfect."

"Yeah, it is," Grayson agreed.

"Almost perfect," she amended as she tilted her head back so she could touch a kiss to his jaw.

"Princess, you are in no condition for sex," he reminded her.

"I know, doesn't mean we can't do other stuff though." The wounds on her back and stomach and the internal damage caused by the bullet meant that sex would be off the table for another couple of weeks at least, but she couldn't wait that long to touch the man she loved.

"Oh yeah? What exactly did you have in mind?" Grayson asked, clearly amused.

"Kiss me, make love to me with your mouth," she said, touching another kiss to his jaw, this time closer to those lips that made her swoon just looking at them.

"I think a little kissing wouldn't break the doctor's orders," he said, his green eyes heating with desire.

Grasping her chin, he turned her face and let his thumb brush a sensual path across her bottom lip. His mouth lowered until it was right above hers and then the tip of his tongue followed the same path his thumb had taken.

"You taste like happiness," he murmured against her lips.

"You taste like love," she whispered back.

Grayson smiled, and she felt his joy deep down inside her soul, and then finally his mouth was on hers. The kiss was soft, sweet, tender, a kiss of love and happiness, one that promised a lifetime filled with both of those things. It was everything she wanted, everything she needed. It erased past hurts and insecurities and replaced them with acceptance and affection.

CHAPTER 15

April 13th

7:59 P.M.

"WHO THOUGHT it was a good idea to let Chaos drive?" Shark grumbled from the backseat of the Hummer.

Chaos laughed, the guys were always complaining that he drove like an old lady just because he wasn't reckless like the rest of them. "Hey, do you want to get there in one piece, or do you want to get there fast?"

"I want to get there fast," Shark muttered.

He laughed again. "Since when do you voluntarily say anything?" Chaos teased his more often than not silent teammate.

"Since he has a Skype date with Claire later tonight," Spider said, a huge grin on his face.

"Wedding planning fun," Night added.

"Wedding planning Hell," Shark complained, but nothing could hide the complete and utter joy in his dark eyes whenever he spoke about his fiancée. "I keep telling Claire that I don't care, we can do whatever she wants for the wedding, all I care about is making her my wife."

"Women like to obsess over every tiny detail, flowers, menus, music, trust the guy who's been married three times, just act interested but let her have the wedding of her dreams, and she'll be happy," Fox said. After losing his first wife to cancer, Fox had met his second and third wife, Evie. He'd messed things up with her the first time and they'd divorced, but he'd gotten a second chance with her, and this time, he was determined to never lose her again.

"Claire's happiness is all that matters to me," Shark said. Claire had returned to work last month, six months after the abduction and horrific torture she'd endured at the hands of a terrorist cell, and Chaos was pretty sure planning the wedding was the only thing keeping her sane, especially with Shark away right now.

"And after the wedding comes the babies, at least if you do it the right way around," Night joked. He'd gotten his friend Lavender pregnant before the two of them fell in love, but the pair couldn't be any happier, and he and Lavender had just announced that she was pregnant with baby number two right before they'd left on this mission.

"Six months between RJ and Anastasia, only three months between our baby number twos, maybe we'll time the third ones to be born on the same day," Spider joked.

"Shark is getting married on May 1st, Chaos proposed to Juliet just before we left, Sullivan is nine months old now, I say we aim for the next round of babies all to be born on the same day," Night said, making them all laugh.

Chaos cast a quick glance King's way to see if the only

single man left on the team felt left out with all the wedding and baby talk, but he was grinning happily at all of them. This was the first mission he'd gone on since he and Juliet got together three months ago, and he hadn't wanted to leave without making things official. His proposal had come on April 2nd, the day they left, so Fox's bet of the first day of spring for him to propose had been the closest. Chaos was sure that their team leader was already thinking up dares for the others to complete once they got back home.

Home.

Now returning home had a whole new importance to him. This was the first time he'd had a woman he was serious about waiting at home for him, and it was hard not to get distracted thinking about her and how she was doing. She was fully healed from the bullet wound that had almost taken her from him, and she had become close with Abby, Lavender, Evie, and Claire, so she wasn't alone, she was also working on getting her home and office organizing business up and running, so she had plenty to keep her occupied. Still, he couldn't wait to get back to her, kiss her, make love to her, celebrate their engagement, and start planning their summer wedding.

"I can totally imagine all five of your women pregnant at the same time, five newborns all arriving on the same day, that would be hilarious," King said as he tossed back his head and laughed heartily.

"No babies in your future, King?" Spider asked.

"Nope," King said adamantly.

"And no special woman?" Night prodded.

"Nope. You guys know I'm not into the whole one woman, lifelong commitment thing. I couldn't be happier for you guys that you beat the odds and found a partner you actually want to spend your entire lives with, but that's not me.

Come on, you know what kind of blood I have running through my veins. Do you really think with my DNA that I could make a marriage work?" King asked.

Chaos was about to remind his friend that he was neither his father nor his mother when something caught his attention. Immediately all thoughts of good-natured banter fled his mind. "Guys, two o'clock, I saw something. A flash of light."

The mood in the Hummer went from light-hearted to focused in a heartbeat.

"Looks like someone is out there," Fox said.

"Something feels wrong," Night said.

"Agreed," Spider said.

"Think they're waiting to ambush us?" he asked, slowing the Hummer down in case the road ahead was littered with IEDs. The last thing he wanted was to get himself and his team blown up by driving over one and have a swarm of insurgents come in to finish them off. They were in Iraq and were supposed to be on their way to meet with a source who claimed to have information about an up-and-coming terrorist cell that was planning several attacks on American soil. The group may or may not be a faction of the same group that had targeted Claire attempting to rebuild after they were mostly killed off.

"I think we should take a different route to the meeting point," Fox said. "Could be nothing, but better safe than sorry."

Chaos couldn't agree more. He didn't intend to do anything that would stop him from coming home to Juliet. He'd promised her that he would always come back to her and it was a promise he intended to keep.

Veering off the road they'd been taking, Chaos headed for a small valley between two of the mountains that were lining the road. None of them talked, they were all on edge now, carefully surveying their surroundings, the same sense of dread that had settled in his gut seemed to be echoed in his friends.

Something was wrong.

This seemingly simple intel-gathering meeting now felt like anything but.

The more they drove, the more stifling the silence seemed to become. He wanted to make a joke, break the tension, laugh off the small flickering light as nothing important, but for the life of him, he couldn't think of a single thing to say. While possibly nothing, the placement of the light so close to the road had trouble written all over it. His gut had kept him alive this long, and at the moment it was telling him that things were about to go bad.

Soon.

In theory, all they had to do was circle around the other side of this mountain, approach the meeting point from a different angle, hopefully bypassing any intended ambush, but another thing he'd learned in this job was that theories got blown to smithereens almost as soon as a mission started.

They were about halfway along the road that should bring them out next to a small river when the first shot came.

It was quickly followed by dozens more.

The next thing he knew the entire mountainside seemed to come alive. There were lights everywhere, at least a hundred men, all armed, all firing at the Hummer, swarming toward them like ants.

A trap.

In trying to avoid an ambush, they'd instead walked right into one.

Someone had planned this perfectly. Waiting until they were right near this point before flashing the light, knowing that they'd suspect a trap and veer off the road, taking this track instead.

Now they were surrounded.

Outnumbered.

There was no way they could drive through all these men to the river or backtrack to the road.

The vehicle offered only so much protection, and that was temporary.

They'd kill some of the men, but that wouldn't change the outcome. There was no way they could kill them all.

Fox was already calling in the ambush, but help would never get here in time.

It was him and his team against over a hundred armed men.

They weren't walking away from this.

Death or capture.

That was the only way this was ending.

Gunfire filled the air, both from their attackers and his team. Bodies were already beginning to fall, staining the night with blood.

While his team continued to fire on the insurgents, he used the car as its own weapon, taking out as many men as possible before they were overrun.

Fighting the inevitable for as long as possible.

I'm sorry, Juliet.

Have you read the first book in this series? Check it out,
SAVING RYDER

ALSO BY JANE BLYTHE

Saving SEALs Series

SAVING RYDER

SAVING ERIC

SAVING OWEN

SAVING LOGAN

SAVING GRAYSON

Broken Gems Series

CRACKED SAPPHIRE

CRUSHED RUBY

FRACTURED DIAMOND

SHATTERED AMETHYST

SPLINTERED EMERALD

SALVAGING MARIGOLD

River's End Rescues Series

COCKY SAVIOR

SOME REGRETS ARE FOREVER

PROTECT

SOME LIES WILL HAUNT YOU

SOME QUESTIONS HAVE NO ANSWERS

SOME TRUTH CAN BE DISTORTED

SOME TRUST CAN BE REBUILT

SOME MISTAKES ARE UNFORGIVABLE

Detective Parker Bell Series

A SECRET TO THE GRAVE

WINTER WONDERLAND

DEAD OR ALIVE

LITTLE GIRL LOST

FORGOTTEN

Count to Ten Series

ONE

TWO

THREE

FOUR

FIVE

SIX

BURNING SECRETS

SEVEN

EIGHT

NINE

TEN

Christmas Romantic Suspense Series

CHRISTMAS HOSTAGE

CHRISTMAS CAPTIVE

CHRISTMAS VICTIM

YULETIDE PROTECTOR

Conquering Fear Series

(Co-written with Amanda Siegrist)

DROWNING IN YOU

OUT OF THE DARKNESS

ABOUT THE AUTHOR

Jane Blythe is a USA Today bestselling author of romantic suspense and military romance full of sweet, smart, sexy heroes and strong heroines! When she's not weaving hard to unravel mysteries she loves to read, bake, go to the beach, build snowmen, and watch Disney movies. She has two adorable Dalmatians, is obsessed with Christmas, owns 200+ teddy bears, and loves to travel!

To connect and keep up to date please visit any of the following

Email – mailto:janeblytheauthor@gmail.com
Facebook – http://www.facebook.com/janeblytheauthor
Instagram – http://www.instagram.com/jane_blythe_author
Reader Group – http://www.facebook.com/groups/janeskillersweethearts
Twitter – http://www.twitter.com/jblytheauthor
Website – http://www.janeblythe.com.au

There are many more books in this fan fiction world than listed here, for an up-to-date list go to www.AcesPress.com

You can also visit our Amazon page at: http://www.amazon.com/author/operationalpha

Special Forces: Operation Alpha World

Christie Adams: Charity's Heart
Denise Agnew: Dangerous to Hold
Shauna Allen: Awakening Aubrey
Linzi Baxter: Unlocking Dreams
Jennifer Becker: Hiding Catherine
Alice Bello: Shadowing Milly
Heather Blair: Rescue Me
Misha Blake: Flash
Anna Blakely: Rescuing Gracelynn
Julia Bright: Saving Lorelei
Cara Carnes: Protecting Mari
Kendra Mei Chailyn: Beast
Melissa Kay Clarke: Rescuing Annabeth
Samantha A. Cole: Handling Haven
Lorelei Confer: Protecting Sara
Anne Conley: Redemption for Misty
KaLyn Cooper: Rescuing Melina
Janie Crouch: Storm
Sarah Curtis: Securing the Odds
Jordan Dane: Redemption for Avery
Tarina Deaton: Found in the Lost
Aspen Drake, Intense
KL Donn: Unraveling Love
Riley Edwards: Protecting Olivia
PJ Fiala: Defending Sophie

Nicole Flockton: Protecting Maria
Alexa Gregory: Backdraft
Michele Gwynn: Rescuing Emma
Casey Hagen: Shielding Nebraska
Desiree Holt: Protecting Maddie
Kathy Ivan: Saving Sarah
Kris Jacen, Be With Me
Jesse Jacobson: Protecting Honor
Silver James: Rescue Moon
Becca Jameson: Saving Sofia
Kate Kinsley: Protecting Ava
Rayne Lewis: Justice for Mary
Heather Long: Securing Arizona
Margaret Madigan: Bang for the Buck
Trish McCallan: Hero Under Fire
Kimberly McGath: The Predecessor
Rachel McNeely: The SEAL's Surprise Baby
KD Michaels: Saving Laura
Lynn Michaels: Rescuing Kyle
Olivia Michaels: Protecting Harper
Wren Michaels: The Fox & The Hound
Annie Miller: Securing Willow
Kat Mizera: Protecting Bobbi
Keira Montclair: Wolf and the Wild Scots
LeTeisha Newton: Protecting Butterfly
Angela Nicole: Protecting the Donna
MJ Nightingale: Protecting Beauty
Victoria Paige: Reclaiming Izabel
Anne L. Parks: Mason
Debra Parmley: Protecting Pippa
Lainey Reese: Protecting New York
KeKe Renée: Protecting Bria
TL Reeve and Michele Ryan: Extracting Mateo

Elena M. Reyes: Keeping Ava
Deanna L. Rowley: Saving Veronica
Angela Rush: Charlotte
Rose Smith: Saving Satin
Lynne St. James: SEAL's Spitfire
Dee Stewart: Conner
Harley Stone: Rescuing Mercy
Sarah Stone: Shielding Grace
Jen Talty: Burning Desire
Reina Torres, Rescuing Hi'ilani
Savvi V: Loving Lex
Megan Vernon: Protecting Us
LJ Vickery: Circus Comes to Town
Rachel Young: Because of Marissa
R. C. Wynne: Shadows Renewed

Delta Team Three Series

Lori Ryan: Nori's Delta
Becca Jameson: Destiny's Delta
Lynne St James, Gwen's Delta
Elle James: Ivy's Delta
Riley Edwards: Hope's Delta

Police and Fire: Operation Alpha World

Freya Barker: Burning for Autumn
B.P. Beth: Scott
Jane Blythe: Salvaging Marigold
Julia Bright, Justice for Amber
Anna Brooks, Guarding Georgia
KaLyn Cooper: Justice for Gwen
Aspen Drake: Sheltering Emma
Emily Gray: Shelter for Allegra
Alexa Gregory: Backdraft

Deanndra Hall: Shelter for Sharla
EM Hayes: Gambling for Ashleigh
India Kells: Shadow Killer
CM Steele: Guarding Hope
Reina Torres: Justice for Sloane
Aubree Valentine, Justice for Danielle
Maddie Wade: Finding English
Laine Vess: Justice for Lauren

Tarpley VFD Series

Silver James, Fighting for Elena
Deanndra Hall, Fighting for Carly
Haven Rose, Fighting for Calliope
MJ Nightingale, Fighting for Jemma
TL Reeve, Fighting for Brittney
Nicole Flockton, Fighting for Nadia

As you know, this book included at least one character from Susan Stoker's books. To check out more, see below.

SEAL Team Hawaii Series

Finding Elodie
Finding Lexie
Finding Kenna
Finding Monica (May 2022)
Finding Carly (TBA)
Finding Ashlyn (TBA)
Finding Jodelle (TBA)

Eagle Point Search & Rescue

Searching for Lilly (Mar 2022)
Searching for Elsie (Jun 2022)
Searching for Bristol (Nov 2022)
Searching for Caryn (TBA)
Searching for Finley (TBA)
Searching for Heather (TBA)
Searching for Khloe (TBA)

The Refuge Series

Deserving Alaska (Aug 2022)
Deserving Henley (Jan 2023)
Deserving Reese (TBA)
Deserving Cora (TBA)
Deserving Lara (TBA)
Deserving Maisy (TBA)
Deserving Ryleigh (TBA)

Delta Team Two Series

Shielding Gillian

Shielding Kinley
Shielding Aspen
Shielding Jayme (novella)
Shielding Riley
Shielding Devyn
Shielding Ember
Shielding Sierra (Jan 2022)

SEAL of Protection: Legacy Series

Securing Caite (FREE!)
Securing Brenae (novella)
Securing Sidney
Securing Piper
Securing Zoey
Securing Avery
Securing Kalee
Securing Jane

Delta Force Heroes Series

Rescuing Rayne (FREE!)
Rescuing Aimee (novella)
Rescuing Emily
Rescuing Harley
Marrying Emily (novella)
Rescuing Kassie
Rescuing Bryn
Rescuing Casey
Rescuing Sadie (novella)
Rescuing Wendy
Rescuing Mary
Rescuing Macie (novella)
Rescuing Annie (Feb 2022)

Badge of Honor: Texas Heroes Series

Justice for Mackenzie (FREE!)
Justice for Mickie
Justice for Corrie
Justice for Laine (novella)
Shelter for Elizabeth
Justice for Boone
Shelter for Adeline
Shelter for Sophie
Justice for Erin
Justice for Milena
Shelter for Blythe
Justice for Hope
Shelter for Quinn
Shelter for Koren
Shelter for Penelope

SEAL of Protection Series

Protecting Caroline (FREE!)
Protecting Alabama
Protecting Fiona
Marrying Caroline (novella)
Protecting Summer
Protecting Cheyenne
Protecting Jessyka
Protecting Julie (novella)
Protecting Melody
Protecting the Future
Protecting Kiera (novella)
Protecting Alabama's Kids (novella)
Protecting Dakota

New York Times, *USA Today* and *Wall Street Journal*

Bestselling Author Susan Stoker has a heart as big as the state of Tennessee where she lives, but this all American girl has also spent the last fourteen years living in Missouri, California, Colorado, Indiana, and Texas. She's married to a retired Army man who now gets to follow *her* around the country.

www.stokeraces.com
www.AcesPress.com
susan@stokeraces.com

Made in the USA
Monee, IL
11 February 2024

53335960R00154